AWARDS AND ACCOLADES FOR THE
CRITICALLY ACCLAIMED AND BESTSELLING
PASSPORT TO PERIL MYSTERY SERIES

"Maddy Hunter's Passport to Peril series is a first-class ticket to entertainment. *Dutch Me Deadly*, the latest adventure of her endearing heroine and zany Iowan seniors, offers nonstop humor and an engaging plot woven so well into its setting that it could take place only in Holland. Despite the danger, I want to travel with Emily!"—Carrie Bebris, award-winning author of the Mr. & Mrs. Darcy Mystery series

Alpine for You
An Agatha Award finalist for Best First Novel and a Daphne du Maurier Award nominee

"I found myself laughing out loud [while reading *Alpine for You*] . . ."
—*Deadly Pleasures* Mystery Magazine

Top O' the Mournin'
An Independent Mystery Booksellers Association bestseller

"No sophomore jinx here. [*Top O' the Mournin'*] is very funny and full of suspense."—*Romantic Times BOOKclub* Magazine

Pasta Imperfect
An Independent Mystery Booksellers Association bestseller
A BookSense recommended title

"Murder, mayhem, and marinara make for a delightfully funny combination [in *Pasta Imperfect*] . . . Emily stumbles upon clues, jumps to hilarious conclusions at each turn, and eventually solves the mystery in a showdown with the killer that is as clever as it is funny."—*Futures Mystery Anthology* Magazine

Bonnie of Evidence

Bonnie of Evidence

A PASSPORT TO PERIL MYSTERY

maddy
HUNTER

MIDNIGHT INK
WOODBURY, MINNESOTA

First Edition
First Printing, 2013

Book design by Donna Burch
Cover design by Adrienne Zimiga
Cover illustration © Anne Wertheim
Editing by Connie Hill

Midnight Ink, an imprint of Llewellyn Worldwide Ltd.

This is a work of fiction. Names, characters, places, and incidents are either the product of the author's imagination or are used fictitiously, and any resemblance to actual persons living or dead, business establishments, events, or locales is entirely coincidental.

Library of Congress Cataloging-in-Publication Data

Hunter, Maddy.
  Bonnie of evidence : a passport to peril mystery / by Maddy Hunter. — 1st ed.
     p.   cm.
  ISBN 978-0-7387-2705-9
1. Andrew, Emily (Fictitious character)—Fiction. 2. Tour guides (Persons)—Fiction. 3. Americans—Scotland—Fiction. 4. Older people—Fiction. 5. Mystery fiction. I. Title. PS3608.U5944B66 2013
  813'.6--dc23

Midnight Ink
Llewellyn Worldwide Ltd.
2143 Wooddale Drive
Woodbury, MN 55125-2989
www.midnightinkbooks.com

Printed in the United States of America

To my Brian, just ... because.

—mmh

ACKNOWLEDGMENTS

Heartfelt thanks to wordsmith extraordinaire and loyal fan, Christina Ward, for providing the title for the Iowa gang's misadventure in Scotland. You rock, Christina!

Thanks to my childhood friend and intrepid high school debating partner, Susan Ainaire Lahti, for introducing the term "geocaching" into my lexicon.

And continued thanks to my diehard fans, whose expressions of delight at the crazy misadventures of my Iowa seniors make it all worthwhile.

Maddy Hunter
October 6, 2012

ONE

THROUGHOUT HISTORY, WHEN PEOPLE realized that the sulfur-spewing crater down the street was an active volcano, they invented both sober and creative ways to deal with the predicament.

The once mighty Incas flung virgins into theirs.

Ancient Pompeians built a resort around theirs.

Battle-hardened Scotsmen plunked a fortress on top of theirs.

Thankfully for the Scots, the volcano had stopped spewing sulfur when they undertook the project.

Tilly Hovick waggled her walking stick at the impenetrable hillfort turned castle, looking like a native in her beret and tartan plaid skirt. "The ancients called it *Din Eidyn*, meaning, 'the stronghold of Eidyn.'"

"Who was Eidyn?" I asked.

She shrugged. "No one knows. But when the Angles invaded the country thirteen hundred years ago, they dubbed the rock Edinburgh, and it's gone by that name ever since."

To say that Edinburgh Castle dominated the cityscape was an understatement. It was so imposing, it looked like the medieval version of an alien mothership perched atop a mountain of stone, and oddly equipped with round towers, cannon embrasures, and an impossibly steep curtain wall. Its turbulent history had been explained to us by the local guide who'd provided our group with a personalized tour of the buildings and battlements, but his accent had been so thick, I'd only caught half of what he'd said.

My grandmother peered up at Tilly in awe. "Was that somethin' you knew on account of you was a professor, or somethin' you seen on the History Channel?"

"I believe it was the first historical fact out of our guide's mouth this morning," acknowledged Tilly.

"No kiddin'?" Nana gave a little suck on her uppers. "George said the fella was speakin' English, but I didn't believe him."

"His burr was quite pronounced," Tilly admitted. "I'm not surprised you couldn't understand him, Marion. If I hadn't cut my anthropological teeth mastering non-labial consonants on Faraulep Island, I wouldn't have been able to understand him either."

We were killing time on the Royal Mile, an inordinately wide, brick-paved street that stretched like a landing strip from Edinburgh Castle all the way to Holyrood Palace, where the Scottish Queen Mary had resided for a handful of years in the sixteenth century. Since our visit coincided with the city's famous festival and military tattoo, we were sharing the street with musicians, jugglers, acrobats, actors, bagpipers, and craftsmen hawking everything from Celtic crosses to tam o' shanters. Normally, I'd be concerned about losing guests in the chaos, especially since my tour group consists entirely of seniors who might be easily disoriented. But thanks to modern technology, my worries have all but been eliminated.

"Time's up," shouted Dick Stolee as the stopwatch on his cell phone beeped. He was carrying the most advanced mobile phone known to man, boasting science-fiction technology in a unit the size of an index card. Not only could he make face-to-face calls using the video feature, he could download the entire Library of Congress onto the e-reader, uplink to the international space station, and with his new and improved user-friendly global positioning system, knew he could visit anywhere in the world and never get lost again, even if he wanted to. The entire Windsor City contingent had purchased their phones at Pills Etcetera at a huge volume discount—knockoff Smartphones with high def, mega-pixel cameras. The only glitch was, when cell service went down, so did the cameras.

"You s'pose Team Number Five found the container?" asked Nana.

"Show of hands," said Osmond Chelsvig, who'd popularized opinion polls long before Gallup or Zogby had ever hit the scene. "How many folks think that having Bernice on Team Five is gonna doom it to failure?"

"Point of order." Tilly raised her walking stick in objection. "In the spirit of fairness, wouldn't it be better to phrase the question in a way that doesn't emphasize such obvious negative bias? We're Iowans. We pride ourselves on being fiercely democratic. We demand impartial results."

Osmond nodded. "Absolutely." He paused thoughtfully and began again. "How many folks *know* that having Bernice on their team is gonna screw up their chances of winning Emily's grand prize?"

Tilly's hand flew into the air. Four others followed.

"Opposed?"

"We don't got no one left to oppose," observed Nana. "Everyone else hightailed it into the Fudge Kitchen."

"The 'ayes' have it," announced Osmond. "Team Five is toast."

Yup. That was unbiased.

Dick Teig pumped his fist with glee. "More opportunity for the rest of us to make it into the final drawing, right Emily?" Dick had to be cautious about broad gestures with his fist because his head was so big, one wrong move, and he could knock himself out.

I'm Emily—Emily Andrew Miceli—glorified chaperone for a core group of a dozen Iowa seniors who regularly sign up for international tours. On this trip, twenty-nine guests from across the Corn and Rust Belts had booked the Scottish tour offered by Destination Travel—the travel agency my husband opened after moving across the Atlantic to settle in my hometown of Windsor City. The prize Osmond alluded to is a promotional offer I thought up to attract more business in a bad economy—a drawing at the end of the tour to award a free trip to the lucky winner. And the only thing a guest would have to do to qualify for the drawing would be to locate a series of objects stashed in obscure places throughout Scotland by avid geocachers.

Decades ago, when children ran all over their neighborhoods armed with lists of nonsensical items to find, they called it scavenger hunting. Today, adults still look for the same nonsensical items, but they've expanded the playing field to the entire world, and they're using Internet websites and sophisticated GPS units to assist their search. Today, the pursuit is called geocaching, and it's become the favorite pastime of every member of the Windsor City

Senior Center, next to texting and synchronized back floating in the new warm-water wading pool.

"Don't get too cocky," I advised the group. "This is only the first site, so I wouldn't count Team Five out just yet."

"Did you miss the discussion?" asked Dick Stolee. "They can't win. *Bernice* is on their team."

I'd divided the group into five teams of five guests apiece and stipulated that each team would have a limited amount of time to find the cache. After all, we were on a tour and had a schedule to maintain. Whichever team registered the most number of finds at the end of the trip would be eligible to enter the lottery for the grand prize, with yours truly drawing the name of the winning team member out of a hat. On paper, it looked like a pretty good system, but as the saying goes, the devil is in the details.

"You wanna see what we found in the first cache?" Nana asked me as she fiddled with her phone. She held up the picture of a narrow alleyway that dipped below street level as it snaked between two buildings. "This here's the alley where it was hidin', but the locals don't call 'em alleys. They call 'em 'closes,' and they're so historic, each one's got its own name on a fancy sign on the entrance. I can't remember what this one's called on account of I forgot to take a picture of the sign."

New York City had alleys, too, but when I'd lived there, the only signs I'd ever seen had read KEEP OUT.

She showed me the next photo—swirls of green and yellow set against a rough gray background. "This is the graffiti what someone spray-painted all over the wall. It musta been the real expensive brand 'cuz I didn't see no signs of chippin'."

George Farkas thumped toward me on his wooden leg. "This one's my favorite." He angled his phone so I could see the image on the screen. I tilted my head left and right.

"What is it? A sewer grate?"

"Steel bars. They're on all the windows in the alley. I thought they added a nice touch to the general ambiance."

Right. Kind of like razor wire added a nice touch to state prisons.

This opened the floodgates for Osmond, Tilly, and the two Dicks to crowd around me, offering up their own photographic masterpieces.

"This is the doorstoop where the container was stashed," enthused Tilly.

"Here's the container," said Osmond, displaying a photo of a plastic box the size of a brick.

"This is the little notebook what was inside," said Nana. "We signed and dated it to prove we was actually here and found it."

"And then we put it back under the stoop for the next team to find," Dick Stolee chimed in. "And we did it way under the fifteen-minute time limit."

"That's all that was inside?" I asked. "A notebook?"

"And a pen," said Tilly. "A very thoughtful gesture on the part of the person who hid the cache. Without a writing implement, you can't sign the register."

"And if you don't sign the register, you don't got no right to score it as a find," added Nana. "The rules say you gotta have proof."

"Does anyone ever leave anything inside for you?" I asked. "A little reward for your efforts?"

"We *are* rewarded," said George. "We get to see our names posted on the official geocaching website in really big black letters."

Nana pulled a face. "That's on account of folks what's in our age bracket don't got good eyesight no more."

"I found a bottle of Jack Daniels in a cache near Lars Bakke's grain elevator a couple of months ago," Osmond reflected.

"And you didn't offer the rest of us a little nip?" barked Dick Teig.

Osmond lifted his ninety-something-year-old shoulders in a helpless gesture. "It was empty."

"Don't look now," Nana said as she shot a glance across the street, "but we got incomin'. And would you look at them long faces?"

The members of Team Five were clumped together at the crosswalk on the opposite side of the street, looking pouty and irritated as they waited for the traffic light to change.

"Do those look like the faces of a team that registered a find?" Dick Teig asked me.

He was right. They looked miserable. *Uh-oh.* "Look," I urged the gang, "if it turns out they didn't find it, would you *try* to be sympathetic when they join us?"

"You bet," said Nana.

"He who laughs last, laughs best," said Tilly.

George lifted his Pioneer Seed Corn hat to scratch the back of his bald head. "What does that mean anyway?"

Dick Stolee snickered as he elbowed my arm. "Did I call that or what? I'm telling you, Emily. The other teams are going to mop up the floor with them."

"So how did it go?" I asked in a cheery voice as the five team members trooped onto the sidewalk.

"Why don't you ask Bernice?" Lucille Rassmuson locked her arms across her chest and pursed her dime-thin lips in what was recognized as the Iowa version of a hissy fit. "She *said* she knew where she was going."

Lucille was sporting a new, easy-care hairstyle for the trip. Gone were the tight, kinky curls of her home perm, replaced by longer, layered strands that hugged her skull like a bathing cap. She'd even tweaked the color, replacing her peach Margarita tint with a soft shade of powdery pink. If her late husband—cigar-smoking, practical joking Dick Rassmuson—had still been alive, he might have passed her on the street and not even recognized her.

"My coordinates were right," Bernice huffed. "We were practically standing on top of the thing! It was Tweedledee and Tweedledum who dropped the ball." She fired accusing looks at the two other women on her team.

"I beg your pardon?" Tweedledee's mouth fell open, drawing attention to her beautifully capped teeth and neatly applied lipstick in the season's most vibrant color. She'd listed her occupation as "retired retail buyer" on her guest information form, and judging from the way she'd added a stylish belt to glam up a simple sweater and designer jeans, I'd guess she'd been a whiz at it. Her name tag identified her as Dolly Pinker from Chicago. "There was no hidden cache in that alleyway. You entered the wrong numbers in your GPS."

"Did not."

"Did so. And you were too pigheaded to admit you were wrong, so thank you very much for helping us to end up with *nothing*. This is all your fault."

"Is not."

"Is so. I want to change teams."

"Me, too," said Tweedledum, whose real name was Isobel Kronk from Gary, Indiana. "I could use a free vacation, but it ain't gonna happen with Wrong Way Corrigan calling the shots." Isobel was hard-edged and rough-angled, with long gray hair, sun-damaged skin, and eyes that snapped with impatience. Her lone fashion accessory was a backpack handbag in an exotic animal print that made it look as if she had a zebra strapped to her back. She owned a scrap metal business in Gary, where she probably spent most of her time crushing car engines between her teeth. "Are we the only team who didn't find the cache?" she asked me. "Our timekeeper refused to tell us."

Unwilling to hammer the first nail into their coffin, I resorted to evasive tactics. "I'm sure the timekeeper simply wanted to tabulate all the results before she released—"

"Everyone scored a find except you," ratted Dick Teig.

Dolly held up her iPhone. "Is this the alley where you found it?" The image on the screen showed a seemingly endless flight of stairs shoehorned between two buildings.

"We didn't have to climb no stairs," said Nana.

Dick Stolee scrunched his eyes in thought. "Are you sure? I remember stairs someplace."

"Show of hands," said Osmond. "How many people remember climbing stairs?"

"Geez-Louise," griped Bernice in her former-smoker's rasp, "would all you whiners just put a sock in it? We didn't find the stupid thing, all right? Get over it. We'll find it next time." The humidity had caused her hair to frizz around her head like exploded electrical wire, giving her the look of a person who'd just had a run-in with chain lightning.

"Will someone *please* switch teams with me?" Dolly begged, making her appeal to the entire Iowa gang. "I'm willing to offer bribes."

"Me, too," pleaded Isobel.

"Hey, team." The lone male member of Team Five waved his hand in the air. "Remember me?" He was of average height, with thinning brown hair, a weak chin, bulbous nose, neck wattle, and a little paunch belly, but his ever-present smile made up for all his shortcomings, making him appear taller, handsomer, more physically fit. His name was Cameron Dasher, and he was proving to be quite the people magnet with his self-deprecating sense of humor and upbeat mood. The unattached ladies on the tour found him particularly attractive—not so much because he was of the same generation and made them laugh, but because he possessed the one quality they were all looking for in a man.

He was still alive.

"What are we? A team of quitters?" Dasher scolded. "Tell me this—how flavorful would our food be if Marco Polo had given up trying to discover a trade route to the East? How exciting would our world surfing competitions be if Balboa had given up searching for the Pacific Ocean? Where would all of us be living today if Columbus had quit trying to find his way to the New World?"

Osmond shot his hand into the air. "Croatia?"

"Come on, ladies," Dasher goaded. "This was only our first try. There's eleven more sites to explore. Where's your fighting spirit? So we messed up the first one. If we stick together, I guarantee we'll find all the rest. We can do this! If you want to quit after just one round, I can't stop you. But if we hang tight, one of us can look forward to a free vacation in our future! Are you with me?"

Eye rolling. Sighs.

Not surprisingly, Cameron had listed his occupation as "motivational speaker."

"What's our team slogan?" he prodded, cupping his hand around his ear.

"Yes, we can," came the grumbled reply from his teammates.

"I can't *heeeear* you."

"Yes, we can," they recited with slightly more gusto.

"Once more with feeling!"

"Yes, we can," they chanted as they tapped into his enthusiasm. "Yes, we can!" Lucille, Dolly, and Isobel high-fived each other. "YES, WE CAN!"

"Yes, we can," chimed Osmond, pumping his spindly arms as he boogied to the beat. Dick Teig whacked him on the shoulder.

"Cool it. You're not on their team."

Cameron Dasher banded his arm around Bernice and gave her a squeeze. "And from now on, Bernice promises to respect all our opinions and not hijack the whole show. Right, Bernice?"

"Good luck with that," wisecracked Dick Stolee.

Bernice glanced from Cameron's hand to his face, melting against him with a breathless sigh. "Whatever you say," she gushed, fluttering her lashes like a silver-screen movie goddess.

Whoa! This guy was good. I wonder if he'd ever consider freelancing as an assistant escort on tours saddled with especially nasty guests?

Bernice's teammates fell suddenly silent, their mantra dying on their lips as they narrowed their eyes and hardened their jaws. *Unh-oh.* It had been awkward enough that every woman on the tour had wanted to be on Cameron's team, but if they started throwing daggers at each other every time he paid attention to one of them, there was going to be trouble.

"It's decided then?" Cameron asked good-naturedly. "We're still a team?"

"Of course we're still a team," Dolly assured as she looped her arm through his, smiling possessively. "And just to set the record straight, it wasn't my idea to change teams in the first place." Honey oozed from her voice. "It was Isobel's."

"Me?" Age might have ruined Isobel's complexion and turned her hair gray, but her hearing still rocked. "What the hell have *you* been smoking? You're the one who—"

Cameron raised his hands in Biblical fashion as if to calm the waters. "Laaadies, laaadies, it doesn't matter who said what first. All that'll matter in the end is how many checkmarks we have in the 'Find' column, so let's put this episode behind us and start with a clean slate tomorrow. Fair enough?"

Bernice and Dolly took wary measure of each other as they lingered at Cameron's sides, looking like two spurs of an about-to-be-snapped wishbone. "Fine," they crooned in unison.

Lucille heaved a sigh and nodded grudgingly. "Okay."

Isobel's mouth strained at the corners as if she were trying to force her lips into a smile, but all she managed was a sneer. "Whatever," she spat, her eyes narrowing to hostile slits.

Yup. There was going to be trouble.

As a troupe of Shakespearean players paraded past us, reciting extraneous lines of prose to any tourist willing to listen, Nana grabbed my arm and dragged me aside, concern etched across her face.

"I know what you're going to say," I offered preemptively. "You're afraid that glaring jealousy issues on Team Five might lead to trouble, and I have to admit, that makes me a little nervous, too, but here's the thing." I raised a determined finger. "It's going to be different this time because Etienne is with us. Guests will *not* be creeping around, trying to knock each other off, with a former Swiss police inspector watching their every move. So, even if the ladies of Team Five get into it with each other, I don't expect it'll escalate beyond snotty name calling or an occasional cat fight." I flashed a confident smile. "I think we're good!"

"Whatever you say, dear."

My smile morphed into a wince. I hung my head. "I'm in denial, aren't I? Those women hate each other already and the tour has just begun."

"I don't wanna be no alarmist, Emily, but we got bigger problems than them four women."

"We do?"

"You bet. Team Five come up with a snappy slogan for themselves. The rest of us don't got one."

I stared at her, non-plussed. "That's a problem?"

"You bet it is. They're makin' the rest of us look bad, so we're gonna have to think of one, too."

"Is that going to be difficult?"

"Emily, dear, we got one Catholic, two Lutherans, one birther, and a vegetarian on our team. How are we s'posed to compromise? That don't give us no common ground to work with."

Ew. She had a point. I just hoped their diversity didn't set them up to get sucked into knockdown-dragouts over issues of a more ideological nature—like, if Catholic priests should be allowed to marry, or, which *Gilligan's Island* character was hotter, Ginger or Mary Ann? That could get really ugly.

I gave her a hug. "Chin up. You'll think of something."

"I just did. I'm gonna let Tilly figure it out."

Nana had three chins, blue hair, and stood four-foot-ten in her bare feet. She'd won millions in the Minnesota lottery a few years back, but the experience had changed neither her outlook nor her practical spending habits. She was the treasurer of the Legion of Mary at church, a card-carrying computer geek, and an enthusiastic subscriber to every TV channel offered by her cable provider. She had only an eighth-grade education, but given her addiction to the Discovery and Smithsonian networks, she was the smartest person I knew.

"*Uh-oh,*" Nana fretted in a sudden panic. "I don't mean to ditch you, dear, but I'm outta here." Like a video playing at warp speed, she raced behind me in her size five sneakers and ducked into a shop displaying a selection of tartans and kilts on headless mannequins.

I stared after her. *What in the world?* And then it hit me.

I turned slowly.

She was barreling toward me with her laptop slung over her shoulder in its trusty carrying case and her fannypack riding her opposite hip like an oversized jellyroll. Her little moon face was flushed from exertion, and her salt and pepper hair was disastrously windblown, but her girlish excitement made it quite apparent that she wouldn't have missed this for the world. The tour guests knew her as "the timekeeper."

Nana knew her as Margaret.

I knew her as Mom.

TWO

"I haven't had this much fun since I alphabetized the IRS forms in the new public library."

Mom was addicted to alphabetical order like a shopaholic is addicted to outlet malls. Nana blames the disorder on a dormant gene that apparently sprang to life when Mom started volunteering at the library after she retired. Her Facebook page lists her favorite pastime as, "Alphabetizing grocery cans in the kitchen pantry." In fact, she gets so giddy during Fareway's annual canned food sale that Dad has to accompany her down the soup aisle to protect her from herself. The one time she sneaked out without him, she bought so many pallets of condensed soup that she had to store them in the machine shed and break out the forklift to stack them in order—an event the family refers to as, "The Highlight of Her Life."

"One down, eleven to go, and if I do say so myself, the first leg went off without a hitch"—she patted her laptop case as if it were a cherished pet—"if you don't count Team Five's objections."

"What were they objecting to?"

"Having too little time. Having no luck finding the cache. Having someone on their team named Bernice Zwerg. But I think my pep talk helped." She flashed a self-satisfied smile. "I mentioned that Bernice was probably too modest to say, but she was the reigning champ of the two-yard dash at the Senior Center and probably had the fastest feet on the tour, so that gave them a huge advantage over the other teams."

"And they believed you?"

"Bernice did. I thought one out of five was pretty good." She switched gears to organizational mode. "I've developed a spreadsheet to keep track of all the contest statistics, Emily, so you'll know at a glance where all the teams stand. Would you like to see it?" She fingered the zipper on her laptop case with an eagerness that bordered on lust.

"How about I wait until you enter more data?" I hedged. "That's when things should get really intense, right?"

"They're intense right now! Three teams are neck and neck in the time department, and if you don't think that's exciting, I'll show you the line graph. It's enough to take your breath away."

I crooked my mouth, giving her a narrow look. "I'm not sure the scorekeeping thing needs to be so complicated, Mom. Can't you just jot down who finds the cache and who doesn't on a piece of notepaper and call it a day?"

She regarded me as if I had zucchini growing out of my ears. "I don't see how that's possible, Em. I'm planning a series of line graphs to illustrate comparisons, and I'm thinking about either bar graphs or pie charts for extraneous statistics. Do you have a preference? I could do both. It'd be no trouble at all. Or I could do a flow chart. They're not as popular as they used to be, but—"

I held up my hand to cut her off. "Whatever works for you, Mom. I—"

"Or I could do a bubble chart. I'd have to buy another software program and spend some time installing it, but I'm sure I can find a computer store somewhere in Edinburgh."

A tic began tap dancing beneath my eye. "Okay, here's the thing. I just don't want you to devote so much time to your contest duties that you miss out on the sights."

"That's not going to happen." She paused, reconsidering. "But if it does, your father is videotaping everything, so I'll get to see what I missed when I get home." She threw her arms around me, giving me an exuberant hug. "I'm so happy you appointed me official scorekeeper, Em. Who knew I'd enjoy it so much?"

Nana had begged me to find an activity to occupy Mom's time for the duration of the trip. As she had so artfully phrased it, "If Margaret don't have nuthin' to do except gawk at stuff, she'll be on me like ice on an igloo, and I'm not forkin' out the big bucks just so's your mother can have an old person to babysit." So I'd told Mom that if I could impose upon her good nature and ask her to accept the burden of monitoring the contest challenges, she'd free me up to spend some needed time with Etienne, for which both he and I would be eternally grateful.

Mom thinks Etienne is the perfect son-in-law. He speaks with a sexy French/German/Italian accent that's a real hit back home, and unlike my first husband, who had a penchant for borrowing my lingerie, the only time Etienne is motivated to touch my underwear is when I'm actually in it. So, in theory, Mom took the job as a favor to Etienne, but in reality, she wanted the job because there's nothing she'd rather do than be burdened.

The digital tone on Mom's wristwatch beeped. "Have you seen your grandmother?" She frowned as she ranged a look around us.

"She went shopping." Alarm suddenly fluttered in my stomach. "Why? What's up?"

"I haven't told her yet, but I'm putting her on a regimen of calcium and vitamin D to strengthen her bones. Chewables. In two fruity flavors. She doesn't want to admit it, Emily, but she's shrinking, so I figured since we were going to be traveling together anyway, the least I could do is schedule her supplements to make sure she takes them." She rotated in a slow circle, her eyes darting left and right. "I wish she wouldn't disappear like this. You might think I'm way off base, but I sometimes get the impression she's trying to avoid me."

"Nana?" I lied. "N*ooo.*"

"Well, if you see her, tell her I'm looking for her."

"You got it."

Her face brightened. "There's Grace, Helen, and Alice. And look, they're carrying shopping sacks. Would you excuse me, Emily? Maybe they've seen your grandmother. Yoohoo!"

"We board the bus in two hours," I called after her. "Leave yourself enough time to get back to the hotel."

She waved her hand in acknowledgment as she made a beeline for the girls.

She wouldn't be late. Tardiness was a physical impossibility for native Iowans. No one can explain when the condition first appeared, or how it spread to the general population, but it affects so many people, the State Water Control Board is testing the drinking supply. If their suspicions pan out, the governor is hoping to plug his state budget deficit by bottling the stuff and selling it to a country where nothing ever runs on time, like Italy or France. If their suspicions are wrong, the governor has vowed to increase government coffers by auctioning off every antique clock in the state's ninety-nine county courthouses. As he's fond of saying, "Why is the State providing Iowans with universal time coverage when the private sector can provide the same service at lower cost? I mean, what are wristwatches for anyway?"

"*Psssst.*"

I glanced over my shoulder to find Nana poking her head out the door of the tartan shop.

"Is she gone?"

I shot her a withering look as I dug out my antacid tablets.

It was going to be a long trip.

During its forty-three years sailing the high seas, the Royal Yacht *Britannia* made 968 official voyages, traveled over a million nautical miles, and called at six hundred ports. Once spotted in such exotic locales as Sydney, Samoa, and Hong Kong, it was decommissioned in 1997 and can now be spotted in Edinburgh harbor—attached to a multi-level shopping center.

Armed with individual audio handsets, the group was oohing and aahing its way through five decks that once boasted a complement of two hundred Royal Yachtsmen and forty-five household staff, whose sole purpose was to serve Queen and country. With the bridge and all its incomprehensible gizmos behind me, I was climbing up and down companionways to tour the more interesting parts of the ship's interior—from the State Dining room, with its table properly set for an intimate party of ninety-six, to the drawing room, with its grand piano, electric fireplace, and plush floral sofas.

According to the recorded voice on my handset, the drawing room could accommodate nearly two hundred people, but there were only a dozen of us standing behind the roped-off area at the moment. Most of the male guests had hurried off to ~~slather~~ slaver over the Rolls Royce housed in the garage on another deck, and the Dicks had professed an urge to inspect the engine room, so Etienne had headed below decks with them, because leaving Dick Stolee in a room filled with pressure gauges and gears was like leaving a chocoholic in a room filled with Cadbury Easter eggs.

"Would you take a picture of us, Emily?" Helen Teig, dressed in a plus-size sweatshirt with plaid Scottie dogs frolicking across her chest, handed me her Smartphone before scurrying back to pose with Grace Stolee, who was wearing the same sweatshirt, only in medium.

"New sweatshirts?" I asked as I focused and clicked.

"It's our team uniform," boasted Grace.

"But they were kinda cheap, so we're worried about pilling." Helen examined her sleeve for fresh examples.

"Do you want to hear our team slogan?" asked Grace as I returned her phone.

I blinked my surprise. "That was fast. Word's already on the street about the slogans, eh?"

"Dick texted us," said Helen, "and it's a good thing, because all the good slogans are going fast, so we needed time to think." She sidled a glance at Grace. "Ready?"

"Do it or lose it!" they chimed in unison.

I smiled stiffly. Slogans? Uniforms? What would be next? World licensing rights? "Catchy," I said.

"Combining two popular slogans into a fresh new saying isn't considered plagiarism, is it?" questioned Grace.

"Mmm … if it *is* plagiarism, you'll be out of the country before the authorities can track you down, so I think you're safe," I assured her.

"Will you be awarding a prize for the best slogan?" tittered Helen.

"Hadn't planned on it."

"Best uniform?" asked Grace.

"Nope."

Helen corkscrewed her mouth into a half twist, her thickly crayoned eyebrows rocketing into disapproving slants. "Oh. That's disappointing."

Grace sucked in her breath as she eyed her wristwatch. "C'mon, Helen. If we don't put a move on, we'll get stuck having to browse through the gift shop with the men hanging onto us. And you know what that means."

Helen rolled her eyes. "'Why do you need that?'" she mimicked in her husband's voice. "'Where are you going to put it? Don't we have enough junk already?'"

Grace's expression turned devious. "What do you say we just skip the other decks and head directly for the gift shop?"

Helen's face lit up.

"If the Dicks ask," Grace called over her shoulder as they charged across the floor, "you haven't seen us."

"But—"

They were out the exit before I could add another word.

But it's the Britannia, I said to myself as I turned back toward the rope partition. Weren't they impressed by the powerful people who might have sipped cocktails here? Ambassadors might have lounged on the flowery country sofas. Prime ministers might have relaxed in the wingback chairs. Heads of state might have tripped over the Persian rugs. I mean, there was real history in these rooms.

"Excuse me, Emily. Could I get you to take my picture?"

Stella Gordon waved her camera at me, causing the charm bracelets on her arm to jangle like leg shackles. "I'd ask Bill to do it, but he's not here."

"Isn't that the way?" I teased. "I think the rap on husbands is that they're never there when you need them, and always there when you don't." I held out my hand for her camera. "Where would you like to stand?"

Stella Gordon was a short woman with hair dyed too black, cheeks rouged too pink, and lips stained too red. She had unfortunate taste in clothing, demonstrating a fondness for blousy polyester prints in loud colors, but her five-inch strappy heels were nothing short of spectacular, shattering the myth that women over seventy were more interested in preventing bone fractures than making their legs look really good.

"Press the shutter halfway down, focus, then click," she directed as she struck a dramatic pose against the rope barrier.

"So where did you lose Bill?" I asked as I focused and clicked. "Did he head off to see the Rolls with the rest of the guys?"

"Hell, no. He stayed behind in the shopping center. How'd the picture come out?"

I handed her the camera so she could check it out herself. "Bill stayed in the shopping center ... on purpose?" Then again. Seventy shops. A bunch of restaurants. I might have stayed behind myself if I could invent a way to avoid excess baggage fees at the airport.

"Of course, on purpose." She studied the image. "Nice job. If I photoshop him into the picture, all his Looney Tunes relatives will think he did the unthinkable and set foot on the Queen's yacht. I can hear the fireworks now." She let out a Wicked Witch cackle. "Now *that* should be worth the price of admission."

I gave her a narrow look. "Why is it unthinkable for Bill to tour the *Britannia*?"

"Honey, you're not up on your Scottish history, are you? What do you know about the Battle of Culloden?"

I'd actually brushed up on my Scottish history by reading a dog-eared bodice ripper Nana had lent me. History was always more entertaining when enacted by bare-chested men wielding really long blades. "*Uhh*—Isn't that the battle where the guy who got defeated, a Scottish prince or something, dressed up like a woman to avoid being captured by the opposing forces?"

"Some prince," Stella said sarcastically. "The coward abandoned his men and ran away from the English as fast as he could with his tail between his legs. What a wuss."

Actually, being able to run away was pretty impressive, considering the length of women's dresses back then.

"Charles Edward Stuart," droned Stella. "Bonnie Prince Charlie. The Young Pretender to the throne of England. The only thing he 'pretended' to be was a man."

Ouch. A little harsh, but she obviously had issues. "So Bill's relatives don't want him to tour the yacht because..." I gave her a blank look. "I'm sorry. I think I missed the point."

Stella groaned at my obvious stupidity. "The ship is *English*. It belonged to an *English* Queen. Do you get the point now?"

"*Uhhh*—No."

"Oh, for the love of—Whose back do you think Clan Gordon and the other highlanders were protecting at Culloden? I'll give you a hint. It wasn't King George's."

My mouth fell open. "The Gordons were at Culloden? No kidding? Bill had relatives who actually fought in the battle?"

"Bill never kids, and he especially never kids about his ancestry." She offered me an acid smile. "It's what makes being married to him such a joy."

"Okay, so Bill is refusing to set foot on the ship because... he's ticked off about the disappearing act Prince Charlie pulled over two hundred years ago?"

Stella rolled her eyes. "Have you listened to the words coming out of my mouth? He's not mad at the wuss. He's mad at the *English* for slaughtering what remained of the Gordons after the wuss ran away. It was only one of the most brutal acts in military history, and the Looney Tunes Gordons aren't about to forget."

Great. Just what we needed to lighten the mood—a guest with a two-hundred-year-old battle ax to grind. "Was Charlie ever caught?"

Stella shook her head. "Hell, no. He hightailed it to France. Spent the rest of his miserable life dithering about which of his many mistresses was the flavor of the month."

Wasn't that always the way? The guy responsible for the disaster gets off scot-free while his underlings get stuck with the cleanup. In the popular vernacular, I believe it's called "Getting the shaft." On Wall Street, it's called "Business as usual."

I shook my head at the unfairness of it all. "Well, I might be totally off base, but if I were a Gordon, I think I might be more ticked off at Prince Charlie than the English. If he hadn't abandoned his troo—"

"The Gordons *looove* Prince Charlie," Stella cooed. "Doesn't matter that he was a screwup. He was Scottish. The last Prince in the line of Royal Stuarts. In their eyes, he could do no wrong." She made a dismissive gesture with her hand. "It's because of that clan nonsense with the blood and the allegiances and all the other blah, blah, blah. Turns 'em into fanatics. So I'll give you a word of warning." She stepped closer and bowed her head close to my ear. "Never, *ever*, belittle Prince Charlie when you're around Bill. He has a teensie problem with his temper, and cheap shots about his hero really set him off."

"How teensie?"

"Pills help, when he remembers to take them."

Oh, God. Prickly heat crawled up my neck. "*Uh*—Did you happen to mention Bill's ... problem ... on the medical history form we sent with your travel documents?"

"Shoot, we never fill those things out. Pain in the butt. We just leave 'em blank so you'll think we're healthy."

My jaw dropped to my chest. "But all our guests are *required* to fill out medical forms. It's absolutely mandatory. No exceptions."

"Sorry. No can do. Our medical history is none of your business. You ever heard of privacy laws?"

"But what if you're walking around with serious health issues? What if you're allergic to bee stings, or shellfish, or peanuts?" I made a calculated leap to worst-case scenario. "What if you go into anaphylactic shock and die before I can figure out what's happening?"

Stella bobbed her head with indifference. "Same warning. If the Gordon clan shows up for my funeral, pass the word along not to say anything unflattering about Prince Charlie. That temper thing? It's hereditary."

I found Nana on the veranda deck, posted in front of the glass partition that provided an interior view of the Queen's bedroom. "Is Bill Gordon on your team?" I asked as I perused the narrow starboard compartment with its modest twin bed and homespun furnishings.

She held up a finger to "wait a sec" as she concentrated on the voice speaking on her audiophone. "Well, I'll be," she marveled when the tape ended, her mouth hanging open in awe. "When the Queen packed up for an official visit, she brung five tons of luggage with her. Can you imagine? I don't got five tons of stuff in my whole apartment. No wonder she didn't go by plane. She never woulda cleared security in time. I'm sorry, dear, what was your question?"

"Bill Gordon. He's on your team, right?"

"Yup. He's one a them birthers."

"*He's* the birther?" I winced. "Great. Is he causing problems?"

"Not for me, but if George ever gets a notion to run for President, he better watch out, on account of Bill says Farkas don't sound like a real American name."

"What kind of name does he think it sounds like?"

"One that don't got a real birth certificate."

"Well, Stella Gordon just finished talking to me about Bill, and I'm afraid he might turn out to be a handful." I raced through the historical information, ending with the pertinent information about how to avoid igniting Bill's temper. "Will you spread the word to the rest of the gang? Forewarned is forearmed."

"You bet. Isn't that somethin'? He never said nuthin' about bein' Scottish. Gordon don't even sound Scottish."

"Maybe you should ask to see his birth certificate."

A gleam crept into her eye. "Emily, do you s'pose there was Maccoulls what fought in that battle Stella was talkin' about?"

Nana was Scottish on her mother's side of the family, but no one had ever dug into the genealogical history.

"Anything's possible," I admitted, "but I'm not sure Bill is the guy to ask. God only knows how he'd react if it turns out your Maccoull ancestors fought with King George and the English *against* the Gordons. You don't need to pick up where the Hatfields and McCoys left off."

"Amen to that." She locked her lips with an imaginary key and dropped it down her bosom.

"Can you handle more upsetting news?"

She went statue-still, her eyes darting to the corners of her sockets. "Your mother's standin' behind me, isn't she?"

I shook my head. "It's worse than that."

"There isn't nuthin' worse than that."

"How about...Grace and Helen have come up with a team slogan already."

"I knew this was gonna happen. Them girls are a lot smarter than they let on. Must be they think better when they don't gotta run roughshod over the Dicks. Them two fellas can be a real brain-drain." She sighed with resignation. "Lay it on me, dear. What'd they come up with?"

"'Do it or lose it.'"

"Dang. That's a good one."

"And did you notice the matching sweatshirts they're wearing?"

"I didn't pay 'em no mind on account of they looked like they was made of polyester. Polyester don't breathe good."

"It's their new team uniform."

"They got uniforms?" Her eyes bulged with panic. "Jesus, Mary, and Joseph. If my team don't wake up, we'll be headin' straight down the tubes. We don't even got a slogan yet!"

Breathless with frenzy, she charged to the left then whirled back to the right before stopping dead in her tracks. "Don't know if I should be headin' up or down. I gotta find Tilly and George. Have you seen 'em? We gotta call an emergency team meetin' before we get blown away."

"I didn't pass them on my way down from the upper deck, so they must be ahead of—"

29

"Emily! Thank God I found you." Tilly pelted toward us from the aft sun lounge, jaw set and cane thumping. "You'd better come quick. Margi's being detained by security."

"What for?" I cried.

"Distribution of a suspicious substance. If you hurry, you can catch them before they haul her off to jail."

THREE

"I DON'T KNOW WHAT was wrong with their noses," Margi Swanson fussed later that night. I'd brought her back to my hotel room for a little TLC after her near brush with disaster at the hands of the *Britannia* security detail, but the incident had turned her into such an instant celebrity with the other tour guests that I'd had a hard time dragging her away from her admirers. "Honestly, Emily, does this smell like a compound that could be used to make a nuclear device to you?"

Seated opposite me in a comfy armchair, she leaned forward to hand me a plastic bottle that was no bigger than my baby finger. Popping open the flip-cap, I squirted a stream of clear gel into my palm and sniffed. "*Hmm*, this is different." I rubbed it into my hands and sniffed again. "Smells like a blend of…baked ham, hickory-smoked bacon, and pork rinds."

"It's the pharmacy's signature scent for the summer," said Margi. "They call it, 'Hog Wild.' Isn't that cute? They formulate it right there at Pills Etcetera, and I buy it in gallon containers and transfer it to one-ounce bottles for travel. Saves me a ton of money. You wouldn't believe what hand sanitizer goes for in specialty shops." Margi still worked part-time for the Windsor City Medical Clinic, so annihilating other people's germs was a big part of her daily routine.

"The pharmacist is working on a new scent for fall," she tittered. "An homage to grain farmers. He's going to call it, 'Harvest Moon.'"

I wondered what that was going to smell like. Corn silage?

"Okay, Margi, here's the deal." I handed back her plastic bottle. "In order to avoid a repeat of today's incident, I'm going to recommend that you only hand out sanitizer to people who know you."

Disappointment rippled down her face in one long, gut-wrenching wave. "But, Emily, people who *don't* know me have germs, too."

"True, but they also have suspicions. How do they know the gel in those bottles won't kill them?"

She lowered her brows over her eyes, fixing me with a grave look. "Because if I intended to hand out poison, I would have bought the bottles with the skull and crossbones on them."

"Of course you would! I know that, and you know that, but *they* don't know that." I paused. "Where do you find travel-size bottles with skulls and crossbones on them?" My nephews would get a kick out of something like that.

"Pills Etcetera. They're in the aisle with all the pirate paraphernalia."

"The pharmacy carries pirate stuff?"

"They expanded their inventory after the tornado remodel." She sighed. "I suppose I could have bought the regular one-ounce bottles and attached warning labels, but I think the print would have been too small to read without a magnifying glass, and I'm not sure the pharmacy sells magnifying glasses in bulk. I could have tried a couple of the big box stores—"

"Margi."

"But if I struck out at Walmart, I would have gotten stuck driving all the way to Ames, and—"

"MARGI!"

She clamped her mouth shut and blinked. "What?"

"If you distribute all your sanitizer to complete strangers, you'll run out, and then you won't have enough left for your friends. You wouldn't want that to happen, would you?"

She inched her lips into a self-confident smile. "I stuffed so many bottles into my suitcase, I'll never run out."

Of course she wouldn't.

"I had to play it safe, Emily. I knew I couldn't replenish my supply with British pounds sterling. Did you get a load of the exchange rate? It'd wipe me out."

I heard a key card being slid into the outer lock, and in the next moment Etienne strode into the room, his piercing blue eyes locking on Margi. "Ms. Swanson! Just the person I wanted to see. How fortunate to find you here."

He crossed the floor with the wiry grace of a panther, every pore in his six-foot, two-inch frame oozing testosterone and some powerful pheromone that rendered women deaf, dumb, and dizzy. His hair was black, his shoulders broad. His dimpled smile had the same effect on the female psyche that sunshine had on flowers. In a perfect world, his picture would appear twice in the dictionary: once under "raw sexuality," and the other under "1 percent body fat."

"Your public is clamoring for you in the hotel lounge," he announced as he crossed the floor toward us. "And bring a pen.

They're demanding your autograph. Who knew that your being suspected of domestic terrorism would cause such a sensation?"

She stared up at him like a puppy dog, her mouth hanging slightly open, her eyes adoring. "Okay."

He offered her his hand, which she stared at, adoringly.

"Ms. Swanson?"

Her gaze drifted to his face. "Uh-huh?"

"Would you like to join the other tour guests in the lounge before it closes? The drinks are on them."

"Okay."

He helped her to her feet and slid her shoulder bag up her arm. "And if I could impose upon your good nature, would you mind distributing your sanitizer to our Destinations Travel guests only? We want your sightseeing experience to include visits to sites other than police interrogation rooms."

She smiled dreamily. "Okay."

I rolled my eyes. It was official. There was no justice in the world.

He escorted her to the door and let her out. "The hotel lounge," he called after her. "Ground floor. Through the glass doors to the right of reception." He rejoined me, looking a bit wary. "Did she seem a bit 'off' to you?"

"She'll be fine once she's outside your force field."

"I beg your pardon?"

"Let's just say that she likes your suggestions better than mine, even when they're the same suggestion. You kinda have that effect on women."

"I do?" Smiling seductively, he pulled me off my chair and pressed me against him, locking his arms around the small of my back. "Well, then, Mrs. Miceli, I have another suggestion."

Oh, boy. I knew what that tone meant.

"But it involves some minor effort on your part, like … not objecting when I do this." He unclipped the barrette at the back of my head and tossed it onto the armchair. Tangling his fingers in my unbound hair, he tilted my head, baring my earlobe. "Or this." He traced the curve of my ear with his tongue, electrifying every nerve ending in my body. "Or this." He lifted my hand to his mouth and kissed each of my fingertips slowly, provocatively, before drawing my freshly sanitized forefinger into the warmth of his mouth and—

"Emily, darling."

"*Mmm*?" I moaned in a hormone-induced haze.

"I have another suggestion."

"Okay."

"Are you hungry?"

"Ravenous," I purred.

He set me away from him and tidied my hair. "Would you hold that thought until after we find a deli? I'm at a loss to explain it, but I have a sudden, uncontrollable urge for a ham sandwich."

By noontime the next day, Edinburgh was a distant memory.

We'd stopped at St. Andrews long enough for everyone to have their picture taken on the course's first fairway, gawk at the *Chariots of Fire* beach, and argue about whether the tide was in or out— an issue that went unresolved due to the fact that Midwesterners know less about tides than Prissy knew about birthin' babies. From there we headed north, noting a startling change in the terrain as we drove—with the rolling hills of the lowlands ballooning into range after range of humpbacked mountains, and hardwood forests giving way to underbrush, meadow grass, bedrock, and endless sweeps of purple heather.

"We'll be stopping for lunch in Braemar, which is home to the Royal Highland Games," our tour director announced over the bus's microphone. "The event is always held on the first Saturday of September, which is why we're able to stop today. During the games, you can't get near the place. And, as we've marked on your itinerary, Braemar is the site of your second geocaching event, so fire up your GPS units."

Our tour director was a consummate professional with years of experience under his ever-expanding belt. His name was Wally Peppers—a chipmunk-cheeked, boy-next-door kind of guy who was so adept at guiding tours that we'd lured him away from his last employer to work for us on a permanent basis. He was intimately acquainted with so many foreign destinations that in many instances, we didn't even need to hire local guides, which saved us oodles of money. Wally boasted a firm lock on middle-age, an eager attitude, and a long, unlucky streak where the ladies were concerned. He'd served as tour director on two other trips I'd taken, so we had history, even though it was a bit checkered.

"How are we supposed to eat lunch and geocache at the same time?" Dick Teig called out.

"You're not," said Wally. "But I'll let Mrs. Andrew explain the logistics. Would you like to give us the particulars, Margaret?"

Mom popped out of her seat faster than a Whac-a-Mole out of its hidey hole. "Day two," she announced with breathless excitement as she opened her official geocaching notebook. "I have it all worked out. Two teams will search first, then eat, and three teams will eat first, then search. And today's search will probably be pretty challenging because we can only allow each team ten minutes to get the job done."

Groans. Boos. Collective whining.

"That's not fair!" shouted Isobel Kronk. "We're challenged enough having Bernice on our team."

"I resent that," snapped Bernice.

"Now, now," Mom placated. "Ten minutes might not sound like a lot of time, but once you enter your coordinates and take off, you'll probably think it's too *much* time."

Isobel let out a sarcastic snort. "Oh, sure. Do you know the Bernice I'm talking about?"

"Is our team going to get stuck going last again?" asked Dolly Pinker. "We're at such a psychological disadvantage when all the teams ahead of us are high-fiving each other about their successful searches. It's totally unfair to put us under that much pressure."

"I agree," Alice Tjarks called out. "You need to make the process more equitable so everyone can take a turn being paralyzed by anxiety."

Mom smiled pertly as we approached the town limits. "I'm way ahead of you. I've put you on a rotating schedule, so Team Five will go first today, followed by Teams One through Four. Team Four will go first tomorrow, and so on. Does that suit everyone?"

"Team Five objects to your use of the term, Team Five," announced Bernice, boosting herself to her feet for effect. "From now on, we want you to call us Team Yes We Can."

"Okey-dokey," said Mom as she made a notation in her notebook.

"In that case, Team Four wants to be called Team Do It Or Lose It," said Helen.

"Gotcha." Mom made another notation. "Any other name changes?"

Margi shot her hand into the air. "Team Three would like to be referred to as Team There Is No Dog."

I frowned. *What?*

"There Is No Dog," Mom recited as she entered the correction in her book.

"Team Two wants to be called Team Two," said Dick Teig. "We're not gonna waste time fartin' around with all this foolishness. If it's not broke, why fix it?"

"Team One wants to be called somethin' with more punch," Nana chimed in, "but we need extra time on account of we got consensus issues."

We downshifted past a Braemar eatery with outdoor picnic tables, then slowed to a crawl past a cluster of quaint shops with steep roofs and chimney pots. "One last thing," Mom continued as we rounded a sharp curve leading toward the town center. "We don't want anyone to develop ulcers on this trip, so I'm going to suggest that all five teams keep mum about their luck finding the cache, and at a specified time each evening, I'll make a formal announcement about the day's results. Does that sound like a good idea, Emily?"

Bless her heart. Mom was all right, despite what Nana said about her. "Great idea," I agreed. "So please remember, people, poker faces. No saying anything to anyone until Mom announces the results every night." Gee, this was working out much better than I ever thought it would.

As we cruised to a stop in the parking lot of what looked like an upscale highland strip mall, Wally took over again. "Mark the time, everyone. Teams Two, Three, and Four should meet back here in an hour and a half to perform their searches. We board the bus again in two hours. And to remind you again, there's a cooler up front here with bottled water that's free for the taking, compliments of Destinations Travel, any time you're thirsty. You'll find lots of places to eat in Braemar, plus craft and gift shops and a really fine tartan store if you're in the market for a cashmere sweater or kilt."

Cashmere? I was always in the market for cashmere, especially if I could find it at bargain basement prices.

The bus emptied in record time. While Bernice and her team members gathered around Mom to receive their coordinates, the other teams scattered, some heading for the elegant stone building with gingerbread trim across the street, some readying their cameras to photograph the rock-strewn river we'd just crossed, and others wandering aimlessly on the sidewalk, looking as if they weren't quite sure where to go. Dad stood on the street corner, in his mismatched John Deere windbreaker and Pioneer Seed Corn baseball cap, videotaping the helter-skelter departures.

"Are we eating lunch, or doing something dutiful?" Etienne inquired as he came up behind me.

I eyed the guests who were still dithering on the sidewalk. "Do those people look like they could use some guidance?"

"Doing something dutiful," he conceded. "Allow me to volunteer. I have a printout of every eatery in Braemar." He kissed the tip of my nose. "And I suspect you might prefer to indulge in an activity that includes the word cashmere."

"You wanna come with me?"

A good-natured smile spread across his handsome face. "It's shopping, bella. I'm afraid I'd rather chew razor blades."

"Suit yourself," I said, adding with a wink, "but to that point, I've heard that the new singled-edged slimlines are really quite tasty."

I tracked down Wally in the parking lot. "Which way to the cashmere?"

"Is your radar broken?" He nodded toward the strip mall. "Right in front of you. And my sources tell me that prices have been slashed to an historic low, so knock yourself out."

Yes!

I scarfed down an energy bar to boost my endurance then crossed the threshold of the tartan shop, pausing for just a moment to inhale the tantalizing smell of highland wool on sale for—I gaped at the sign—forty percent off the original price? *Uff-da*! And I only had two hours to shop? *Whose* stupid idea had it been to spend a measly hundred and twenty minutes in Braemar anyway?

And then I remembered.

Oh, yeah. Mine. Damn.

"Emily? Would you mind coming over here and giving me your honest opinion?"

I darted a look around the store, spying Alex Hart in front of a curtained fitting room in the far corner, waving me toward him.

"Well, would you look at you," I said as I joined him. I looked him up and down then twirled my finger for him to turn around.

"What do you think?" he asked, holding his breath expectantly.

"I think if every man looked as good as you do in a kilt, we'd see the rapid demise of three-piece suits in corporate America." The tartan he'd selected was a brilliant rose and navy blue that neatly hugged his flanks from waist to knees, accenting his flat stomach and narrow hips, and exposing his dough-white legs.

"Oh, thank God." He fanned his hand in front of his face in obvious relief before pausing to give me a tentative look. "You're sure you're not saying that just to be nice?"

"No. Really. It's you."

"I bet she's just being nice," taunted a voice that floated out from the adjacent room.

"Oh, hush," Alex scolded the voice's owner. "And can you believe the prices, Emily? Forty percent off! I'm in heaven."

Alexander Hart was a nuclear engineer who'd looked pretty dull on paper, but who, in person, was anything but. He was a fastidious dresser, neatly tucked in and buttoned up, who sported polo players on his shirts and knife-edge creases on his slacks. His salt-and-pepper hair was razor cut, his face clean shaven, and his fingernails buffed to a gleaming shine. His career might revolve around mathematical equations and proofs, but his "life" apparently included frequent visits to high-end clothiers and Asian manicurists.

He studied his reflection in the wall mirror, turning to observe his backside. "Are you sure this thing doesn't make my butt look big?"

"Give the girl a break," protested the disembodied voice. "She has better things to do than check out how much junk's in your trunk." The fitting room curtains suddenly parted and out stepped Erik Ishmael in all his highland glory. "Ta da!" He nailed a manly pose despite the fact that he was wearing a wool skirt. "I think it has my name written all over it. What do you think?"

"I think you should stop showing off," quipped Alex. "Emily doesn't care that your bare torso once graced the cover of hundreds of romance novels. Your legs aren't ready for prime time. You need a wax job."

Erik lifted his kilt above his knees to peer down at the tangle of dark hair that matted his legs. "Forget it. Not happening. But you know what might work?" His expression brightened. "A can of shaving cream and a bag of disposable razors. Plus several boxes of bandages. Razor nicks bleed all over the place."

Alex rolled his eyes. "I hope you're fond of prickly stubble because you know it's all going to start growing back in less than an hour. And it'll probably itch. Did you remember to pack anti-itch cream?"

Erik flashed me an anguished look. "My ancestors were part gorilla. Seriously. But at least they weren't albino." He lowered his gaze to Alex's legs. "He looks like he's descended from a family of popsicle sticks."

Erik Ishmael's modeling days had probably ended a decade ago, but I could see why he'd been able to make his living in front of a camera. His face was sharply angled, as if the underlying bone were chiseled from granite, creating hollows and rises that a camera lens would have adored. His eyes were dark and almond-shaped, his hair long and purposefully tousled, his complexion a warm café au lait color that seemed a blend of every exotic ethnicity from Spain to the South Pacific. I didn't know how many covers he'd posed for, but if women chose books for their covers alone, the ones featuring Erik Ishmael had probably sold a bazillion.

"Why don't you do what the Scots do?" I suggested, nodding toward a mannequin that boasted full Scottish regalia, from jacket and brooches, to hose and leather brogues. "Buy yourselves some knee-length socks. They even come with nifty little tassels. How cute is that?"

They stared at me. They stared at the mannequin. They stared at each other. "Socks!" they echoed in perfect unison, as if the ability to predict what the other was going to say was second nature to them. "Group hug, group hug." They surrounded me like two slices of marble rye around a half-pound of pastrami, giving me a heartfelt squeeze before hurrying to the mannequin for a closer look.

"Love the socks," said Erik. He bent down to smooth his fingers over the ribbing. "Feels like wool and poly blend. You think I can wear them with my sandals?"

Alex shook his head. "Not if you want to be seen with me, you can't. How much are the shoes?"

"Doesn't matter. They're ugly. I wouldn't wear them if they were giving them away." They were black, tongueless oxfords with lacings that crossed the top of the foot and wrapped around the leg to tie at mid-calf, kinda like what a business exec might buy if he were looking for just the right shoes to wear with a tutu.

Alex sighed woefully. "You're right. Ugly *and* impractical. I wouldn't wear them either."

"How about modified hiking boots?" I piped up. "That's what our local guide wore yesterday, and I thought he looked rather fetching."

Delight flitted across their faces. They looked at me. They looked at each other. "Shall we keep her?" asked Alex.

"I'd love to," Erik said in a conspiratorial tone, "but I think her husband might notice."

"The cad. So, Emily," Alex inquired, eyes leaping with excitement, "what else would you recommend to complete our ensembles?"

"*Whoa!* I'm not an expert in—"

"Scottish fanny pack?" asked Erik. He toyed with the tasseled pouch that hung from the mannequin's belt and rested at groin-level, like a furry cod piece. "The Scots call this thing a sporran. Or how about a Scottish bread knife?" He tapped the sheath of the long-bladed dagger suspended from the mannequin's waist. "Or a Scottish shawl?" He fingered the length of tartan cloth that was draped neatly over the mannequin's left shoulder.

I looked from Erik to Alex. "Are you sure you wouldn't rather eat lunch?"

Alex regarded me, wide-eyed. "Eat, rather than shop? Are you insane?"

I smiled involuntarily. *Wow.* That clinched it. I loved these guys.

We made it back to the bus just in time for both men to receive their coordinates from Mom and traipse off into the great unknown for ten short minutes with their individual teams. Much to my astonishment, each team finished its search within the allotted time, without any pouting, sniping, or name calling, so we were able to reload the bus and head for Inverness right on schedule. I figured this had to have been an easy find, because everyone seemed to be in a good mood. They were lending their voices to Wally's singalong, chatting each other up across the aisle, and talking to family back home on their cell phones. I guess success bred contentment. Even Isobel Kronk, who'd gone ballistic about Bernice's GPS failure yesterday, seemed happy.

And not just happy.

As she exchanged quips with Cameron Dasher across the aisle, she looked absolutely exuberant.

Almost too exuberant.

And for whatever reason, that worried me.

FOUR

DAD WAS FIRST OFF the bus at our hotel, so he made good use of his time by videotaping everyone else getting off, just in case Mom happened to miss it. I paused in front of him, mugging for the camera like a six-year-old, because seeing Dad wield a piece of photographic equipment reminded me of the silly pictures he'd shot of me on the last family vacation we'd taken together, when I was six years old.

Dad loved travel. He just preferred that other people do it so he wouldn't have to do it himself.

"Hi, Dad." I waved idiotically.

"Hi, hon."

"Having a good time?"

"Yup."

"Are you getting geared up to shoot some jaw-dropping footage of Nessie?"

"Yup."

Our hotel was perched on a grassy hillock overlooking the shores of Loch Ness—a family-owned-and-operated boutique hotel that was undergoing extensive renovations, which explained why we'd been able to scoop up every room in the place.

With sawdust you got a discount.

The advertisement touted the building's importance as a historic landmark dating back to the sixteenth century, but we'd been assured the rooms had been upgraded and indoor plumbing installed since then. The stone exterior gleamed chalk white, with an authentic thatched roof overhead and flower-glutted window boxes adding splashes of color. Loch Ness lay at the bottom of the hill, its rock-ribbed shores surrounded by ancient forests and spotty patches of barren earth, its frigid waters slicing through the glen for twenty-two miles, like a long, severed finger.

"Line up at the front desk to receive your room assignments," announced Wally as we crowded into the lobby with its exposed half-timbers, cozy furniture groupings, and wall plaque claiming that *Mary Queen of Scots Slept Here.* "Dinner is scheduled to be served in the dining room at seven, so let's plan to meet in the library at six-forty-five so Margaret can share today's geocaching results with you. Keeping you in suspense throughout dinner might be hard on your digestive systems. Any questions?"

Cameron Dasher raised his hand. "Does this place rent out watercraft? Canoes? Rowboats? Something that would let us explore the lake on our own?"

"*Uhh*—" Wally shot a questioning look at the clerk manning the front desk.

"Mrs. Dalrymple considered boat rentals," the young woman informed us in a lilting burr, "but decided against it. Ye wouldn't believe the cost."

"What about inner tubes?" asked Dolly Pinker. "They're all the rage at indoor water parks. Floating down a concrete canal in a giant inner tube gives you such a wonderful sense of what the great outdoors can be like without insects flying up your nose."

Isobel Kronk snorted her disdain. "Inner tubes are for sissies. I want horsepower between my legs." She sidled a provocative look at Cameron. "Jet skis are the only way to go. *Vroooom!*"

"Pills Etcetera is having an End of Summer Clearance Sale on waterwings," Margi added helpfully. "Aisle six, if anyone's interested."

"The boats weren't the difficulty," confessed the clerk. "It was the pier. There's a drop-off so near the shore that a dock can't be anchored without using deepwater equipment. Mrs. Dalrymple said if that be the case, they might as well drill fer oil, but of course, she wasn't wanting ta do that." She made eye contact with every guest before lowering her voice to a dramatic whisper. "As ye might imagine, she was leery of whit she might be disturbing at the bottom of the loch."

A hush fell over the lobby. Hearing tales of the Loch Ness monster was one thing; standing near the creature's legendary domain was something else entirely.

"How deep is that drop-off?" Dick Teig inquired.

"Around seventy-six meters."

"What's that in English?" he asked.

"Approximately two hundred-fifty feet," said Etienne.

Whistles. Gasps. Eye-widening.

Dick Teig was disbelieving as he glanced out the lobby windows toward the manicured lawn that swept toward the loch. "You're telling me that a few feet from the end of the lawn down there, the water is two hundred-fifty feet deep?"

The clerk smiled enigmatically. "It's one of the more shallow spots. Mrs. Dalrymple is fond of telling her guests that Loch Ness is so deep—eight hundred feet in some places—that the entire population of the world could fit into it three times over."

More gasps. Collective jaw dropping.

Lucille waved her hand in the air. "Does that calculation take into account the population of the United States? It might not be all that obvious to you foreigners, but we Americans tend to be a bit … bigger boned than folks in the rest of the world."

"She means we're fatter," said Bernice.

"It's not important how many bodies fit into the lake," Wally interrupted in his tour director's voice, "as long as none of the bodies belong to any of you. I'll caution you to heed the warning though. If you wander down to the loch to take pictures, be sure to watch your footing near the water's edge. The grass can be slippery, and that first step is a doozey."

As the desk clerk began dispensing room keys, I sauntered over to the lobby's enormous picture windows for a better view of the infamous lake. A brick walkway zigzagged down the hill from the hotel's patio to the shoreline, where umbrellaed tables and Adirondack chairs awaited guests hoping to catch that once-in-a-lifetime glimpse of Nessie. But I saw no cleverly disguised guardrails, no quaint fences, no neatly clipped hedges to prevent people from tripping over their shoelaces and stumbling headlong into the lake, with its two-hundred-and-fifty-foot plunge to the bottom.

Unh-oh. This wasn't good.

I guess the hotel felt obliged to keep the view from the Adirondack chairs unobstructed for visiting tourists, just in case Nessie decided to rear her much celebrated head.

My stomach executed a slow roll as I considered the potential for disaster. My only saving grace was that the wind had picked up and the blue sky was being devoured by billowing, soot-gray clouds that threatened an evening of mist and unrelenting rain.

Hallelujah.

I arrived at the library fifteen minutes early to find most of the group already there. Several optimists idled at the windows with binoculars pressed to their eyes, apparently trying to convince themselves that the loch was visible through the fog, while others staked out spots in front of the floor-to-ceiling bookshelves, perusing titles whose leather spines looked to have been bound about the time Gutenberg invented the printing press. I didn't see Mom, but Dad was here with his camcorder, capturing the heart-pounding action of people staring at fog and old books. Nana, George, and the rest of their geocaching team were gathered in a far corner, locked in heated discussion over something that was causing Bill Gordon's already florid cheeks to grow even redder. Etienne and Wally were still in the lobby, kibitzing with the front desk clerk about where we should go tomorrow should our Loch Ness cruise be canceled due to foul weather.

"Hey, check this out," Isobel Kronk instructed us, apropos to nothing. She hovered over an over-sized tome that she'd set on one of the room's many reading tables, her forefinger stabbing a line of text halfway down the page. "According to this *History of the Scottish Clans*, the chieftain of my family's clan became the Duke of Argyll. Pretty impressive, huh? Wait 'til my kid hears there's royalty in the family. He might have to switch from drinking beer to something more snooty, like wine coolers."

"Is the Duke of Argyll the fella who started that nice line of clothing and accessories for both men and women?" asked Margi. "I love his socks."

"The Duke of Argyll?" Bill Gordon's voice boomed out from the corner, prompting all eyes to swivel in his direction.

He was ruggedly built in an "over-the-hill" kind of way, with a bristly red beard, chest as broad as a beer barrel, and a head full of coarse, ginger-colored hair that was shot through with silver. His brows stretched in wild disarray above his eyes, like thorns in an overgrown thicket. His fists were big as mallets. His body language hinted that he was long on pomposity and short on patience, which probably explained why he looked as if he were about to set his hair on fire.

Breaking away from his team, he strode to the center of the room, where he drilled Isobel with a menacing look. "That would mean your clan name is Campbell."

Stella Gordon plopped onto a settee and tossed her head back, offering the heavens a mournful look. "Here we go."

Margi gasped. "Are you the soup people, too? Oh, my goodness. I *love* your new cheeseburger chowder with loaded baked potato flavor." She squinted thoughtfully. "Or is that the generic brand?"

"My maiden name was Campbell," Isobel said proudly, her gaze fixed on Bill. "What of it?"

"If you're a Campbell, you're no friend of mine."

Isobel looked him up and down, as if he were an engine that needed crushing. "Gee, pops, I'm devastated. But the feeling's mutual, I'm sure."

Bill stood statue-still for a moment before whirling around to address the room in a voice that swelled with righteous anger. "Shall I tell you the tale of the crooked Campbells?"

Unh-oh. I was getting a bad vibe that the tale of the crooked Campbells was going to be a lot more grisly than the tale of say, Benjamin Bunny.

"They're land-grubbing charlatans," he spat, "from the first to the last. There was never a good one born, and not nearly enough that's dead. They instigated. They persecuted. They outright lied. And the highlands ran red with blood because of them."

Isobel braced her fists on the table, eyes slatted, lips pinched. "I wasn't alive back then, and neither were you, so here's a little advice. GET OVER IT."

"The Gordons will never get over it! Hating Campbells is in our blood. We'll never forget Glen Coe, or Argyll's betrayal, or the massacre at Culloden. We know you for what you are, you traitorous, murdering sons of bi—"

"Mom should be here at any minute," I broke in, glancing desperately toward the door. "So if you'd all please find a seat, we'll be ready to hear the results when she—"

"Where are you digging this crap up?" Isobel shot back at Bill. "Glen Coe? Culloden? Who's ever heard of this stuff?"

Stella tossed her head back, groaning. "You should attend one of their family reunions. It's all they talk about."

"You have the nerve to stand there and tell me you've never heard of Glen Coe?" Bill accused. "You've never heard how Campbell foot-soldiers repaid the hospitality of the MacDonalds by slaughtering every man jack of them? Not on the battlefield, mind you. They didn't fight like real men. They slew them as they rose from their beds, unaware and unarmed. And when they were done with the men, they punished the womenfolk and their babes by burning every house in the glen, leaving them with no food or shelter, in the middle of winter. Leaving them to die in the ice and snow. But the Campbells didn't care about innocent children, the bloody savages. They couldn't stop boasting about what they'd done." His tone grew ominous, his eyes threatening. "There's a special place in Hell for you and your kin."

"My mother was a MacDonald," Dolly Pinker announced with a stunned expression that deteriorated into utter contempt as she regarded Isobel. "Are you telling me that *her* relatives murdered *my* relatives?"

"Jud*aaa*s *priest*," snapped Isobel. "Does anyone else want to crawl out of the woodwork to pile on?"

"Did this happen this past year?" asked Helen, shock in her voice. "Because I don't recall seeing it on cable news, unless Dick was flipping through the channels so fast I missed it."

"February twelfth," droned Stella as she stared mindlessly at the ceiling. "Sixteen ninety-two."

"Three hundred years ago?" cried Isobel.

"Don't try to spin your way out of it," raged Dolly. "You're guilty. All you Campbells are guilty. Ruthless lowlifes. I knew there was a reason I didn't like you."

A muscle bunched in Isobel's jaw—kind of like the thing that happens to the Incredible Hulk just before he explodes out of his shirt and turns green. "Don't take this the wrong way," she seethed, looking Dolly straight in the eye, "but if my relatives knocked off your relatives, they probably had good reason."

Dolly's mouth fell open. Her eyes bulged. She began to wheeze. I didn't know if she was expressing indignation or having an asthma attack, but I didn't dare wait to find out.

"Okey-dokey," I jumped in. "How are we doing finding those seats?" I hurried toward the library table, directing people toward nearby chairs and sofas as I ran interference between Isobel and Bill.

"Would this be a good time to remind folks of an old French proverb?" asked Cameron Dasher as he joined Isobel at the table. He gave her hand an encouraging squeeze. "'He who boasts of his descent is like the potato; the best part of him is under ground.'"

Stella Gordon's laugh ricocheted through the room like a misfired bullet. "Did you hear that, Bill? He just compared you to an Irish root crop. Sounds like he infiltrated one of your family reunions."

"No, no," Cameron corrected, brushing off the accusation. "I'm merely suggesting how pointless it is to use one's relatives as bludgeons to beat up on perfectly wonderful people like Isobel. It's pretty counterproductive, don't you think? What does it accomplish?"

Bill speared Dasher with a hostile look, his gaze settling on the name tag pinned to Dasher's shirt. "Your name's Cameron? Well, aren't you a sorry excuse for a Cameron—siding with the likes of a crooked Campbell against a gallant Gordon and a brave MacDonald. We have a name for traitors like you."

Cameron remained so cool and unflappable, he reminded me of a talking version of my dad. "Hate to disappoint you, but I don't have an ounce of Scottish blood in me. My parents were both photographers. Camera? Cameron? Get the connection?"

"Of course, he does," I quipped as I locked my hand around Bill's arm and steered him across the floor to safer territory. "Sit," I insisted, plunking him down on the sofa between Nana and Tilly.

"So are the Campbells the soup people or not?" asked Margi. "Doesn't anyone besides me want to know?"

"Well, would you look at that," Nana marveled as she glanced toward the doorway.

Erik and Alex marched into the library like the color guard at a sports event, jaws set, eyes forward, shoulders squared, looking as comfortable wearing their kilts as my ex-husband had been wearing my undies. They'd selected matching white oxford shirts to complement their tartans, and finished off the look with furry sporrans to hold their personal effects, spotless hiking boots, and short-bladed knives stuffed down their calf-high socks. When they reached the center of the room, they posed straight-faced for several seconds before Erik broke out of character and winked. "Gentlemen, you would not *believe* how liberating it is not having to adjust the 'boys' all the time to get them back in alignment. This is what I call real comfort. Shame on you ladies for keeping it a secret for so long. A guy would have to be crazy to squeeze into flat-front pants again after enjoying this kind of freedom."

"Right," scoffed Bernice. "Let us know how your 'boys' fare after you give 'em a taste of support hose with tummy control."

"Campbell tartan?" Bill roared as he leaped off the sofa, spittle flying from his mouth like water from a garden sprinkler. "I'd rather pluck out my eyes than look at Campbell plaid!"

Stunned silence ensued, followed by quiet reflection. "I'd rather eat dirt than watch another one of Helen's stupid chick flicks," mused Dick Teig.

"I'd rather die than let Grace wax my chest again," confessed Dick Stolee.

Note to self: *expand present portfolio by investing heavily in men's health service.*

"Get out of my sight. The two you!" Bill raved, his ears turning as red as cooked beets. "If you don't, I swear I'll come over there and rip those tartans off your bodies so fast, you won't know what hit you."

"Hey!" Nana grabbed his belt and yanked him back onto the sofa. "You're blockin' my view."

Erik wagged a cautioning finger at Bill. "You better watch out what you pray for, buttercup. I bet you wouldn't be so anxious to rip off our togs if you knew our undercarriages were"—he paused for maximum effect—"X-rated."

Gasping from the ladies. Eye rolling from the men.

A half-dozen snack-size bottles of hand sanitizer flew through the air at them. "You'll probably need those," said Margi.

"They're not wearin' no undershorts?" spluttered Nana.

"They're being historically accurate," Tilly asserted as she craned her neck for a better look. "It wasn't uncommon for highlanders to go about their daily business with their undercarriages fully vented. In fact, trousers might have been considered too confining, especially if one believes certain rumors that have been passed down through the centuries."

"What kind of rumors?" I asked.

"Typical testosterone-driven hype. The early Scots were reputed to have equipment under their hoods that was so excessively… manly, some of the more impressive fixtures might have ended up as exhibits in scientific museums if someone had thought to preserve them."

"No kiddin'?" Offering Bill Gordon a contrite look, Nana seized a fistful of his shirt and propelled him back to his feet. "Sorry about the misunderstandin'. You go right ahead and rip them kilts off those young fellas. Just give me a sec to turn on my camera."

"I'm here at last!" Mom dashed into the room all aflutter, armed with her laptop, her notebook, and a file folder full of papers. "The suspense must be killing you, so I'll get right to it." Dumping everything on the nearest reading table, she cleared a space for her laptop, powered it up, consulted her notebook, then took a deep breath in preparation for—

Her eyes strayed to the sudden clutter. Unable to stop herself, she trailed a finger across one of the glossy magazines she'd shoved out of the way. "*Ew*," she cooed, "current periodicals." She did a quick scan, smiling beatifically. "And they're not in order."

I could hear her heart go pittypat all the way across the room.

"Dinner's in twelve minutes," carped Isobel Kronk. "Could we get this show on the road before they start serving?"

"You bet," said Mom, forcing her attention back to the computer. "Here we are. The results are as follows, and I'll ask you to please withhold your applause until the very end. Team Yes We Can, formerly known as Team Five, went first. I'm thrilled to report they redeemed themselves admirably after their disappointing first try and found the cache in an astounding six minutes and thirty-five seconds."

Isobel pumped her fist as relief and satisfaction played across her face, making her harsh features almost attractive. "What'd I tell you?" Cameron encouraged his teammates. "Aren't you happy we didn't give up?"

Dolly and Bernice didn't look too happy, but I figured their sullenness had little to do with cache results and everything to do with where Cameron had chosen to sit—shoulder to shoulder with Isobel at the library table.

Mom continued her tally. "Team One, still known as Team One until further notice, went second, and they found the cache in seven minutes flat." She offered a heartfelt smile to the group. "For those of you who are unaware, my mother is on Team One. Wave to everyone so they can see who you are, Mom."

Oh, God.

"Nepotism!" yelled Bernice. "Blatant nepotism!"

Mom inched her gaze back to the magazines, her internal struggle between duty and desire playing out on her face until she looked as if she were about to implode. "I'm sorry. Would anyone mind if I alphabetize these periodicals before we continue? It should only take a few minutes. They're just so … out of order."

"Everyone minds," shouted Dolly Pinker. "Just get on with it, would you?"

"Nepotism!" Bernice accused more emphatically. "Blatant nepotism!"

Dick Teig shot her "the look." "We heard you the first time, Bernice. We're ignoring you."

Ignore Bernice? Damn. Why hadn't *I* thought of that?

Returning reluctantly to the business at hand, Mom picked up where she'd left off, at warp speed, in one long breath. "Teams-TwoThreeandFourfoundthethingtoo. Goodjob. We'redonehere." She slammed down the cover of her laptop and scooped up the magazines, cradling them in her arms while she shuffled through them.

Mumbling. Confused looks. Blank expressions.

"What'd she say?" asked Stella Gordon.

"She said everyone found the cache," Dad explained from behind the viewfinder of his camcorder.

"She's lying!" Isobel Kronk hammered her fists on the table as she sprang from her chair, frothing with outrage. "None of you found it. You couldn't have!"

"My team sure found it," argued Dick Stolee.

"Did not," countered Isobel.

"Did so," challenged Dick Teig.

Boos. Shouting. Cat calls.

I let out my signature whistle, sending hands flying upward to muffle distressed ears. When the room was quiet again, I nodded. "Thank you." I leveled a look at Isobel. "Would you mind telling us why you think no team other than yours found the cache?"

"Sure," Isobel said without apology. "Because I took it."

FIVE

"YOU WHAT?" DOLLY PINKER shot to her feet, hands on hips, condemnation in her voice. "Oh, my God. You *cheated*?"

"It wasn't cheating," Isobel defended. "It was a simple maneuver to level the playing field."

"In Iowa we call that cheating," said Dick Teig.

"In Wisconsin they call it the gubernatorial agenda," said Osmond.

"Don't you dare give me any grief," Isobel fired back at Dolly. "I did it for the team. *Our* team. Remember? The one you wanted to desert after we got screwed out of our first find because of *her*?" She stabbed a menacing finger at Bernice. "How else are we supposed to stay in the hunt?"

"By playing by the rules," Cameron announced flatly.

"Bull!" Using her finger as a gavel, Isobel pounded out her points on the table in front of Cameron. "Don't give me rules. Do mortgage companies play by the rules? Do politicians play by the rules? No! No one plays by the rules anymore, so spare me the sanctimonious lectures. Stretching the rules is what it's about these days."

"I've heard enough." Dolly fell back into her chair. "She's off the team."

"I'm not aware that anyone died and put you in charge," Isobel challenged.

I guessed this was where I should step in. Great.

"Okay, then," I said as I clasped my hands in a gesture meant to evoke the wisdom of King Solomon. Not everyone would make the connection, but I figured it looked more self-assured than scratching my head. "*Uhh …* we've kept the rules of the contest deliberately simple to avoid confusion, and to be perfectly honest, we never thought to write up a contest manual because we never expected anyone to … *uhh …* modify the existing rules."

"They never expected anyone to *cheat,*" Bernice translated.

"So this will be a test case," I continued, directing a look at Bernice that cautioned her to "zip it." "I'll have to explain the circumstances to my husband and Wally, and then the three of us will have to decide what we should do about the situation, if anything."

"I think she should be booted off our team," Lucille Rassmuson piped up.

"To hell with that!" fumed Bill Gordon. "The entire *team* should be booted. No contest for them."

"Don't even think it," Dolly warned. "The four honest members of our team don't deserve to be punished for the flagrant rule violation by one dishonest member. Isobel needs to take a hike, but if you try to come after the rest of us, I'll be making an overseas call to my lawyer. Our government has rules prohibiting discrimination. In case you weren't aware, it's un-American."

"We're not *in* America," taunted Bill, "so the rules don't apply. Besides which, how do I know any of you are *real* Americans? Can you prove it? Do you have the right documentation?"

"What's the wrong documentation?" questioned Margi.

Yup. This was going well.

"I like to win just as much as the next guy," Cameron explained to the rest of the room, embarrassment evident in his voice, "but not like this. What were you thinking, Isobel? I don't want to side with the opposition, but fair is fair. You've probably earned our team some kind of penalty, but I'm not sure what."

His words found their mark, because Isobel Kronk suddenly looked as if she'd been slapped, and slapped hard. I watched her bottom lip quiver for a heartbeat before she brushed aside the obvious hurt by acting as if she were immune to it. "Some friend you turned out to be, *Cam*"—his name shooting out of her mouth like a nail out of a nail gun. "Are you sure you're not Scottish? Because you seem to have a real aptitude for stabbing people in the back."

"Don't you dare criticize Cameron," Dolly chided. "He found that last cache singlehandedly, in record time, despite the flak that our resident bellyacher was throwing at him."

Lucille smiled broadly. "She's talking about Bernice."

"Okay, time out." I motioned for quiet as I navigated my way around furniture and guests to take center stage. "I'm confused. If Cameron's team found the cache first, and Isobel removed it—"

"Stole it!" Bill Gordon bellowed.

"—*removed* it from its hiding place so no one else could find it, then what, exactly, did the other four teams find?"

Everyone flew into motion at the same time, digging into pockets, purses, and fanny packs to retrieve their cameras and mobile phones. Alex Hart was quickest on the draw, yanking his camera out of his new sporran with the skill of a marsupial yanking a joey out of its pouch. He punched a button then handed the camera over to me. "I can't speak for anyone else, but that's what our team found."

I studied the screen, trying to analyze what I was looking at. "A shoebox-shaped plastic container."

"It was one a them real good ones," offered Nana. "The kind what won't decompose even if you nuke it."

"The register was noteworthy," said Tilly as she regarded the photo she'd taken with her own Smartphone. "It was a glittery pink notebook, with kitten and pony stickers covering the front, which might indicate that the person who placed it there was a teenage girl."

"Or not," I quipped as I cradled my hands around the metallic pink housing of Alex's camera.

"I got a good shot of the page we signed and dated," said George, brandishing his phone in evidence. "Marion did the honors for Team One because she has the best penmanship. She even managed to jot down a nice comment about the scenery."

"I took a picture of the comment," enthused Dick Teig as he accessed his zoom function. "It says, 'Out.'" He held it up so everyone could see.

"I have a picture of that, too!" exclaimed Margi. "Do you think it's code for something?"

"It's code for—there wasn't no time to write no more, so I had to leave off the last half of the word," said Nana.

"Which was—?" I asked.

"Outstandin.'"

"I think 'outlandish' would have been a better word," said Dick Teig.

"Outdoorsy," countered Grace. "Definitely, outdoorsy."

"You're both wrong," quibbled Helen. "'Outdated' is the word you want. I mean, didn't you notice? The whole town looked like it was about a thousand years old."

Tilly stared at her, deadpan. "That's because … it is."

"Is the pink register the only thing everyone found in the container?" I persisted.

"Our team found a travel size bottle of Hog Wild hand sanitizer," Grace revealed. "Three guesses where *that* came from."

Margi lifted her shoulders and smiled impishly. "Seemed like the polite thing to do. Kind of like a little hostess gift."

"I could have used some sanitizer after I pried that container out of its hiding place," admitted Dick Stolee as he inspected his fingernails. "It was a great location, but those rocks were gross. Have you ever seen so much slime-green algae in your life?"

Bernice sat up in her chair as if she'd been poked by a cattle prod. "Rocks? What rocks?"

Erik Ishmael leaned over in his chair to show her the image on his camera screen. "These rocks."

She studied the photo for a half-second before dissolving into a fit of snarky laughter. "Hate to break it to you losers, but the container wasn't hidden near any rocks. Your team went to the wrong place."

"Did not," snapped Margi.

"Did so," mocked Bernice. "*This* is where the container was hiding." She held up her phone, flashing the picture to anyone sitting close enough to see. "In a hollowed-out tree trunk camouflaged by lots of weeds. Weeds, not rocks."

"Shoot." Helen regarded the photo on her Smartphone in dejection. "I've got rocks."

"Me, too," lamented Osmond.

"So do I," said Alice Tjarks. She sighed. "Does this mean we didn't find the cache after all?"

How did the saying go? If disinformation is repeated often enough, people are brainwashed into thinking it's the truth? "Did you sign the pink register?" I asked Alice.

She nodded. "I was the official signatory for Team Two. I even took a picture. See?" She turned her Smartphone outward. "My signature, the date, and the time. And you can see where Team One signed just above me, with Marion's comment."

"Did you happen to take a picture of Team Five's signature?" I pressed. "If they were first up, they would have signed before you."

Alice shook her head. "The entry above Marion's wasn't written in English."

"It was written in Lithuanian," Tilly spoke up. "Left by two geocachers named Jadvyga and Pranciskus. Rough translation, 'These rocks are very slimy.'"

"Aha!" I lasered a look at Bernice. "So your team didn't sign a register?"

"There *was* no register," Dolly answered for her. "There was a box in a tree trunk, and no register, which I thought was odd, but now that we know people are stealing things, should we be surprised?" She directed a haughty look at Isobel, who flipped her long gray hair over her shoulder before bracing her fists on the table, looking supremely smug.

"Would you like to know *why* there was no register in the box?" Isobel asked. "Have you figured it out yet? Because our intrepid leader—the guy who found the cache *singlehandedly,* in record time, took us to the wrong location. Nice going, Cam." She slapped him on the back. "You found the wrong damn container."

"No. That's not possible." He looked utterly bewildered. "I . . . I followed the right coordinates. I—"

"Turkey," Isobel jeered.

"Point of order!" Lucille Rassmuson raised her hand, looking as puzzled as Cameron. "Which container did Isobel steal? The one with the pink register or the one with the knife?"

I leveled a quizzical look at the members of Team Five. "Knife?"

"Don't get your panties in a wad," Isobel shot back in a growly voice. "It wasn't real."

"It looked real to me," argued Dolly.

"That's because you're a putz."

If Dolly's eyes hadn't been weighted by so much volumizing mascara, they would have flown out of their sockets. "*I'm* a putz? Oh, that's rich, coming from the freaking genius who decided to rig the contest by stealing the wrong container. You want to find the real putz? Try looking in a mirror."

"I have a makeup compact if you'd like to borrow it," Margi offered helpfully.

"Hold it!" Lucille heaved herself to her feet, making herself visible to everyone in the room, while at the same time insuring she was first out of the blocks in the upcoming race for the dining room. "So if Isobel stole the wrong container, whose container *did* she steal? Won't the owner be mad when he goes back to get it and discovers it's missing?"

"No one's going back for it," Isobel ranted. "It's a piece of junk. Who wants a crummy box with a crummy knife inside anyway?"

"You mean, besides you?" asked Bernice. "How do we know you haven't bamboozled us? How do we know your crummy knife isn't worth a whole lot of money that you don't want to share with the rest of us?"

"Cameron found it singlehandedly!" Dolly reminded us as she slanted a flirtatious smile at Dasher. "If it turns out to be worth a fortune, he's the one who should receive all the proceeds. And then he can dole out whatever monetary settlement he chooses to the team members he deems worthy." She gave her hair a little pouf. "You know. The ones who aren't thieves."

"Morons," grumbled Isobel as she reached for her zebra print backpack.

Uh-oh. This wasn't good. Not only was Isobel stealing other people's property, she was stealing Bernice's lines.

She slapped the backpack onto the table, unzipped the closure, and riffled through the contents like a petulant child before yanking out a metal box that was the size and shape of a hardback novel. She slammed it down in front of her. "Here it is. The ill-gotten treasure that's worth a fortune. Good luck finding someone dumb enough to pay you."

The metal was so eroded with rust that it looked to be suffering from a fatal case of psoriasis.

"Looks pretty old," I said as I stepped closer for a better view.

"It took a little elbow grease to pry the lid off," said Cameron. "It wasn't completely rusted shut, but it was getting there. I'd guess it hadn't been opened in a really long time."

"Is the knife still inside?" I asked Isobel.

She wrestled the lid off and banged it onto the table with a noisy clatter. "The knife," she said, eying my dad sourly as he tip-toed in for a close-up shot.

"Do you mind if I pick it up?" I asked.

"I don't give a flip what the hell you do with it." She gave the box a shove toward the edge of the table. "It's not doing me any good. You can give it away for all I care."

"I'll take it!" Dolly and Bernice cried out at the same time.

I waited indulgently while Dad stood over the box, zooming in, and out, and in, and out. "Done?"

"Yup," he said, panning seamlessly to a floor shot as he skulked off in Mom's direction.

I plucked the knife out of the box, surprised by its heft. The blade was as long as my hand, double-edged, and narrowed into a point like a Viking spear. The hilt was intricately carved into a pattern that mimicked the corkscrew twists of a licorice stick. An inch below the hilt, a band of uncarved wood circled the grip, its smoothness marred by a series of deep scratches.

"Hold it up so the rest of us can see it!" demanded Bill Gordon.

I elevated it above my head and rotated in a slow circle.

"Well, would you look at that?" marveled Nana.

"Is something about the dagger familiar to you?" Tilly asked her.

"Nope. I was just noticin' that the fog's lifted."

"Have you found the 'Made in China' designation on that thing yet?" Stella Gordon wisecracked.

I examined the dagger more closely, noticing that the blade was tarnished in long streaks near the tip—like sterling silver in need of a good polishing. Oddly, though, the oxidized streaks were rust brown instead of gun-metal gray. "I'm not seeing where it was made anywhere," I confessed, "but it's a great looking knockoff, right down to these smudges that I suspect are supposed to be blood stains. I bet someone used it as a prop for a play or something."

"But why was it stuffed in a tree trunk?" asked Lucille.

I shrugged. "Before there was geocaching, there were scavenger and treasure hunts. Maybe this was an item that the participants never found."

"Didn't I say as much?" squawked Isobel. "It's like a piece of space junk."

Margi sucked in her breath. "You think aliens left it?"

Isobel drilled me with a hard, unflinching look. "I hope this is the end of your interrogation, because whether it is or not, I'm heading for the dining room."

"One more question," I ventured as I returned the dagger to its box. "Out of curiosity, how did you manage to abscond with the cache without your teammates seeing you do it?"

"By lying to us," Dolly accused. "She said her ankle bracelet fell off, so she wanted to run back to look for it."

Isobel fished the bracelet out of her jeans pocket and dangled it from her finger. "It wasn't a lie."

"Hah!" spat Dolly. "You probably broke the clasp yourself, just to have an excuse. Putting it on display proves nothing."

"It proves that Campbells are all cheats and liars," yelled Bill.

"Seven o'clock!" announced Dick Stolee as he launched himself out of his chair. "Soup's on."

Oh, God.

The exodus started with subtle movements—head bobbing, weight shifts, foot shuffling—and gradually erupted into a full-blown stampede as Lucille raced full-throttle for the door with Dick Stolee hot on her heels. I leaped out of the way to avoid being knocked down by the exiting mob, flattening myself against the library table until the room had emptied itself. Etienne and Wally ran into the room like firemen in search of a fire, eyes wild, and breath heavy.

"What was that?" asked Etienne, gasping.

"The Iowa response to the dinner bell." I peeled myself away from the table and dusted off my hands. "They've gotten so much more orderly. I hardly recognize them anymore."

"You call that orderly?" squeaked Wally.

I smiled. "You should have seen them before."

He shook his head. "I'll referee in the dining room. See you in there."

Etienne walked across the room and placed a lingering kiss in the hollow below my earlobe. "In the interest of preserving the health of arthritic knees and fragile hips, do you suppose we might suggest that guests proceed to the dining room with a bit more decorum?"

"Good luck with that."

"I was afraid that might be your response." He lowered his gaze to the table, nodding at the dagger. "A rather fierce-looking bauble. Scotsmen do love their dirks, but the packaging needs updating."

I groaned. "It has a very interesting backstory, which I'll share with you *after* dinner." I replaced the lid then leaned over and blew rust flecks off the surface. "I bet Isobel will be forever cleaning this stuff out of her backpack."

"Excuse me?"

"Nothing. Shall we go in to dinner? I'm in desperate need of a drink."

The hotel dining room had the look of a primeval great hall with its exposed beams, heraldic shields, and wall plaques mounted with the heads of any dead thing sporting antlers. The tables were set for either four or six guests and were strategically arranged to allow great views of the loch from any location on the floor. Most of the guests had staked out their seats already, leaving only a few empty spaces, so Etienne, Wally, and I were going to have to split up, which wasn't a bad idea logistically.

Maybe the three of us could preserve peace among the feuding factions.

"You have two choices," Etienne said in a low voice. "You can either sit with your mother, or Bernice. Do you have a preference, or would you rather flip for it?"

"I'd rather sit with you."

"Not an option."

I ranged a look over the dining area. "I could sit with Dad. Do you see him?"

"He's not at the table with your mother."

"No kidding? Wow. He escaped. How'd he manage that?"

"Actually, bella, I don't see your father anywhere."

"He's not here?" I looked left and right. "That's odd. I wonder where he is?"

"I GOT IT ON TAPE!" Dad cried as he charged into the room, waving his camcorder. "I couldn't believe it! Right there! Right in front of me!" He skidded to a stop, hair mussed, face red, chest heaving with exertion. "I saw Nessie!"

SIX

THE STAMPEDE OUT OF the dining room made the recent stampede *into* the dining room look as if it had happened in slow motion. In the mere blink of an eye, chairs were upended, tables abandoned, goblets toppled, napkins discarded.

"Out of my way!"

"Ow! Get off my foot!"

"Move it! It's almost dark and my camera doesn't have night settings!"

Panting. Shoving. Grunting. Then silence.

Mom and Nana remained at their tables, looking as stupefied by the empty room as they were by Dad's announcement. Dad stood beside me, his knees shaking as badly as his hands. "How about we sit you down?" I said as I grabbed his arm and ushered him to a nearby chair.

Etienne nodded toward the doorway. "Shall I—?"

"Yes! Don't let them out of your sight. And if you see a life preserver along the path, grab it. Someone's probably going to need it."

This was one of the unexpected benefits of marriage—knowing what your spouse was going to say even before he said it. I didn't know the physiological mechanics of how this phenomenon happened, but I figured it would be a great perk fifty years from now, when neither one of us could remember what we were about to say.

"Geez," choked Dad as he sank into the chair, his eyes glassy with shock. "Geez." He gave his head a shake. "I've never seen anything like it. Not in my entire life. It scared the bejeebers out of me."

This was a pretty strong statement coming from Dad, who was completely fearless when dealing with truly frightening stuff like spiders, snakes, and dentists. I hovered over him, hoping I could restore calm by patting his shoulder. "You want to show me the goods?"

"Sure, hon, but—" He slid the wrist strap off his hand, shoved a dinner plate aside, set the camera on the table, then stared at it as if he were a botanist observing a new species of plant. "I only know how to record. I haven't learned how to play anything back yet."

"Well, you've come to the right place." I'd become something of an expert at solving the complex technical and electronic problems that arose with guests' ever-changing audio and video equipment. The secret was knowing how to ask the right questions.

I shot a desperate look at Nana. "Do you know how to operate this thing?"

"Nope. But if it's got a battery, I can probably figure it out."

"I know I packed the owner's manual," said Mom as she riffled through her fannypack. "I thought reading it might help your father fall asleep on the plane ride over, but I don't remember him giving it back to me." A look of horror crept into her eyes. "Oh, my God, Bob, I hope you didn't leave it in the seat pocket in front of you."

Nana toddled over, grabbed the camcorder, flipped open the touch screen, then studied it for a long moment before fiddling with some widgets and buttons that produced a soft *whirring* sound. "Now we're cookin'," she said, waiting for a good portion of the tape to rewind before hitting the Stop button. She looked over at Mom. "You wanna see the creature what's been hauntin' Loch Ness for thousands of years?"

"The three of you go ahead," Mom insisted as she dumped the contents of her fannypack onto the table. "Bob's manual has to be here someplace. I'm just going to double check real quick."

"*Mom.*" My voice became a high-pitched squeak. "It's the Loch Ness monster."

"Which makes it doubly important for me to find the manual." She began sorting through her stash of papers with her usual systematic thoroughness. "If your father becomes famous, we're going to have to know how to download the tape to the computer so we can post it on YouTube."

Dad nodded his agreement, apparently delighted by the idea. "What's YouTube?"

"It's little videos of people's pets, weddin' receptions, and summer vacations," said Nana as she set the camcorder back on the table. "Kinda like TV shows what forgot to add plots." She pressed the Play button.

I squeezed Dad's arm and held my breath, beside myself with excitement.

Pavement. Shoes. Dad's shoes. Dad's shoes standing on the pavement. Car engines revving in the background. Voices. A horn tooting. Dad's shoes walking over the pavement. Over a curb. Over a crack in the pavement. Past a patch of grass.

I squinted at the screen, waiting for the money shot. "Obviously not the monster yet."

Dad looked perplexed. "Did I shoot this? I'm going to have to work on content."

Bluejeans. Dad's bluejeans. Dad's bluejeans standing on a bridge with the sounds of rushing water below.

"That's gotta be the bridge what we seen in Braemar," said Nana. "You can tell on account of it sounded like we was standin' on Niagara Falls."

Dad gaped at the screen, looking more confused by the minute. "Where's my footage of Nessie?"

"It's probably there someplace," I encouraged as we were treated to a stationary image of the floral upholstery covering the back of our bus seats. "I bet you just got a little mixed up in these shots and switched the camera off when it was supposed to be on, and on when it was supposed to be off. This happens to *everyone* when they're using a new camcorder for the first time. Doesn't it, Nana?"

She stared at me as if I had two heads.

"You just wait and see," I continued. "You probably got yourself back on track without even knowing it."

Green screen. Bouncing green screen. The sleeve of Dad's green John Deere jacket. Dad swinging his hand back and forth. Dad making me dizzy with the back and forth thing.

Okay then. Big negatory on the getting back on track theory.

"Dang. This is brutal," said Nana as she pressed the Fast Forward icon on the touchscreen.

Bricks. A brick walkway. Dad's shoes running on the brick walkway. Panting. A hideous bubbly, gurgling noise that sounded more ferocious than the dreaded screech of a prehistoric raptor.

"Ohmigod!" I cried. "Was that Nessie? Is that what she sounds like?"

Dad shook his head. "It's my stomach. I'm pretty hungry."

Blue screen.

I looked at Nana, startled. "That's it?"

She picked up the camcorder and punched Fast Forward, to no avail. "That's it. End of tape."

"The end?" Dad sat bolt upright in his chair, as if electrified. "But it can't be the end. Where's Nessie? I got a clear shot of her. I know I did. I even zoomed in for a close-up." He took the camera from Nana and snugged his eye against the lens. "She's gotta be in here somewhere."

"It's like Emily said," Nana agreed. "You was in Standby mode when you was s'posed to be recordin', and you was recordin' when you was s'posed to be in Standby. User error." She slapped him on the back. "It'll getcha every time."

"But if you saw her once, there's an excellent chance you might see her again," I chirped in an attempt to cheer him up.

He nodded in slow motion, face glum, voice dispirited. "I suppose." He set the camera down in front of himself and patted it wistfully. "She had lovely eyes for a monster."

"Found it!" whooped Mom. She popped out of her chair and rushed over to us, gripping a small booklet in her fist. "I said a prayer to Saint Anthony. Works every time. So—" She was all smiles and beatific joy as she clutched the manual to her bosom. "Do you have something to show me?"

A troupe of wait staff paraded into the dining room at just that moment, laden with trays that smelled suspiciously like dinner. Greeted by an empty dining room, however, the lead waiter slowed his steps in apparent confusion, which caused the waiter behind him to pull up short, the waitress behind that guy to lose control of her tray, and the last guy in line to run full speed into her back, setting into motion the mother of all chain reactions.

BOOM! Cruuunch. Clatter, clatter, tinkle.

Plates somersaulted upward, then down. Trays fell. Food spilled. China shattered. The door to the kitchen banged open, spewing out a handful of startled cooks in chefs' hats and aprons.

"*Ooh yah cun'!*" shouted one, hands clapped to his cheeks.

"*Eejits!*" yelled another, hands clapped to his head.

"*Bawheids,*" wailed a third as he danced around the mess.

Nana whipped her cell phone out of her pocket, snapped a picture, and began texting.

"Please tell me you're not planning to post that online," I cautioned her.

"Nope." She pressed Send. "I'm givin' George a head's up that supper's gonna be late."

"There are no dibs on tables!" Wally announced as he marched the group back into the dining room under what looked like obvious protest. "Sit wherever there's an empty chair. If it's not where you were sitting before, enjoy the change of venue."

"It's not completely dark yet," sniped Bill Gordon. "We could have stayed out there a few more minutes."

"You all saw what happened." Wally stepped aside to allow the crowd to pass. "It's too dangerous."

"Only for people who are too dumb to watch where they're going," taunted Bernice.

"Something happened?" I repeated as people streamed by me.

"Where's the guy who saw Nessie?" asked Erik Ishmael. "Hey, bud," he called out when he spied Dad. "Did you get her? Did you really get her?"

"You bet he did," Mom answered proudly. "We're going to post it on YouTube after dinner."

"Bob's going to be famous," predicted Alice Tjarks.

"Not if the rest of us take better pictures tomorrow," Isobel Kronk shot back as she passed by our table. "How do we know if his images are any good? Maybe they're too dark, or too grainy."

"Or too invisible," offered Nana.

"Cameron?" shouted Dolly Pinker. "Where's Cameron? Can you remember where we were sitting?"

"Find a table that'll accommodate all of our team," he instructed. "We need to mend fences and regroup. Again."

Dick Stolee stopped suddenly to regard the mayhem near the kitchen. "Tell me that's not our dinner."

A round of spontaneous applause broke out as Etienne entered the room, escorting a waterlogged Dick Teig, whose shoes were squishing like wet whoopee cushions. His left hand clung to the life buoy that circled his neck in dog collar fashion. His right still clutched his cell phone, which he raised above his head in triumph. "I'd like to thank arthritis-strength ibuprofen for helping me to keep my phone dry." He beamed at his audience, water streaming down his face in rivulets. "I never even came close to losing my grip. Is that stuff effective, or what?"

My mouth came unhinged, falling to my chest. "That's amazing," I marveled as I gaped at him.

"Helen signed him up for that new Treadin' Water for Dummies course at the Senior Center," confided Nana. "Probably saved his life."

"I'm talking about the life preserver." I gawked at the ring buoy circling his neck. "How'd he ever fit it over his head?"

"She absconded with the wrong container?" Etienne couldn't disguise the amusement in his voice.

"It's not funny!" I slid my toes down the long, bare sinews of his leg, tickling the downy hairs of his shin. "The other guests are very upset. They're demanding Isobel's ejection from the team, the team's ejection from the contest, and Isobel's head on a platter. When we wake up in the morning, we could be facing a full-fledged rebellion." I snuggled against his flank, burrowing my head into his naked shoulder. "Whose idea was this contest anyway?"

The kitchen staff had taken so long preparing backup meals after the tray fiasco that by the time we finished dessert and coffee, people were already nodding off, including Wally. So we arranged to meet him before breakfast to discuss the Isobel controversy, then headed up to our own room, where it took us less than a minute to brush our teeth and collapse into bed.

"I believe we both share responsibility for the contest idea," he whispered as he roved idle fingers through my hair. "No more brainstorming for us."

"Seriously, Etienne, how are we going to handle this diplomatically? We're not in this business to punish guests who use poor judgment, but if we just blow it off, we'll be accused of not being fair to the other guests. *Why* do people do things like this?"

"Because they can, darling."

A sliver of light lanced through an opening in our pulled drapes, brightening the ceiling with a ghostlike luminescence. I sighed. "The real fly in the ointment is that what she ended up taking doesn't affect our contest one bit, so do we declare no harm, no foul? Or do we throw the book at her for malicious intent?"

"You've been watching *Law and Order* marathons with your grandmother again, haven't you?"

"Do you suppose Wally has ever run into a situation like this before?"

"He's probably—"

"And if the three of us decide to give Isobel a slap on the wrist, what kind of slap can we give legally? Could she sue us?"

"Emily—"

"*Oh, my God!* What if she makes things so difficult for us that this turns out to be the last trip ever for Destinations Travel? Could she do that?" I stared at him in the dark, my mind spinning like a whirl-a-gig.

"I suspect you might be blowing this a bit out of propor—"

"And what about Dad? What in the world did he see? He obviously saw something because he was more upset than I've ever—*Oof.*"

I expelled a breath as Etienne pressed me down into the bed, his mouth a hair's breadth above mine, his heart pounding against my rib cage. "Emily, darling," he rasped, "you talk too much." He drew my lip into his mouth, then with seductive slowness, worked his way down from there.

The phone woke us from a dead sleep just before dawn. Etienne caught it on the first ring.

"Miceli."

I jackknifed to a sitting position as my stomach launched itself into my windpipe. Etienne listened intently, saying nothing for at least half a minute, while I worried the corner of my mouth.

"Thanks for the call. We'll be right there."

I winced, bracing myself for the worst. "It's bad news, isn't it?"

He nodded. "That was Wally. We no longer have to fear being sued by Isobel Kronk. She's dead."

SEVEN

It HADN'T BEEN AN easy death.

Isobel lay face up on her bed, pajamas twisted around her body in a tortuous mess, eyes fixed on the ceiling, hands clutched around her throat, head thrown back as if her last earthly act had been a desperate gasp for air, mouth contorted, hair wrapped like a scarf around her throat, bedcovers ripped from their moorings. I saw no weapon, no wounds, no blood. I couldn't guess what had killed Isobel Kronk, but whatever the cause, it happened while she was alone in her bed.

Etienne sprang into police inspector mode almost immediately, while I sank down on the luggage bench to stop my knees from wobbling. I'd seen my share of death, but Isobel's struck me as oddly poignant. She'd acted so coarse and rough-edged. Who knew she'd be the type to wear satin pajamas emblazoned with kitties in tutus? Monster trucks, maybe. But kittens in toe shoes? She'd probably bought them especially for the trip, and now she'd never get to wear them again.

Kitty pajamas. They were almost enough to make you forget that she'd stolen the cache, thrown the contest into disarray, and tried to ruin everyone's chances at winning the prize.

Inexplicably, kitty pajamas almost made her seem likeable.

"I've never had a guest ta die in my hotel before," said Morna Dalrymple in a strained voice. "It's very upsetting."

The owner of the Crannach Arms Hotel sat arrow straight in the room's only armchair, her gaze averted from the bed, her hands clasped in an obvious attempt to prevent them from trembling. Wally sat perched on an ottoman beside her, offering moral support, while Etienne lingered by the dresser, doing his best to establish a timeline. "I apologize for the questions," he said in an even tone. "I know it's not the way you'd hoped to begin your day, but I suspect the emergency services people will appreciate any information we can give them when they arrive."

"Seventy-six years on this earth, and I've never begun a day in such a manner."

For a woman of her age, Morna Dalrymple looked as ethereal as a woodland fairy, with silver hair hanging in a braid to her waist, a sharp, upturned nose, oddly pointed ears, and a complexion so milk-bottle white, she would have made Count Dracula look tan in comparison. Her face was remarkable in that she sported neither crow's-feet nor laugh lines, which I suspected meant one of two things: either botox was the number one beauty treatment in Scotland, or she'd somehow managed to live for seventy-six years without ever having to squint or smile.

"Would a glass of water help?" Etienne inquired.

"A shot of whiskey would help, Mr. Miceli, but I'll not trouble ye ta fetch it fer me." She inhaled a deep, calming breath. "Go on now with whit ye were asking."

"You indicated Ms. Kronk called down to the front desk."

"She did. About twenty minutes ago. But the lad on duty couldn't make out whit she was saying fer all her coughing and wheezing, so he left the desk ta run up the two flights of stairs ta her room, and this is how he found her. Poor lad. This is the stuff of nightmares."

"Was the door locked or unlocked when he arrived?"

"Locked. He pounded on her door, but when she didn't answer, he used his special passkey ta let himself in."

"Do you know if he checked the body for a pulse?"

"*Wheest*. He was too frightened ta touch anything. He ran down ta my apartment ta fetch me, but when I saw her with my own eyes, I dared not touch her either." Her voice dropped to a whisper. "I'm superstitious enough ta be fearful of whit killed her."

Etienne waited a beat. "What do you suspect killed her?"

"Demons," she said in a wicked witch vibrato. "It was the work of demons."

I hung my head. *Oh, God.*

"Thank you for sharing that," Etienne said with good grace. "Could you tell me what you did after you decided not to check her vital signs?"

"I called nine-nine-nine, then rang up Mr. Peppers ta tell him whit had happened."

"And where were you when you made the call?"

"Standing there by the bed. The lady had knocked the phone off the nightstand, so I picked it up and set it ta rights again." She threw Etienne a sharp look. "Ye wouldn't expect me ta run all the way down ta the front desk ta make the call when I could as easily use the phone in front of me, would ye?"

Morna Dalrymple had obviously never seen *Law and Order.*

"I'll not quibble with anything you've done, Mrs. Dalrymple," Etienne conceded. "You're to be commended for your quick reactions." He nodded at Wally. "Anything of note in Isobel's medical history form?"

Wally pulled a couple of sheets of paper from the file folder on his lap. "She was apparently claiming to be healthy as a horse because except for her name, age, gender, and the name of her primary care physician, the rest of her medical form is blank. No serious health problems. No age-related conditions. No prescription drugs. No nothing."

"So she would have us believe," said Etienne, sounding unconvinced. "Excuse me for a moment." Crossing the floor in front of me, he disappeared into the bathroom.

"Whit's he doing?" asked Morna, craning her neck to follow him. "I hope he has the decency ta close the door while he does his business."

I exchanged a tentative look with Wally. "What if Isobel lied on her medical form?" I asked, recalling my recent conversation with Stella Gordon aboard the *Britannia.* "What if she had a serious medical condition, but failed to report it because she decided it was her business and no one else's?"

Wally let out a cynical bark. "Like that ever happens."

I narrowed my eyes. "What's that supposed to mean?"

"Everyone lies on their medical forms, Emily. Female guests lie about their age. Male guests lie about their virility drugs. No one is sworn to tell the truth, so everyone lies. It's an ego-boosting thing."

I sucked in my breath, mortified. "My guys would *never* lie. It wouldn't even *occur* to them!" Well, it might occur to Bernice, but even she was bright enough not to fudge something as critical as her medical history.

"Isobel Kronk suffered from some type of allergy," Etienne announced as he rejoined us. "There's an epinephrine pen on the counter in the bathroom."

Wally eyed me pointedly. "What'd I tell you?"

"Oh, my God. She died from anaphylactic shock?" Wait until I saw Stella Gordon. I'd warned her that something like this could happen if guests weren't forthcoming on their medical forms. I'd used this very example!

"It was shock, all right." Morna bobbed her head sagely before ranting in her witch's voice again, "The shock of having a legion of demons fly out of her mouth ta strangle her."

I heaved a sigh. Why did I get the feeling this was going to be a very long day?

"Anaphylactic shock is a possibility." Etienne stood at the foot of the bed, regarding Isobel's lifeless body. "I just wonder what she was allergic to. Food? Latex? Insect bites?"

Morna's features bunched together as if cinched by a drawstring. "What kind of insect bites would ye be talking about?"

"Stings, mostly," said Etienne. "Bees. Wasps. Various types of ants."

"If it makes any difference, the windows were open earlier, but I closed them."

Etienne nodded. "I'll make note of it."

"I don't think you're understanding me," she continued. "The windows were open. We have no bug screens on our windows at the Crannach Arms."

Aha! "So a bee or a wasp could easily have flown in?" I asked.

"Scotsmen have no aversion ta bugs," she said with a hint of snark, "much ta the dismay of our visitors from North America. Window screens are an American contrivance that you'll find nowhere in yer travels here."

Note to self—*Items for immediate purchase: Insect repellent. Fly swatter.*

"But it wasn't a bug that killed the lady," Morna cautioned us.

"Right," said Wally as he heaved himself off the ottoman. "It was demons. If I'm no longer needed here, I'll head back to my room to make a few phone calls. I have a number for her son, so I'll let him know what's happening, and maybe he can fill me in on the allergy situation."

Etienne checked his watch. "Sounds good. I'll wait here for the emergency services unit. It'll give me time to jot down some notes."

"They're coming all the way from Inverness," Morna warned him, "so yer in fer a long wait." She boosted herself to her feet and tightened the belt on her robe with a firm tug. "I'd like ta leave now. Mrs. Miceli and I will be in the library if ye have any more questions."

"We will?" I straightened so fast, my bones cracked.

"Yes, we will. I'm an old lady. I've had a harrowing morning, and I want a cup of tea."

We entered the library as the sun was peeking over the horizon, its light gilding the loch with streaks of liquid gold. I wandered to the window while Morna called the kitchen with instructions to deliver a breakfast tray to the library.

"My dad swears he saw Nessie last night," I said when she'd hung up.

"He's not the first; he won't be the last."

"He said she had lovely eyes for a monster."

Her expression was unreadable. "Did he take a photograph?"

"He tried, but it didn't come out. Technical difficulties."

"I never say this too loudly, Mrs. Miceli," she said as she joined me at the window, "but … it's all a myth."

I reeled backward, as if I'd just been sucker-punched. No Nessie? "But—"

"My family has operated an inn on this spot fer over four hundred years. If a sea creature lived in the loch, don't ye think we would have seen it by now?"

I was hit with the same wrenching disappointment I'd felt when Victoria's Secret announced the discontinuation of their Click Miracle bras. "But—"

"It's because of the tourist dollars." She glanced out the window, raising her hand to shield her eyes against the blinding light that reflected off the loch. "Without Nessie, our local economy would take a tumble ta pre-Nessie days. Do ye have any idea whit that would mean?"

I could take a wild guess. "Goodbye boomtown, hello Greece?"

"Worse."

My jaw dropped. "Worse than Greece?" *Wow*. I didn't think that was possible.

"Ye should talk ta the pensioners in the area. Before the Nessie craze, we couldn't give camera film away. Now we charge a thousand percent markup on four gigabyte memory cards, and everyone's clamoring fer them. Do ye know how much revenue we can earn by raising our profit margins on photographic accessories alone?"

"But… my dad saw *something* last night. He's a practical, no-nonsense, salt of the earth conservative who believes in less government and more tax cuts. He could never be mistaken for someone with a functioning imagination. So if he didn't see Nessie, what *did* he see?"

"It's a myth, Mrs. Miceli. If he claims he saw Nessie, I would encourage him ta spread the word ta the rest of yer tour group. And then perhaps ye would direct them ta the hotel's gift shop, where we're currently running a shoppers' special on six gigabyte memory cards… and bottled beverages."

A rattling *clink* of china drew our attention to the door, where a kilted waiter bounded into the room balancing an oversized breakfast tray above one shoulder. "I hope we've not kept ye waiting too long, Mrs. Dalrymple." He set the tray on the library table, removed a cover from a plate of morning pastries, tidied the linens, then nodded his satisfaction. "Enjoy."

Morna Dalrymple swept her hand toward the table. "Would ye pour, Mrs. Miceli? My hands aren't as steady as I'd like."

While I poured tea, Morna circled around me, pausing in front of Isobel's abandoned metal box. "*Wheesht*. Manky thing. I don't

90

know where it came from, but it belongs somewhere other than my library."

"It came from a tree trunk in Braemar," I said as she removed it from the table.

"Is it yers?" She shook it, raising a clatter like pebbles in a tin cup.

"It belonged to Isobel Kronk. Kind of. Until she realized it wasn't what she thought it was."

"Whit is it?"

"A dagger. Open it. Maybe you can suggest what I should do with it."

She pried off the lid, grimacing at the rust flaking onto her fingers. "She should have left it in the tree trunk." She studied the knife for a long moment before lifting it from the box and turning it in her hand, like a museum curator assessing her latest acquisition.

"The handle is pretty remarkable, isn't it?" I said as I sipped my tea. "The Chinese are doing such innovative things with high polymer plastics."

Morna smoothed her fingertip along the carved spirals of the grip. "It's not plastic. It's wood. Fine-grained wood. Maybe boxwood." She angled it toward the natural light spilling in from the window, her brows winging upward in surprise. "And there are markings."

I nodded. "My guess is, someone attacked it with a penknife. My nephews do stuff like that when they're bored."

She removed a pair of glasses from the pocket of her robe and settled them on her face before crossing to the nearest floor lamp to study the dagger in brighter wattage. "A quick and terrible death … ta any foe … who would possess what is mine."

I peered at her over my teacup. "Excuse me?"

"The inscription below the hilt. 'Tis whit it reads. 'A quick and terrible death ta any foe who would possess what is mine.'"

"There's an inscription?" I stared at her, nonplussed. "Seriously?"

"The letters are a bit blurred, but not so much as ta make the words unreadable."

I set my teacup down and hurried over to her. "So what's wrong with my eyes that I only saw scratches?"

"It's not yer eyes that's the problem. It's yer upbringing. Ye had no one to teach ye the old tongue." She glided her index finger over the marks with a respect bordering on religious awe. "The words aren't in English, Mrs. Miceli. They're in Gaelic."

Well, duh. "So it actually looks authentic to you?" Why did that possibility fill me with such dread? Oh, yeah. Because Bernice and Dolly would probably be at each other's throats trying to claim a piece of it.

"It's more than authentic. Do ye see the owner's name here?" Morna tapped her finger beneath a series of vertical squiggles. "This dagger belonged ta none other than Hamish Maccoull."

I did my utmost to look impressed before asking, "Should I know who that is?"

"Ye should, but ye probably don't. Hamish Maccoull was only the most feared chieftain of all the highland clans. He's lacked the name recognition of yer Hollywood favorites like William Wallace and Robert the Bruce, but—"

"Did you say Maccoull?" I suddenly broke in. "Maccoull spelled M-A-C-C-O-U-L-L?"

"How else would ye spell it?"

"My grandmother is a Maccoull. Well, her married name is Sippel, but her mother's maiden name was Maccoull. Could she be related to this Hamish Maccoull and his clan?"

"Every Maccoull, the world over, can trace his ancestry back ta Hamish Maccoull. If yer gramma's a Maccoull, she can claim Hamish as kin."

I clasped my hands with excitement. "This is so awesome! She was just saying today how little she knows about her family tree. You know how that goes. One member of a family emigrates to America to begin a new life, and over time, he loses contact with everything and everyone he left behind."

"Then she's not familiar with Hamish's story?"

"I'm pretty sure she's never heard his name before."

"I have a book." Handing the dagger over to me, she contemplated her floor-to-ceiling bookshelves before crossing the room to the rolling ladder and sliding it halfway across the wall. "She's welcome ta borrow it while she's here." Hitching her robe to her knees, she climbed onto the first rung of the ladder and pulled a hefty tome from its slot before stepping back down. "It's an oral history of his life, handed down from family member ta family member, until it was finally put down on paper … a hundred years after he died."

I regarded the dagger with new eyes and greater appreciation. "Does it mention how his dirk might have ended up in a tree trunk?"

She set the book on the library table, splaying her hand over its faded leather cover. "If memory serves, the dirk was used ta kill him."

My eyeballs froze in their sockets. My breath froze in my throat. *Unh-oh.* "So the stains on the blade could possibly be—?"

"Hamish Maccoull's blood."

"Oh." I deposited the dirk gently onto the table and fluttered my fingers in the air. "You don't happen to have any hand sanitizer, do you?"

"It was his enemies who slew him," she said fiercely. "In his later years, Hamish tired of bloodshed. He married off his daughter ta the son of a rival chieftain, hoping ta secure the peace, but the son used the girl like no honorable man should use a wife, so she ran away, only ta be tracked down and punished like no new bride should ever be punished."

A chill crawled up the back of my neck. "What happened to her?"

"Her husband bound her ta a rock at low tide and left her. When the tide rose, she drowned."

My mouth fell open. "He killed her?"

"Highlanders have never been known fer their temperate responses ta imagined wrongs."

"But to kill her? For running away?"

"At least she died in one piece."

My eyelids flapped up like broken window shades. "Excuse me?"

"The preferred method of punishment at the time was ta have the offender drawn and quartered."

Euw!

"'Tis said Hamish's grief knew no bounds, his wrath no limits. He gathered a raiding party ta avenge the girl's death, but they were cut down on the road by the husband's clan, and Hamish stabbed in the heart with his own dirk. The whole raiding party was slaughtered but fer one man, who made it back ta the compound, and lived long enough ta give witness ta whit he'd seen. When the Maccoulls showed up ta bury their dead, they found Hamish's claymore by his side, but his dirk had gone missing, and was never seen again."

"Until now?" I asked in a tentative voice.

Morna opened the book, causing the spine to crackle as if it hadn't been opened in centuries. She turned to the last page. "The dirk disappeared, but the Maccoulls hoped not forever." She trailed her finger below the spidery text and read aloud. "'Remember well the look of the blade, fer it will come back into our hands one day, when they who dared steal it realize, too late, that their villainy sealed their doom. Those who ignore the admonition will pay with their blood.'"

"Admonition. Is he talking about the inscription on the handle?"

Morna nodded, reciting the words from memory. "'A quick and terrible death ta any foe who would possess what is mine.'"

"So, Hamish carved the inscription onto his dirk as a kind of 'sit up and take notice' warning to potential thieves? Like what we do today when we stick a sign in our front window, announcing the name of the security system we've just installed?"

"Hamish Maccoull meant the words as more than a warning, Mrs. Miceli." Morna Dalrymple eyed the dagger as if it had just grown a viper's fangs. "He meant them as a curse."

EIGHT

"Say what?"

"The dirk," Morna repeated. "It's cursed."

I waited a beat, fighting back a grin. "You actually believe that?"

Her expression grew stony. "Are ye saying ye don't? Why do ye think Hamish Maccoull was the most feared chieftain in all the highlands?"

I'd seen *Braveheart*. I knew exactly why people were afraid of these primitive types. "Scary face paint?"

"He had the eye." She tapped her finger high on her cheekbone. "He could as easily kill ye with a look as with his claymore, and fer added effect, he'd throw in a curse." She suddenly wiped her hands down the sides of her robe, as if to cleanse her palms of toxic contamination. "You'll want ta return this ta the place ye found it."

"Drive all the way back to Braemar? We can't do that. We have to head north tomorrow."

She skewered me with a wary look. "If ye want ta avoid more death," she said, pronouncing the words with exaggerated slowness, "ye'll do as I tell ye."

"*More* death?" I frowned at what she was implying. "Are you suggesting that Isobel's passing can be blamed on the dirk?"

"Was she the one who found it?"

"Well, yah. But—"

"Is she dead?"

"Yah. But—"

"Pull yer head outta the sand, girl. She died because she stole Hamish Maccoull's dagger. It was his curse that killed her."

I lowered an eyelid and stared at her through the slit. "I thought she died because a legion of demons flew out of her mouth and strangled her."

"That's before I knew of the dagger. We're in Scotland. Curses always trump demons. Ask anyone."

"Pardon me, Mrs. Dalrymple." The waiter who'd delivered the breakfast tray appeared at the library door, confusion running rampant on his face. "An emergency van has pulled up ta the front door. They're asking about ... a body?"

"Room twenty-four. Mrs. Miceli's husband is waiting fer them. Tell them I'll join them presently."

With a tired sigh, Morna Dalrymple threw her shoulders back and cranked her neck to left and right, as if preparing herself for the ordeal ahead. "But they'll have ta wait until I change inta something decent. I'll not be welcoming visitors ta my inn wearing my nightgown and robe."

She made her way to the door, pausing halfway across the room to issue a parting decree. "Please tell yer grandmother ta peruse the Maccoull book with my blessing. The text is in English, so she should have no problem. As fer the dirk, ye'll do me the favor of removing it from the premises. Immediately. I'll not have the cursed thing in my hotel."

❧

"So what'd you do with it, dear?"

"I ran into our bus driver downstairs and asked him to stow the box in a safe place on the bus."

I'd stopped by Nana's room on the way back to my own to give her and Tilly a heads up on our most recent calamity.

"I hope he don't get nosy and snoop inside," Nana fretted as she unwound a turban of toilet paper from around her fresh perm. "What if he opens the lid? That curse could escape and sock the rest of us."

"I believe that's Pandora's box you're referring to, Marion." Tilly lingered by the window, observing the emergency van that was still parked in the front of the hotel. "All the evils of the earth flew out into the world. This is different. I don't believe curses are capable of flight."

"There's always a first time." Nana folded her one-ply into a neat stack and plumped her curls in the dresser mirror.

"C'mon, Nana," I chided from my perch on her bed. "Since when do you believe in curses?"

"Since that Kronk woman dropped dead of one."

I wagged my finger at her. "You see? This is how rumors get started. I told you. Etienne found an epinephrine pen in her bathroom, which means she was severely allergic to something."

"You bet she was," Nana agreed. "Curses."

I shot a pleading look across the room. "Tilly, would you please tell my grandmother there's no such thing as a curse?"

"It's all nonsense, Marion." She made a shooing motion with her hand, as if scattering a swarm of midges. "Why, when I was living among the Dani in New Guinea, one malcontented woman was forever invoking curses on her fellow tribesmen. 'May your head fill with black bile and explode with the sound of a thousand roaring rivers. May your man-meat wither like a dead snake and drop onto your feet.' Quite poetic stuff for a diehard headhunter, actually."

"So what happened?" asked Nana.

"Well, as a consequence of the woman's constant incantations, the tribal chief decided to relocate his village to another part of the jungle."

Nana gasped. "He picked up stakes and left the troublemaker behind?"

"Unfortunately, no. He was married to her, so he ended up taking her with him."

A moment of silence, followed by, "That don't make no sense. If he had to drag her along with him, how come he moved?"

"Too much cranial viscera on the ground. You couldn't walk outside your hut without tripping over someone's jawbone or Mr. Winky. It was especially treacherous during the rainy season."

Nana turned slowly in my direction and arched a defiant eyebrow. I glared at Tilly, wild-eyed. "Did I miss something? Didn't you just get through telling Nana that curses are nonsense?"

"I did. That's because they are."

"So what's with the exploding heads?"

"Oh, that." She shrugged. "Pure coincidence. I'm sure it was just a fluke."

Nana polished her glasses on her robe and slid them onto her face. "Well, we better hope we don't get surprised by no fluke when our driver is sittin' behind the wheel of our bus, toolin' down a hill that drops off on either side and don't got no runaway truck ramp."

A digital chiming caused Nana to snatch her Smartphone off the dresser. "It's George," she said, eyeing the screen with a crooked grin.

"Text message?" I asked, wondering if the rumor mill had already begun pumping out misinformation.

"It's a picture." She flashed it in my direction, allowing me a glimpse of what appeared to be naked flesh.

"A picture of what?" I asked with sudden apprehension.

"George's best feature."

"OH, MY GOD! Are you sexting?"

She pressed a finger to her lips, smiling impishly. "Don't tell your mother," she whispered. She punched the screen. "You wanna see a close-up?"

"No, I don't want to see a close-up! Oh, my God. Does George know you're willing to share his private ... *stuff* with the general public?"

"It's not the whole public, dear. It's usually only Tilly."

"You show it to Tilly?"

"He don't mind. He's real proud of them body parts of his."

"*Euuuw*." I fell backward onto the mattress as if shot, forearm over my eyes, tongue lolling out of my mouth. "Mom's gonna find out. I *know* she'll find out. Oh, God. I can't think about it."

Nana jacked my forearm off my face and poised her phone an inch above my nose. "See?"

It filled my field of vision like a mini IMAX—the pert, fleshy protuberance with its fluid dips and angles, its unapologetic nakedness, its exquisitely turgid shape. I blinked at the image. "Why did George send you a picture of his nose?"

"It's his best feature."

I propped myself on one elbow, giving her a narrow look. "Has anyone explained to you that the whole purpose of sexting is to transmit images of body parts that are actually—how do I say this—physically provocative?"

Nana lifted her brows. "You mean, like George's Mr. Happy?"

"Yes, like George's Mr. Happy."

She gave me a hangdog look and sighed. "He had a notion to do that once, but it didn't work out so good."

"What stopped him? Fear of public exposure?"

She shook her head. "The screen wasn't big enough."

"Movement down below," Tilly announced from the window. "They must be preparing for transport."

I popped off the bed and tore across the floor in a footrace with Nana, arriving a half length behind her. Man, I really needed to think about working out.

"Oops, false alarm." Tilly shifted her weight as she leaned more heavily on her walking stick. "It's only one of the technicians lighting up a cigarette."

I marked the time on the nightstand clock. "Yikes, it's getting late. I need to run back to the room to throw myself together, and you'd probably appreciate my clearing out of here so you guys can finish getting dressed. I'm just glad you were awake when I knocked."

"Tilly and me's been awake for a long time, dear."

"Jet lag?" I asked as she escorted me to the door.

"Brainstormin'."

"At this hour of the morning?"

"We still don't got no team motto, so we're tryin' to come up with somethin' before we forget we need one."

"Any success?"

"We was thinkin' about 'You go, girls,' but we figured the fellas wouldn't be too keen on it."

"Yah, guys don't generally like being referred to as girls. But speaking of mottos, what's with Team Three's 'There is no dog'? Do you have any idea what that means?"

"It don't mean nuthin'. It's what happens when you stick an atheist and a dyslexic on the same team together."

As she opened the door to the hall, I nodded at the book I'd left for her on the dresser. "I hope you'll have time to skim at least a few pages of Mrs. Dalrymple's book before we have to leave tomorrow."

"Isn't this somethin'?" whooped Nana. "All these years not knowin' nuthin' about my Scottish kin, and now I get a chance to read a whole book about one of the big kahunas on the family tree. What'd you say his name is?"

"Hamish Maccoull."

"Hamish Maccoull." She rolled the name around on her tongue as if it were a favorite candy. "That's a real nice name."

"*Uhh* … There's just one small detail I should probably tell you before you begin reading."

Her eyes brightened in anticipation. "They're gonna make it available for download on Amazon?"

"Not exactly. Your relative Hamish? He's the one who placed the curse."

Wally made the announcement to the whole dining room an hour later, before the breakfast buffet opened.

"Could I have your attention, please?"

Chatter waned. Cups stilled. Heads turned.

"I'm sorry to have to start out your day on a sad note, but I have some tragic news to share with you. Early this morning, Isobel Kronk passed away quietly in her room."

Gasps. Whispers. A table-rattling belch. "Don't know where that came from," Dick Teig apologized. "Sorry."

"I've spoken to her son," Wally continued, "and we're making arrangements to have her body flown back to Indiana."

"She looked good at dinner last night," Lucille Rassmuson called out, pausing thoughtfully before adding, "Although, why she wanted a rats nest of gray hair straggling down her back is beyond me."

"Her complexion was suffering from serious sun damage," said Stella Gordon. "If I'd been in her shoes, I'd have opted for a submental necklift and laser skin resurfacing rather than a trip to Scotland."

"She had very nice teeth," commented Mom.

"They were probably capped," said Bernice.

"Do you know what caused her to die so suddenly?" Alice Tjarks inquired.

Margi fired her hand into the air, wrist flopping, fingers flying. "I know! It happens to patients at the clinic all the time." She paused for effect. "Her heart stopped."

Even from my table at the back of the room, I could see Wally's eyes begin to glaze over. "That's true, Ms. Swanson, but in this instance, there might have been a trigger that precipitated the event."

Helen Teig gasped. "She was shot?"

"No!" Wally choked out. "Her son confirmed our suspicions that she was allergic to wasp and bee stings, so the medical examiner is theorizing that she might have been stung and suffered a fatal reaction. He'll know more after the postmortem."

"Is this going to have any effect on the contest?" Bill Gordon demanded. "Because I don't think it should. My heart's bleeding about Isobel kicking off, but it wasn't our fault, so why should the rest of us be made to suffer because of it?"

Scattered applause. A subdued, "Here, here."

Gee, it was heartening to see how broken up Bill was about a death in our midst.

Wally's expression grew pinched, his voice tight. "Since the local authorities are in charge now, there's little more we can do, so they've encouraged us to continue our schedule as planned. But I expect each of you will want to remember Isobel in some small way today, either with a moment of silence, or in some other way that'll be meaningful to you."

"I remember her, all right," griped Bill. "I remember how she tried to screw the rest of us and cheat her way to a win."

"That's water over the dam now," Alex Hart pointed out, his emotional stability and calm making him sound even more reasonable than Doctor Phil. "She can't ever do it again, so why don't we just forget about it and move on? Besides, she wasn't a very adept cheat. She stole the wrong thing. Remember?"

Bill smashed his fist on the table, giving us all a start. "Her team should be punished! How do we know they weren't in cahoots with each other?"

"Because we weren't!" Cameron Dasher protested. "She admitted to everyone last night that she acted on her own. Did you miss that part of the conversation?"

"And you expected us to believe her?" Bill snorted.

"I believed her," said Alice Tjarks, raising her hand in support.

"So did I," admitted Mom.

"Me, too," said George.

Osmond popped out of his chair. "Show of hands. How many folks think Isobel was telling the truth about acting on her own?"

I watched heads turn left and right as people tried to gauge how everyone else was going to vote before they cast their own.

"It doesn't matter if you think Isobel acted alone or not." Wally boomed out his pronouncement as if he were channeling the Great Oz. He motioned Osmond to sit down. "We started the contest with five teams, and we'll end with five teams. I've spoken to the Micelis about this, and we're all in agreement. There was no harm done yesterday, no matter how outraged you are about what

Isobel did, so as far as we're concerned, the issue is resolved. However, I'm troubled by another issue."

He paused meaningfully to scan the faces in the room. "Isobel left her medical form blank, so we didn't know about her allergy. Maybe if we *had* known, we might have been able to help her. So if, when you were filling out your medical histories, it slipped your mind that you have a life-threatening condition, I'd encourage you to get your information up to speed. I always have the forms handy, so if you remember anything you'd like to add, or delete, speak to me in private, and we'll get it taken care of. The important thing is for the information to be as accurate as possible in case of medical emergency."

Spines stiffened. Eyes shifted. Guilt marched with heavy feet across the suddenly self-conscious faces of everyone at my table—Dick Teig, Margi, Osmond, Dad.

Dad? I stared at him in disbelief. Oh, my God! Dad had lied on his medical history?

Stella and Bill Gordon, on the other hand, sat rigidly stone-faced, apparently convinced that nothing Wally was saying applied to them.

"I want to go on record as opposing your radical secular social-ist decision not to disqualify Isobel's team from the contest," Bill protested.

"Opposition duly noted," said Wally. "But instead of dwelling on Isobel's misconduct, maybe you should all start gearing up for your next challenge."

The onslaught of negative vibes crackling throughout the room slowly ebbed, replaced by a low-level buzz that swelled to a chirpy titter. "You're still going to let us geocache?" asked Grace Stolee.

"You can count on it," Wally assured her. "The current situation is out of our hands, so there's no reason we can't proceed as planned. I've written the day's itinerary on the whiteboard in the lobby, so please check it out after breakfast. In a nutshell—geocaching at Urquhart Castle first, a late morning stop at the Loch Ness Exhibition Center, an afternoon cruise on Loch Ness itself, and then dinner in Drumnadrochit, where you'll be entertained by a trio of bagpipers and treated to a smorgasbord of original Scottish delicacies such as Cullen Skink, Clootie Dumplings, Rumbledethumps, and Dundee Cake."

Margi looked stricken. "Those things don't sound like they're going to taste very good, except for maybe the cake. Will we be able to order off the menu?"

"There's no menu," said Wally. "It's a fixed meal."

"Why are we having a smorgasbord in Scotland?" asked Helen. "Are they going to serve Swedish food?"

"Is skunk Swedish?" asked Alice, who gave her hearing aid a little tap.

"I think skunk is one a them Southern delicacies," Nana piped up. "Kinda like chitlins, or roadkill."

"Why do Scottish dumplings have cooties?" asked Lucille. "Shouldn't we notify the Board of Health?"

"Maybe they don't got no Board of Health," said Nana.

"Which would explain why all their food is contaminated," concluded Grace.

Wally opened his mouth to respond, then closed it again, looking suddenly unnerved and twitchy, as if he were suffering from shell shock. Poor thing. He was probably more accustomed to dealing with guests whose conversations actually made sense.

"Could I say something?" I asked, standing up so everyone could see me. "Just to clarify about dinner this evening in Drumnadrochit—"

"I'm sorry I'm late!" Dolly Pinker breezed into the room in leopard print jeans and a spandex top that dipped halfway to her navel and clung to her body like plastic wrap. "I'm so disoriented. My alarm didn't go off, so when I finally woke up, I had to hurry, hurry, hurry." She let out an exhausted breath as she scanned the room at large. "So, have I missed anything?"

Wally nodded. "There's good news and bad news."

"Isobel Kronk died last night," Bill Gordon called out without preamble.

Dolly fluffed her hair, looking oddly disaffected by the news. "Oh, really? Imagine that." She turned her attention on Wally. "So ... what's the bad news?"

NINE

URQUHART CASTLE, INEXPLICABLY PRONOUNCED Urkut, occupies a prime slice of real estate on a rock-ribbed promontory overlooking the waters of Loch Ness. Built in the early 1200s, it boasts all the features of a contemporary five-star resort—killer location, breathtaking views, impeccably groomed landscaping, proximity to local attractions. The only things it lacks are a roof, walls, floor, windows, and indoor plumbing.

"What do you mean, it's a ruin?" groused Bernice as we pulled into the coach section of the parking lot. "Who the devil wants to look at a pile of crumbling rocks?"

"Apparently, thousands of curiosity seekers," Wally replied over his mike, "because this is one of the most popular tourist sites in Scotland. It has a pretty bloody history, which is covered in the video presentation at the visitor center, so if you're a history buff and have a strong stomach, I'd recommend you watch it."

"The MacDonalds of the Isles were staunch defenders of Urquhart Castle seven hundred years ago," Bill Gordon said in a booming voice. "And I'm proud to say, the MacDonalds and my kin were like this." He raised his hand above his head and twisted his index and middle fingers around each other like creeping vines.

"Would you give it a rest?" his wife complained. "No one cares about your damn relatives."

As our driver maneuvered into a vacant space and killed the engine, Wally slid out from his front seat and stepped into the aisle. "The visitor center is state-of-the-art, with great views of the loch from the veranda. There's also a coin-operated observation telescope so you can catch a close-up of Nessie should she decide to rear her head. Team Four is first up today, which is our Do It or Lose It team. While they're on the hunt, I suggest the rest of you browse in the gift shop or grab a cup of coffee in the café. I'll let you know when it's your turn to head out."

"Team Yes We Can only has four members now," Bernice shouted from the seat behind me, "so I think you should award us more search time in order to compensate for our devastating loss of manpower."

I bent my head toward Etienne and rolled my eyes. Classic Bernice. Yesterday, she was screaming for a member to be cut loose from her team; today, she was demanding favored status because of it.

"I don't really think Team Five requires extra time," Cameron Dasher called out from across the aisle. "We might be down a teammate, but I think our four remaining team members are pretty formidable. We're ready to go toe-to-toe with anyone, without special favors. Right, team?"

"Yes. We. Can!" chanted Dolly Pinker from the front of the bus.

"Yes. We. Can!" Lucille chimed in from behind me.

Cameron turned around in his seat. "Bernice? What do you say? Are you with us?"

She grumbled something under her breath. "Yes we can," she muttered in a stubborn, tight-lipped monotone.

"Okay, then." Wally nodded his thanks toward Cameron. "That's settled. We'll be here for two and a half hours, which should give you plenty of time to complete your challenge and explore the castle grounds. I know geocaching isn't supposed to take place on sites that charge admission, but everyone is making a special exception for Urquhart. The National Trust is happy for increased attendance to help defray the cost of the new visitor center, and geocachers seem thrilled with the physical layout of the search area, so it's a win-win situation. Mrs. Andrew will give each team its GPS coordinates on the veranda overlooking the grounds, so as soon as Team Four works their way through the building, we can begin. Good luck, everyone."

Amid excited chatter and foot shuffling, people flooded the aisles en masse, kind of like a herd of camels trying to crowd into a pup tent at the same time. Helen and Grace, gung ho in their matching Scottie dog sweatshirts, were first down the rear stairs, followed by Lucille Rassmuson, who'd gotten into the whole team identity thing by crossing out the slogan, "Iowa: It's Easy to Spell" on her sweatshirt, and writing below it in permanent black marker: "Teem Yes We Can."

"Do you suppose Mrs. Rassmuson realizes she spelled 'Team' incorrectly on her shirt?" Etienne asked me as we waited for the aisle to clear.

"Yeah, she knows. And she's learned a valuable lesson."

He grinned. "What? There's still a niche market for liquid white-out?"

I grinned back. "Water-based markers are much more forgiving."

We exited the bus at the back of the pack and followed the group across the lot and down a flight of stairs, to a low circular building that could have doubled as a World War II artillery bunker. "This is the visitor center?"

I gaped at the structure, which covered an area only slightly larger than a child's wading pool. Were they kidding? How could a building this small possibly have enough restroom stalls to accommodate a busload full of seniors with internal plumbing issues?

"It's the entrance, bella, like the conning tower on a submarine. There's a lift inside that'll take us down to the main floor."

I eyed him curiously. "You never mentioned you'd been here before."

"I haven't." He flashed a sexy grin that showed off his dimples. "I Googled it."

The main floor was a sleek blend of pale wood and glass, with circular columns supporting the ceiling, and recessed pot lights that slanted illumination downward like laser beams. I watched the group scatter in four different directions while Etienne detached his phone from its holster, looking as if he wished it would ring.

"Important call on the docket?"

"Medical examiner. He said he'd keep me apprised of his findings, but I'm probably being too optimistic to think he'd have enough results to call me back this quickly. I'll just have to stay busy to keep my mind off it."

Which, I'd come to discover, was the workaholic's solution for everything. "I know something that'll keep you busy." Leaning in to him, I lowered my voice to a seductive whisper. "At least … it'll keep your hands busy."

He bobbled his phone as if his fingers had suddenly gone numb. Finding his grip again, he secured the device back in its holster and asked out of the side of his mouth, "What did you have in mind?"

I nodded toward the opposite end of the room. "Margi looks as if she needs someone to take her picture. Would you do the honors? You'll probably make her day."

"Very clever, Mrs. Miceli." He smiled sardonically. "I'll get you for that."

I gave him a little finger wave as he headed across the floor. "I'm counting on it!"

With Wally managing the geocaching activities and Etienne playing photographer, I was freed up to do a little exploring on my own, but where to start? Video presentation? Outdoor veranda? Castle proper?

Rather than waste time doing the eenie, meenie, miney, moe thing, I reverted to my default setting: the gift shop.

"What do you mean, do I really need a new necktie?" Alex Hart balked as I crossed the threshold. He and Erik Ishmael were browsing through the woolens on a display table just inside the door, looking like natives in their new kilts, hiking boots, and nifty sporrans. "Do I ever complain about the number of wristwatches you buy?"

"That's different," scoffed Erik. "I'm building a collection."

"Well, so am I, only I wear mine around my neck instead of my wrist." He snatched a red tartan tie from the table and held it near his cheek. "Royal Stuart. What do you think? Does it fight with my complexion?"

"You don't need another freaking necktie. I've given up enough closet space to your clothes fetish."

"And I've given up enough dresser space to your jewelry fetish. So there."

"You don't even wear neckties!"

"So?" Alex rubbed the Royal Stuart wool between his thumb and forefinger, as if testing for softness. "They're pretty. I like to look at them."

Erik arched a brow at me. "He's impossible to reason with when he gets in these moods."

"My husband would sympathize," I commiserated. "I tend to hog all the closet space, too."

Erik fisted his hand on his hip, exasperation flooding his face. "So how do you handle the issue and remain happily married?"

"You build a new house with lots of walk-ins." I smiled pertly. "Problem solved."

Alex laid the necktie back on the display table and made a great show of dusting off his hands. "See? I put it back. Happy now?"

"So do you guys live in a house or an apartment?" I inquired.

"House," claimed Alex, as Erik said, "Apartment."

They crossed glances. Erik laughed. "We actually live in a detached condo," he explained. "Technically, it's a house, but it's so small, it feels more like an apartment."

"So it's a house with a pintsize footprint. How very green of you. New condo? Old condo?"

"New," claimed Erik, as Alex said, "Old."

They lifted their brows and pinched their lips together, refusing to look at each other. "It all depends on your definition of old," Alex explained. "It was built ten years ago, which in my estimation, is pretty old. Erik obviously disagrees."

"A building that's only ten years old is practically brand new," argued Erik. "Just saying."

I glanced from one to the other. "Are you sure the two of you actually live together?" I teased.

For a heartbeat, their eyes snapped with an emotion as raw as the one effected by silver screen legends before they morphed into werewolves, but it was gone as quickly as it appeared, replaced by guffaws and dismissive gestures.

"You see?" Erik stabbed an accusing finger at Alex's face. "I told you we needed to spend more time together. People don't even realize we're a couple anymore." He turned to me, pleading his case. "It's all his fault, Emily. He spends so much time with his nose stuck in his computer that he doesn't talk to me anymore. I told him to retire, but *noooo*. He thinks the whole nuclear industry will collapse without his input."

"It will," Alex averred. "I'm indispensable."

"Were you involved in that accident at Three Mile Island decades ago?" I asked, summoning the entire depth and breadth of my knowledge about the country's nuclear power industry. Well, that, and two old movie flicks with Jack Lemmon and Cher. "Didn't the core almost melt down, or something? Is that the kind of thing you handle?"

"Have you ever seen *The China Syndrome?*" Alex asked me.

"Yes! Back in college. It was part of a thrillerfest extravaganza on a weekend when the football Badgers had a bye. It was *so* realistic."

"What I do is nothing like that." He ranged a quick glance around the rest of the gift shop. "I'm not seeing anything else in here that even vaguely tempts me, so why don't we queue up for the video?" he asked Erik.

"Love to. Would you excuse us, Emily?"

They hustled out the door as if they were migratory birds fleeing a hurricane—a hurricane, I suspected, named Emily. I wasn't stupid. I could recognize a last-minute escape when I saw one. What I didn't understand was—What was up with the discrepancy in their answers about their life together? And why did that bother them to the point of prompting such a quick exit?

"Your eyes are younger than mine," Bill Gordon announced as he approached me. He thrust a piece of cardboard wrapped in cellophane into my hand. "How much does this thing cost?"

The "thing" was a replica of a two-handed sword miniaturized to the size of a fingernail file. I turned it over, spying the price in microscopic font in the corner. "Ten pounds sixty, it says here."

"Are you kidding me? What are they trying to do? Make up the country's financial deficit on the backs of us tourists?" He snorted with self-righteous indignation. "What does the writing on the front say?"

"*Uhh*—'The Claymore was a common weapon among the highland clans, designed to facilitate sweeping slashes and powerful thrusts. Unlike other swords of the period, it was unique for its sloping cross-guards that terminated in … quatrefoils and a high collared … quillon block, with the … langets following the … blade fuller.'"I frowned. "I hope that means something to you because it means nothing to me."

"Anything else?" he asked.

"'Made in China.'"

"Are you *kidding* me?" He snatched it from my hand, stormed across the room, and tossed it back into a display basket. "The next time you decide to charge a crapload of money for a souvenir," he railed at the cashier, "make sure the damn thing is made in Scotland! Shysters," he grumbled as he blew by me on his way out the door.

"It looked like a really nice replica," I called after him. "Even if it *was* made in China."

He turned back to me. "Authentic Scottish blades *are not* made in China. They're made in Scotland, by authorized Scottish armorers."

"Yeah, but if the replica fills a gap in your collection—I assume you have a collection?"

His eyes grew fierce, his voice menacing. "I have a replica of every sword and dagger wielded by clan Gordon to slay Campbells, and Mackelvies, and Loudouns, and Maccarters, and Conochies, and Maccoulls, and—"

"Maccoulls?"

He lowered his brows, squinting malevolently. "Yes, Maccoulls. Why? Do you know any?"

I shook my head. "Nope. It just sounds like Maccoull should be ... Irish."

"It's not. The Campbells were ruthless, backstabbing scaffs, but the Maccoulls? The Maccoulls taught them everything they knew."

I assumed "scaff," in this context, wasn't intended as a compliment.

"Stella!" he yelled across the room. "I'm heading to the can."

"Why are you telling me?" she yelled back. "Do I look like your mother?"

I made a mental note to warn Nana against mentioning Hamish Maccoull or the rest of her Scottish ancestors to Bill. If the Gordons had a history of slaying Maccoulls, Nana could be in the crosshairs, and with Bill being so rabid about keeping the whole revenge thing alive, I was a little nervous about how far he might go to promote his clan's honor.

I inhaled a calming breath. It was a good thing Isobel's death wasn't suspicious, because if it was, I knew the first person I'd be asking for an alibi.

I power-shopped my way through the rest of the store, picking up souvenirs for my nephews, and selecting postcards that I convinced myself I'd actually fill out. Stella Gordon got in line behind me at the cashier's counter, carrying the claymore that Bill had thrown back into the bin.

"I'm not sure you were paying attention," I said as I eyed the merchandise in her hand, "but Bill was adamant about not wanting to buy that."

"He's adamant about a lot of things. That doesn't mean he's right."

"He seriously objected to its being made in China."

She rolled her eyes. "What isn't? If I don't buy this for his weapons collection, once we're home, he'll be kicking himself from here 'til Sunday for letting it slip through his fingers. And guess who becomes the captive audience for his griping? Me. So I'm buying it. I like to think of it as a preemptive measure to shut him up."

I handed the clerk my credit card. "I don't think I've ever seen anyone quite as ... passionate about his heritage as Bill."

"Fanatical, you mean. He's like a bloodhound, sniffing out people with Scottish blood so he can pick a fight if they were born on the wrong side of the tartan. You know what I wish?"

I signed the receipt and gathered up my purchases. "What?"

"I wish every person on this tour with Scottish roots would disappear so I could enjoy the rest of my vacation."

I stiffened, uneasy with her implication. "You mean that rhetorically, of course."

"Oh, for crying out loud. What do you think I'm going to do? Wave my magic wand, say 'Poof', and zap a whole busload of people into oblivion?"

I couldn't speak to her methodology, but if eliminating guests was her goal, she had a pretty good start.

I bypassed the theater on my way to the veranda and bumped into the Dicks as they were exiting the cafe. I stood back, looking them up and down with a critical eye. "Well would you look at the two of you? You've been shopping, I see."

"This wasn't our idea," griped Dick Stolee as he tugged his kilt around his waist. "This is all your fault, Emily. You built too much free time into the Edinburgh schedule and the wives went nuts."

"So how do you like wearing a skirt?" I needled.

"How do you think I like it?" he snapped. "I look like a girl." He tugged the fabric in the opposite direction. "Damn fool thing. It's itchy."

"Not enough undergarments," speculated Dick Teig. "What are you wearing? Boxers or briefs?"

Dick Stolee registered a blank look as he patted down his flanks. "Damn. I knew I forgot something."

Euw.

"I kinda like the whole pantless thing myself," confessed Dick Teig as he rotated his hips, causing the pleated wool to swish back and forth. "But so help me, Emily, if you ever breathe a word to Helen, I'll deny I ever said it."

The girls had bought them identical kilts in a Black Watch plaid, with identical sporrans to carry incidentals. The outfits fell apart below their knees though, with Dick Stolee sporting black dress socks and white canvas sneakers, and Dick Teig running around in white athletic socks and wingtips. Not the best fashion accessories to achieve that rugged, devil-may-care highland look.

"So are these your team uniforms?" I asked.

"The wives tell us they are," groused Dick Stolee.

Swish, swish, swish. "The ventilation is great," said Dick Teig as he continued to rotate his hips. "That Erik fella sure called it right. My boys finally have room to breathe! And wait until I see my chiropractor again. He told me if I'd stop parking my backside on my wallet, my sciatica would improve, and doggone, he was right. Look at this." Stretching his arms out in a T, he executed a series of torso twists that sent his stomach swinging with near seismic bounce. "It doesn't hurt anymore!"

Dick cringed. "Oh, Jeez."

"I might never wear pants again."

"Will you stop?" snapped Dick Stolee. He peered around the room as if all eyes were on him. "You're embarrassing me."

Dick Teig hiked his kilt to his knees and stared down at his shoes. "I'm not sure about the wingtips and athletic socks though.

What do you think, Emily? Would dress socks look better? Helen bought some really nice ones at the dollar store."

"I'm gonna take in the video," huffed Dick Stolee as he nodded toward the theater.

"Great idea," I encouraged. "I bet the whole area will come alive once you learn the history behind the ruins."

"I'm not going in there to hear about the ruins," he dead-panned. "I'm going in there because it's dark." He arched a brow at his friend. "You coming with me, or would you rather stay here, discussing your ensemble with Emily?"

Dick Teig looked suddenly desperate. "I've gotta use the men's room. Anyone seen it?"

"By the gift shop," I said, pointing in the right direction. "That-away."

As he struck out across the floor, Dick Stolee stood beside me, watching him go, which was a little unusual, since the two men rarely allowed themselves to be out of each other's sight.

"You're not going with him?" I asked.

He shook his head.

"Sooo ... unlike the female of the species, men don't have to go to the restroom in twos?"

"I wouldn't mind going, but ... " He threw a careful look around him before leaning toward me and asking in a self-conscious voice, "Can I go in there dressed in a skirt?"

After calming Dick's nerves about acceptable dress code in a Scottish men's room, I headed toward the exit doors and stepped out onto the blacktopped terrace that fronted the building. In the distance I could see the battered ruins of the castle, perched on a bluff like a crumbling section of the Great Wall of China, looking oddly formidable in its decrepitude. It was as long as a Florida strip mall, with a solitary watch tower poking up from its gutted remains, and a footbridge welcoming tourists through an arched gate that might once have run slick with boiling oil. Nana and Tilly stood at the veranda, checking out the grounds with their binoculars, while George manned the observation telescope, looking much like a submarine captain draped over his periscope. Mom sat at a patio table to my right, entering information onto her laptop while seemingly oblivious to Dad, who was locked in conversation with Wally at the far end of the terrace.

I fired up my camera to snap a few candid shots of everyone, but had to scoot out of the way when Cameron Dasher barreled out the door with Bernice, Lucille, and Dolly chasing behind him like tin cans behind a car with a Just Married sign. They were next up to search for the cache, so I was glad they were here and raring to go, but if I'd been Cameron, I might have decided to hide in the men's room to be free of his entourage, if even for a few minutes.

"Will you take a picture of me with Cameron over by the railing?" Dolly shoved her camera at me. "And just so you know, my right side is my best side."

"You already had your picture taken with him in the café," sniped Bernice. "It's my turn." She slapped her Smartphone into my palm. "Don't use the zoom, Emily." Then, in a whisper, "Cameron looks better at a distance."

"Funny," taunted Dolly, "I would have guessed *you're* the one who'd look better at a distance."

"Goes to show what you know." Bernice turned smug, jutting her chin into the air. "I used to be a magazine model."

"Which magazine?" asked Dolly. "*Antiques Journal*?"

"Why don't I take a picture of your whole team?" I suggested in the hopes of defusing the situation.

Dolly squinted at me with impatience. "Because photos of the whole team aren't going to make it into my photo album."

"Stand a little closer," Nana instructed. "That's right. Say 'Cheese.' Oh, you're gonna like this one, Lucille. This Scottish light takes twenty years off your age. Stay right there, now. I wanna take one with my cell."

We glanced sideways to find Cameron and Lucille smiling enthusiastically as they posed against the veranda. Dolly sucked in her breath and grabbed her camera back. "Witch," she muttered in an undertone, her eyes throwing daggers at Lucille. As she stormed toward them, Bernice snatched her phone from my hand and charged after her.

"Don't you think we should have a picture of the whole team?" Dolly suggested to Cameron as she staked claim to his free side, snuggling close against him.

"Now, that's the spirit." He wrapped one arm around her shoulders and the other around Lucille's, looking suddenly chagrined when Bernice planted herself in front of him, arms crossed as she tapped her foot. "Well, come on and join us, Bernice," he encouraged. "You're part of the team, too."

"I don't think everyone got that memo." Posing stiffly in front of him, she gritted her teeth in a less than flattering smile.

"Hold that pose," said Nana, snapping the picture. "Wow. This is a real nice one. What do you think, Emily?"

I hurried over to her, nodding my approval at the photo. Somehow, the camera had managed to turn Bernice's gritted teeth into a thousand watt smile. Gee. She really *was* photogenic.

"We done yet?" asked Nana.

"One more," said Bernice as she burrowed backward into the half-inch space between Dolly and Cameron, propelling Dolly out of the picture with an able thrust of her hip. "Okay, Marion. Shoot."

"Hey!" balked Dolly as she stumbled off-balance. "I was standing there first."

"Well, you're not standing here now."

"Can we switch sides?" asked Lucille as she gave up her plum spot to join the fray. "I look thinner on my right side."

As they jockeyed for position around Cameron, I realized that the three of them had turned cozying up to him into a competitive sport, with no rules, no boundaries, and no holds barred. *Geesch.* I hope they didn't get too carried away. I'd hate for a guest to avoid traveling with us again because he'd been pestered to death on his first go-round. Too bad men didn't live longer. If they did, maybe their participation on tours wouldn't be such a novelty, and maybe men like Cameron wouldn't have to beat their admirers off with a stick.

I rolled my eyes as the ladies leapfrogged around each other.

Nana snapped a picture of the chaos, then angled her camera screen toward me. "You s'pose if I show them girls what a nuisance they're makin' of themselves, they'll leave the poor fella alone? I don't wanna say nuthin' unkind about the dead, dear, but can you imagine how much worse it'd be if there was still four women fightin' over him instead a three?"

I stared at Nana, my breath catching in my throat. "What?"

"Team Four's heading back," yelled George from the observation telescope, prompting Nana to shuffle over to him for a look-see.

Mom popped out of her patio chair. "Team Yes We Can! You're in the batter's box!"

As Cameron struggled to herd his teammates in Mom's direction, I remained rooted to the spot, Nana's words still echoing in my head: *Can you imagine how much worse it'd be if there was still four women fightin' over him instead a three?*

"Stay very calm and try not to overreact, bella," Etienne said as he drew alongside me, "but we've run into a patch of bad luck."

I looked up at him, intuiting what he was going to say even before he said it.

"I just received a call from the medical examiner. He's unsure what caused Isobel's death, but he's certain it wasn't anaphylactic shock."

Damn.

TEN

Four hours later, having departed Urquhart Castle and completed our tour of the Loch Ness Monster Exhibition where, to the accompaniment of laser lights, digital projections, and eerie music, we spent a quick sixty minutes traveling from the dawn of time to the third millennium—we were ready to undertake the next step: venturing onto the loch itself.

"What do you mean, you're not going on the cruise?"

I'd yet to warn Nana against mentioning her Maccoull ancestry to Bill Gordon, so as the other guests proceeded to hike down the gravel path to the sightseeing boats, I'd pulled her aside to issue my alert, only to be blindsided by her unexpected pronouncement.

She shrugged the shoulder that wasn't weighed down by her oversized pocketbook. "It's on account of my memory, dear. I forgot to pack them pills what's s'posed to keep me from losin' my cookies all over the person sittin' next to me on the boat."

"You don't get motion sickness."

She tucked in her lips and regarded me impishly. "No kiddin'?"

"When the decks were awash on our Hawaiian cruise, you were in the ship's lounge, tossing back Shirley Temples like there was no tomorrow."

"That don't mean I won't get sick today. I got more years on me now. My system's more delicate. I can't handle them big waves like I used to."

I glanced at the loch to find it calm as bath water. I narrowed my eyes at her. "What's the real reason you're ditching the cruise?"

"It don't have nuthin' to do with you, dear, so don't you go takin' it personal. We just decided that old bones and high seas don't go together real good."

I rolled my eyes. "Who's 'we'?"

"You gotta have names?" She gave me a downtrodden look as she ticked them off on her fingers. "Me, George, Tilly, Margi, Osmond, Ali—"

"The whole gang is staying on shore?"

"We're not taking no chances. You don't get to be older than dirt by bein' stupid." She paused. "Well, the Dicks did, but they're the exception."

"Nana! What is stupid about cruising the most famous lake in the world? And don't tell me your bones are old because I'm not buying it."

She twitched her mouth self-consciously before blurting out, "There's a monster down there, Emily."

"No, there isn't."

"Yes, there is, and your father seen it."

"No, he didn't."

"Then what'd he see?"

Damn. She had me there. "I don't know what he saw, but I'm thinking it might have been one part ocular anomaly and one part figment of his imagination."

"He don't got no imagination."

"Okay, imagination isn't his strong suit, so maybe what he thought was a sea creature was just a really big floater." I smiled, hoping to convince myself as much as Nana. "He should probably see an ophthalmologist when he gets home."

"He don't need no eye doctor. He needs folks to believe him."

"I believe him." I nodded emphatically. "Kinda. I mean, I believe he saw something." I paused reflectively. "Can floaters appear in the shape of sea serpents?"

"Emily, there wasn't nuthin' in that monster exhibit that proves there isn't no Jurassic Park creature livin' in this lake."

I thrust my finger into the air in a "Eureka" kind of gesture. "Mrs. Dalrymple confided to me this very morning that the only reason the legend of Nessie persists is to boost the local economy."

"No kiddin'?"

"Yup. Her ancestors have lived on the shores of Loch Ness for four hundred years, and not one of them has ever reported seeing a sea creature."

"Maybe them's the folks what needed the eye doctor."

"So what do you say? Will you change your mind and come with us?"

"Can't. We already voted nine to two to stay on shore instead a goin' down with the ship."

I gave her an exasperated look. "The ship is not going down."

"Tell that to the folks what was on the *Titanic*."

"There's a difference. Loch Ness doesn't have icebergs."

"It's got a monster. That's worse. You just make sure they got enough life jackets to go around on that boat, Emily. I don't want nuthin' happenin' to you."

As she shuffled down the path in front of me, I noticed something odd. "Why are you listing thirty degrees to starboard? What's in your pocketbook? Bricks?"

She stopped short and snorted with impatience. "This is all your mother's doin'." Swinging her pocketbook in front of her, she unsnapped the top and opened it wide to show me a jumble of brown plastic bottles with labels that read "Milk Thistle" and "White Willow Bark."

"*Uff-da*. Are these the elusive supplements she bought to prevent you from shrinking?" I frowned at the cache. "How many bottles do you have in there anyway?"

"Sixteen."

"Well, duh? No wonder you're listing." I regarded her quizzically. "How come you didn't leave them in your room?"

"'Cuz Margaret says I gotta take 'em with every meal, and I can't figure out no way to ditch her at meals, so I gotta haul the dang things around with me. If I'da known I was gonna be tossin' back a steady diet of weeds 'n trees on this trip, I mighta stayed home!"

I'd rarely seen Nana out of sorts, so her mood worried me a little. Oh, God. I hoped the situation didn't escalate to the point where she and Mom would be forced to have "words." What would I do? Whose side would I take?

I scratched a sudden itch at the back of my neck and tried not to think about it.

By the time we reached the waterfront, my guys had already spaced themselves out along the shore like ducks in a shooting gallery, their Smartphones focused on the impossibly calm waters of the loch as if in anticipation of a YouTube-worthy event.

Plink, plink, plink.

Heads and cameras swiveled toward the sound.

"D'you hear that?" shouted Osmond, who'd recently been outfitted with hearing aids so high-tech, he could have heard belching if the Mars rover had developed acid indigestion. "Look! The water's rippling!"

"It's Nessie!" cried Margi.

"It is not," crabbed Bernice. "It's those moronic Dicks skipping stones."

The remainder of our traveling twenty-nine were filing onto our waiting boat, the *Highland Queen*—an ancient-looking tub with paint peeling off its wheelhouse and benches flanking the aft bulwarks to accommodate outside seating. Etienne spurred me on with a "hurry up" gesture as I ran onto the dock.

"I thought I was going to have to send out the bloodhounds," he chided with good humor. He nodded toward the photographic frenzy taking place on shore. "Do they realize they're literally in danger of missing the boat?"

"They're not coming."

"Why not?"

"Because of the monster. They're apparently not interested in becoming her mid-afternoon snack."

"You can't be serious."

I cocked my head and gave him *the look*.

"*Merde*. You're serious."

Cursing held so much more allure when uttered in a foreign language.

I craned my neck to see who was gathered on deck, noting the absence of two critical guests. "Have you seen Mom and Dad?"

"Your mother decided to stay on the bus to tally the geocache results."

Not a bad idea. At least Nana would get a breather. "Is Dad with her?"

"Your father has staked out a seat in the wheelhouse to be near the new multifunction fish finder with bottom tracking performance, GPS, sonar, and an 83/200 khz transducer."

I stared at him, deadpan. "I don't know what that is."

"Neither do I, but your father does. He plans to videotape the monitor while you're cruising in case the device picks up the image of a sea serpent."

I sighed. "But he doesn't know how to use his camcorder."

"He does now. He apparently stayed up all night reading the manual."

"If yer coming with us, lass, yer'd best climb aboard." From the deck, a lanky man in bib overalls and a skipper's cap bent over to extend his hand to me. "Up ye go."

Bridging the significant gap between dock and boat, I hopped aboard then turned to Etienne, who was wearing a resigned expression as he backed away from the vessel. "Hey, where are you going? Aren't you coming with us?"

"And leave the camera hounds on shore by themselves?" He smiled. "Not on your life. Bring back a picture of Nessie if you run into her."

The engine revved anemically before sputtering to a deafening roar. As the lines were cast off, Etienne blew me a kiss, then sauntered back to shore, turning to wave as we were enveloped in a smelly cloud of diesel exhaust.

"This reeks!" Dolly fussed as we motored beyond the dock. She regarded me accusingly. "Are we going to have to sit here and inhale toxic fumes the entire trip?"

"Maybe when we're up to speed, you'd prefer to waterski," Stella Gordon wisecracked.

Dolly narrowed her eyes, her stare growing frigid. "Don't get smart with me."

"Or you'll what?" challenged Stella.

Oh, God. "You might try sitting in the wheelhouse," I offered helpfully. "The fumes might not be so bad in there."

Dolly pursed her perfectly painted lips and raised her perfectly plucked brows a quarter-inch. "I don't want to sit inside." She sidled closer to Cameron Dasher on the bench and smiled. "I'm perfectly happy right here. I just don't want to smell these noxious fumes."

"What's the matter?" taunted Stella. "Do they clash with your perfume?"

"Quiet, Stella," barked her husband. "She's one of the brave MacDonalds. Leave her alone."

Stella curled her lip into a sneer as she regarded her husband. "Bite me."

We were sitting on opposite sides of the deck—the Gordons, Dolly, and Cameron occupying the starboard bench, while Erik, Alex, and I sat to port. Everyone else was in the wheelhouse, where they were probably enjoying a more audible version of the narration that was blaring over the loudspeaker like a soundtrack of angry bees.

"... *bzzzzt* ... thirty-seven ... *bzz* ... kilometers long and ... *bzzzzt* ... *bzzzzt* ... more fresh water than ... *bzzzzt* ... and Wales ... *bzzzzt* ... *bzzzzt* ... except Loch Morar ... "

Cameron Dasher threw up his hands and laughed. "The speaker system is apparently even older than the boat. Do you suppose we're missing anything important?"

Bill Gordon swung his bulky torso around and peered over the side of the boat. "It's probably telling us that Loch Ness has the murkiest water in the world. If the *Titanic* sank in the middle of this lake, a guy in a deep diving submersible with Hellfighter military spotlights blazing from two feet away wouldn't be able to see it."

I flinched. I wish he hadn't said that.

"*bzz ... bzzt ...*"

"Is that true?" asked Dolly.

Bill folded his arms across his chest like an all-powerful genie. "I just told you, didn't I?"

"He's full of crap," droned Stella.

"I don't think he's full of crap at all." Dolly offered Bill an ego-boosting smile. "I think he's quite intelligent to keep all those facts in his head."

"Try being married to him," snorted Stella. "You'd see firsthand how intelligent he is."

"*bzzzzt … low visibil … bzt …*"

Dolly gasped. "What a terrible thing to say! Poor Bill, having to sit here and listen to your nastiness." She hardened her gaze at Stella. "If you can't treat your man any better than that, you don't deserve to have one."

"You hear that, Stella?" crowed Bill. "It's what I've been telling you for years. You don't deserve me."

"Feel free to leave." Stella flashed an acid smile. "I'd welcome the deprivation."

"Always with the put-downs," railed Bill. "I should have listened to my mother. She warned me what would happen if I married outside the clan. *She* knew. She begged me to find a real Scot, someone like Dolly here, a *MacDonald*. But *noo*, I had to be stupid and get myself hoodwinked by a gold-digging Hungarian."

"… peat content … *bzzzzt … bzzzzt …*"

"She married you for your money?" bristled Dolly.

"Yah," Stella droned. "The whole twenty-six dollar and fifteen cent fortune he kept in his cookie jar."

"You were eying my weapons collection," accused Bill. "You knew it was going to be worth millions even back then."

"It *could* have been worth millions," Stella shot back with no small amount of sarcasm, "if you'd been bright enough to keep the documentation. Duh."

Dolly regarded Stella with a disapproving sniff. Leaning sideways, she patted Bill's forearm in a sympathetic gesture. "You're being such a gentleman about this. Honestly, Bill, if she were my wife, I'd wash her mouth out with a big bar of French-milled soap."

"Now there's an idea," he agreed.

Stella Gordon said nothing. She didn't have to. The muscle pulsating in her jaw said it all. Popping up from the bench on her five-inch heels, she spun away from Bill, and 'mid a heavy jingling of bracelets, stormed toward the wheelhouse.

"…increasing speed…*bzzzzt*…change in…*bzzt*…*bzzt*…*bzz*…"

"Something tells me that Stella and I aren't going to be best friends," Dolly confided as the boat altered course, "but I just couldn't sit here and let her talk to you that way, Bill. Where I grew up, a woman learned to show proper respect toward menfolk. And if she didn't, she ended up an old maid."

"Would that have been so bad?" I asked, having been exposed to some pretty extraordinary "old maids" when I was growing up. "Is that the absolute worst thing that could have happened to a woman back then?"

"Well, dying was worse, but—" Dolly heaved a sigh. "Actually, I think being an old maid was even worse than dying."

As we motored down the middle of the lake on a course that paralleled the shoreline, the skipper opened up the throttle, causing the bulwarks to shake with a fierce vibrato, and a strong crosswind to send my hair whipping helter-skelter around my face. Erik and Alex bent over their laps to prevent their kilts from flying up. Cameron raised the collar of his jacket. Bill hunkered lower on the bench. And Dolly let out an ear-piercing shriek as her perfectly coifed hair exploded in the air like a can of number six spaghetti.

"Oh, my God!" Her hands were suddenly all over her head, slapping down the product-laden strands.

"You want to borrow my hat?" asked Cameron, as he pulled a slouch-cap out of his jacket pocket.

"*bzzz*…*bz*…*bzzzzt*…"

135

"No! I want—" The ends of her intricately tied scarf flew up in an opposing gust, smacking her face like a whip. She turned her head away and caught the tails in her fist, but when she turned back, I noticed her lips were an entirely different color than the cherry-red they'd been two seconds before.

Dolly noticed, too.

"Dammit!" she cried when she spied the smear of cherry-red lip gloss on her petal-pink scarf. "Look at this!" She ripped it off her neck and pouted at the stain. "First time I've worn it, and it's ruined!"

"I have a stain remover pen," Alex spoke up, adding in a small voice, "back at the hotel."

"All I have on hand is sanitizer," I lamented.

"I've got water," said Bill as he dug a lime-green plastic mini bottle out of his fanny pack.

"Water won't do any good," she fussed. "It's silk! Do you know what water does to silk?"

"Why are you yelling at me?" huffed Bill. "I'm only trying to help."

"Well, you *can't* help. No one can help! My hair... my scarf..." Imploding in a fit of pique, she flung her scarf over the side, and shielding her head from the wind, ran across the deck to the wheelhouse.

"Damn females," groused Bill. "Just when you think you've found a sane one, she goes postal on you. I'm lowering my opinion of the MacDonald women. Ill-tempered shrew."

Cameron blew a long stream of air out of his mouth as he regarded the wheelhouse. "I'm not sure it's a good idea for Dolly and Stella to be anywhere within sight of each other right now, Bill.

How about you track down your wife and make nice with her so we can avoid a repeat performance."

"Me? Apologize?" Bill guffawed. "Ain't gonna happen."

Cameron's voice deepened with frustration. "Hey, I've got skin in this game, too, and I'm already down one team member. I don't want to lose another one to unintended injury."

"Survival of the fittest," boomed Bill.

"How chivalrous of you," quipped Erik. He splayed his hand over his heart. "It's what makes you sensitive types so endearing."

Bill Gordon threw a squinty look across the deck at him. "Are you making fun of me?"

"Wouldn't think of it, buttercup."

Bill's face morphed into an angry red knot. "You *are* making fun of me."

"Settle down, Bill," soothed Cameron. "He's just needling you a little."

"The hell he is!"

"Would you *please* lighten up?" chafed Alex as he directed a tart look at Bill. "Have you tried yoga? Maybe some relaxation techniques? How about anger management courses? I hear you can even find them online these days. Or here's a thought. Maybe you could just put a cork in it so the rest of us could be spared your ugly American routine."

Yup. I'm sure that helped.

Bill leaned forward, face florid, teeth bared, voice rabid. "Looking at the two of you makes my eyes hurt."

Erik grinned. "So look at something else, buttercup."

"So help me God, if you call me that one more time, I'll—"

"So what do you think of the scenery?" I jumped in, yelling to be heard over the static hiss of the loudspeaker. "Is this how you imagined Loch Ness would look? Hills? Rocks? Water? Would anyone like me to take their picture?"

Bill drilled me with a hostile look. "The scenery sucks," he spat as he heaved himself off the bench and lumbered toward the wheelhouse.

Cameron shrugged good-naturedly. "I guess he's not into having his picture taken."

"Pictures!" whooped Alex as he dug his camera out of his sporran. "Should have thought of it sooner." He turned to Erik. "If you can get that wild mop of yours under control, I might even take one of you."

While the two men fussed with hair and camera settings, I shot across the deck to kibitz with Cameron. "I'll cut right to the chase," I said while we enjoyed a lull in the action. "Are Bernice, Dolly, and Lucille driving you crazy?"

He seemed surprised by the question. "Have I given you the impression that they're driving me crazy?"

"No. But there's nothing wrong with my eyesight. They haven't let you alone for a minute. Aren't you feeling ... smothered?"

"Are you kidding? Ask me the last time I had three women hanging on my every word. Look at this face, Emily." He angled his head to profile his bulbous nose and disappearing chin. "Guys who look like me don't turn women's heads. Guys who look like *them*"—he nodded at Alex and Erik—"are the ones with the wow factor. So I'm not feeling smothered by any means. In fact, I'm practically giddy with all the attention."

"You're sure they're not bothering you? Because I could try to have you switched to another team."

He bowed his head toward mine. "I'll tell you a secret. I grew up with five older sisters, so finding myself in a harem feels pretty normal to me."

"Five sisters? Wow. That's a lot of PMS under one roof."

"My friends thought I was the unluckiest kid in town to live in a house with so many females, but the truth is, I really liked my sisters. Still do. Girls are okay."

"My brother has five sons."

Cameron cringed. "Boys can be savages. Girls are so much more . . . civil. It's a real selling point."

I sighed. "I wish Isobel had been a little more civil. Talk about stirring up a hornet's nest."

"She mellowed a bit at dinner last night. She admitted she was wrong to take the cache, and she apologized for jeopardizing our chances at the grand prize, which was a lot of crow for her to eat, but she made the effort. She even volunteered to resign from the team, but I don't know if she was serious or just floating the idea to prove how sorry she was about what she'd done. We were actually pretty cohesive again when we left the dining room, even though Dolly and Bernice were still making noises under their breath. But my whole point is, if my team had been made up of five men, there would have been no apology, no compromise, and no good will. It'd be like dealing with five Bill Gordons in a never-ending pissing contest. So I'll keep my ladies. They're a lot nicer to hang out with."

"Lower your right shoulder and lift your chin a little," Alex instructed as he set up his shot. "Th*aaa*t's it. Nice one. Now let's get a shot of that famous profile. Good. Good. Can you manage a little more of a Heathcliff vibe? Less smolder and more anguished brooding?"

"This is as anguished as it gets," muttered Erik without moving his lips. "Will you just take the damn picture?"

Cameron grinned as he regarded the duo. "Is the guy with the famous profile a celebrity or something?"

"I guess you could say that. He's a cover model for romance novels. At least, he used to be. I don't know how long he's been out of the business."

"Okay. Maybe that explains it."

"Explains what?"

"Why he looks so familiar. I swear I've seen him before, but I can't place his face. You suppose I've seen him on the cover of a paperback romance?"

"How many romance novels have you read?"

"None, but my sisters were addicted. It's all they ever read. So I've seen my share of bare-chested hunks over the years."

"That would be quite a coincidence, wouldn't it?" I said, laughing. "You, traveling through Scotland with the hero of one of your sisters' romance novels? Maybe you should snap your own picture of Erik so you can show your siblings what he looks like with his shirt on."

Cameron threw a wary look crossdeck and nodded. "Yeah. Maybe I should."

For the next fifteen minutes, as we motored down the loch's long, narrow finger, I snapped occasional pictures of the hilly shoreline.

There was so much sameness in the scenery, however, that other than taking a few pictures of Alex and Erik and one of Cameron that he thought good enough to make into a Christmas card, I didn't feel impelled to go hog wild with the photography. By the time the skipper turned the boat around and headed back to shore, I'd seen more than enough of Loch Ness to satisfy my curiosity. I was just a little bummed that Nessie had kept such a low profile. Dad would be so disappoint—

Commotion in the wheelhouse. A loud thump. Shouts. A piercing scream. A high-pitched whine. A grinding of gears. And in the next instant we were careening toward shore like a rocket in hyperdrive.

I was catapulted off the bench and hit the deck hard on my hands and knees.

"Grab the throttle!" came the yell from the wheelhouse.

"Is he dead?"

"It's stuck!"

"Gimme a hand, someone!"

"Ohmigod! He's dead!"

"I can't budge it!"

"Outta the way! Let a real man give it a try."

Gasps of horror.

"You broke it!"

"It wasn't my fault!"

"Brace yourselves!"

"You mean, we can't stop?"

Air *whoosh*ed out of my lungs as Cameron heaved his body on top of mine. "Stay down! I'll try to—"

"We're all going to die!"

CRRRRRRRRRRRUNNNNNNNNNCH!

ELEVEN

"IT WAS NESSIE," DAD said breathlessly as we watched the ambulance tear out of the parking lot, siren blaring. "She showed up as a gigantic blip on the monitor. And she was right under the boat! But the skipper was too busy giving his spiel to notice what was happening on the fish finder."

"So you pointed it out to him?" I questioned.

"Yup."

"Which explains why we suddenly headed toward shore at warp speed?"

Dad crooked his mouth. "Not exactly. The throttle got pushed forward when the skipper passed out on top of it. And then it jammed, so we couldn't slow down. And that Gordon fella didn't help any when the knob came off in his hand." He glanced toward the waterfront, where boat company personnel were milling around the wreckage of what used to be their main dock. "How many knots do you suppose we were doing when we hit that thing?"

I followed his gaze, a fist clenching in my stomach. "I don't think I want to know."

"Guess it's not such a bad thing that Iowa's landlocked," he said upon reflection. "No docks to run into."

Despite ramming the dock at warp speed, we'd all managed to survive the crash with only minor scrapes and bruises. The only person needing transport to the hospital was the skipper, and this, only as a precautionary measure. His vital signs had been so good that the paramedics had ruled out a heart attack and suggested his sudden fainting spell might have been a vasovagal episode triggered by extreme emotional distress.

I guess this was the first time he'd ever seen a blip the size of Delaware on his fish finder.

"I caught the whole thing on video," Dad affirmed as he cradled his precious heap of camcorder scraps against his chest. "I could even show you what the blip looked like"—a piece of plastic casing slipped between his fingers and clattered onto the ground, prompting him to peer down at it—"if my camera was still in one piece."

"But you're not the only one who saw the anomaly. The captain saw it, too, right? So you can back each other up?"

"Yup. The skipper'd even be able to replay the actual footage for us"—another piece of camera casing fell to the ground—"if his fish finder was still in one piece."

The captain's new multifunction fish finder had been the only casualty in the accident, having crashed to the deck upon impact and disintegrated into a thousand slivers and shards. *The Highland Queen* herself had escaped damage, save for a few more chips gouged out of her already peeling paint. She might be an eyesore, but she was apparently an indestructible eyesore.

"Could I have your attention, please?"

At the sound of Wally's voice, we glanced toward the bus, where guests had congregated to compare their war scars and one-up each other with exaggerated tales of heroism and survival.

"Considering what many of you have just experienced, I'm not sure you want to proceed with the rest of the day's schedule." He stepped up into the well of the bus so we could see him better. "I'd like to see a show of hands to gauge how many of you would prefer to return to the hotel rather than have dinner at Drumnadrochit."

"What's for dinner if we go back to the hotel?" asked Bill Gordon.

"Will we have to wait all night for the food to be served again?" Dick Stolee called out.

"Skunk isn't on the menu at the hotel, is it?" Alice inquired.

"Mrs. Miceli?" a voice urged nearby.

I turned around to find our coach driver standing behind me with a sheepish look on his face. He was pleasantly rotund with a shaved head, amiable personality, and narrow necktie that was splattered with what looked like tomato soup stains. His name was Calum, but I had yet to figure out if that was his first or last name. "Could I speak ta ye privately fer a minute?"

"You bet." Leaving Dad to puzzle over the voting procedures on his own, I followed Calum to a more secluded area of the parking lot, where he took a deep breath before blurting out, "It's gone."

I guess I was supposed to know what that meant. "It?"

"The thing that was inside the tin box ye wanted me ta stow on the bus fer ye. It's not there anymore."

"The dirk?" I gasped. "The dirk is gone?"

"Is that what was inside?"

"Yes! A dirk. A really *old* dirk."

"Sorry. I put the tin in the cooler I keep up front, and when I went ta get a bottle of water a few minutes ago, the lid was off and the tin was empty."

I waited a beat, staring at him dumbstruck. "You stored the box in a cooler that can be accessed by everyone?"

He shrugged. "Seemed as good a place as any. Ye told me ta 'stow' the thing, so I did. Hey, it's a coach, not a passenger train. Space is at a premium. If ye'd wanted it kept totally out of sight, I assume ye would have asked me ta *hide* it instead of stow it. There's a world of difference in the meaning of those two words."

All the coach drivers on the tour circuit, and we had to hire the one with superior knowledge of four-letter transitive verbs.

"Nuts." I trained a look across the parking lot. One of the guests had obviously made off with the knife, but the question was, which one? "Did you happen to see any of the guests open the cooler?"

He shook his head. "We're down a few bottles of water, but I haven't noticed who's been taking it. Since it's free fer the taking, there's no reason ta keep track. But I have ta tell ye, Mrs. Miceli, I rarely have theft on my coach, so this surprises me."

I'd like to say it surprised me, but after what Isobel had pulled, I felt as if the floodgates had been thrown wide open. "Our thief certainly worked quickly."

"Probably happened this morning when guests were boarding. The thief opens the cooler thinking ta stock up on water ta wash down some pills and ends up taking yer dirk as well. Do ye know why any of yer guests might want the thing?"

I thought back to the scene in the library last night, when Bernice and Dolly nearly came to blows over which one of them should take ownership of it. "There are a couple of people who might like to prove it's worth something, but I'm not about to accuse either one of them of stealing without some evidence to back it up."

"How do ye feel about circumstantial evidence?" He pulled a plastic bottle out of his jacket pocket. "Keep yer eyes out fer a guest who's carrying a 23-milliliter bottle of our Thistle brand water, and ye might find yerself a thief."

The bottle was an ergonomically shaped mini in a bilious shade of lime green.

Exactly like the one Bill Gordon had yanked out of his fanny pack less than an hour ago.

"What do you suggest we do, bella? Strip search the man?"

"No! I don't want to see him naked. I just want to apply enough pressure to make him cough up the knife."

Etienne and I were headed down the staircase to the library, where, at any moment, Mom would be announcing the day's highly anticipated geocaching results. We'd arrived back from Drumnadrochit only a half-hour ago, so we were in something of a mad dash. We were thrilled that the majority had voted to stick with the schedule, however, because between the cuisine, the bagpipers, and the steady flow of Scotch whiskey, most of us had found a way to cope with the fright of our disastrous boat cruise.

Etienne slowed his steps as we approached the ground floor. "Have you any idea if Mr. Gordon is familiar with the history attached to the dirk?"

"Don't know, but he apparently collects ancient Scottish weaponry, so he might be more knowledgeable than any of us realize. I'm betting that if the knife stays missing, it'll eventually show up as the centerpiece of Bill Gordon's collection."

"Even with the dreaded curse looming over it?"

I rolled my eyes. "Trust me. Bill Gordon is the kind of guy who's a lot more interested in the monetary value of an artifact than in a dubious curse invoked by a man who's been dead for three hundred years." I flashed a toothy smile. "You can quote me on that."

He opened the stairwell door. "I might warn you against being too cavalier about the world of metaphysics, bella. Mysterious things can happen, many of which we're never able to explain."

I stepped into the lobby area and threw a long look toward the library. "Well, if you ask me, the only mysterious thing about Hamish Maccoull's dirk going missing is where Bill Gordon has hidden it."

"I should think you'd be happy to be rid of the thing."

That brought me up short. "Why would I be happy to be rid of an historic relic that belonged to Nana's most notorious relative?"

"Because, my darling"—he gave my chin a little pinch—"it's cursed."

"Comin' through!" shouted Bernice from the far end of the corridor. She was charging toward us with arms pumping, a body length ahead of her fellow team members. "Look lively, you slackers. It's wind sprints that'll keep us competitive."

Etienne and I jumped out of the way as they barreled past us—Cameron, red-faced from exertion, Lucille, huffing and puffing, and Dolly, swiveling her shapely hips in a speeded-up version of a beauty pageant walk.

"Mr. Dasher!" Etienne called when they'd passed.

Without breaking stride, Cameron U-turned back in our direction, followed by Lucille and Dolly, who U-turned with him. "You don't need to follow me, ladies," he gasped out as he paused beside us, head bent and hands braced on his thighs. "Catch up with Bernice. Save me a seat."

The women hesitated for only a heartbeat before sprinting toward the library as if they were a couple of crazed Bridezillas participating in the "Running of the Brides" wedding dress sale in Filene's Basement.

"I haven't had time to thank you for what you did for Emily today," Etienne said as he cupped his hand around the back of my neck and drew me close. "I don't know what I would have done if anything had happened to her. So, thank you. I'm in your debt." He extended his hand to Cameron who appeared to have to muster all the energy he had to shake it.

"No problem. Glad I could whip off my Average Joe shirt to reveal my true identity."

"Which is?" I asked, grinning.

He pulled the neck of his shirt away from his body and peered down his front, as if studying his undershirt. "It's supposed to say 'Aging Superhero,' but I can't be too sure since I'm not very good at reading things upside down."

I leaned over and pressed my lips to his cheek. "Etienne's right. Thanks for watching out for me."

"Don't stop there," he insisted. "Plant one on the other cheek, too. We're in Europe. It's acceptable."

"Cameron!" Lucille motioned to him from the entrance to the library. "C'mon! The seats are filling up fast. We're really late."

He raised his hand in a "Be right there" gesture. "What can I say?" He shrugged. "It's tough being the tour's designated hottie, but duty calls. See you in there."

"Have you recalled where you might have seen Erik Ishmael before?" I asked to his retreating back.

"Hey, I've been wracking my brain about that, but nothing's sticking." He tapped his fist against the crown of his head as if to jog something loose. "Have you ever seen your postman in the grocery store without his uniform and mail bag? You know you've seen him before; you just can't figure out where. That's what I'm dealing with."

Etienne's phone chimed softly. Fishing it out of his trouser pocket, he checked the caller ID before raising a finger for me to wait for him. "I need to take this, bella. Miceli," he said as he strolled away from me. He paced for a good five minutes while he conversed, his mood subdued when he returned.

"Not the news you wanted to hear?"

He forced a stream of air between his teeth. "That was the medical examiner. No results on Isobel's postmortem yet because he's having to send slides to another facility where the equipment is more high tech. He tells me he's never run into anything quite like this before, so he's rather mystified."

"He's never run into anything like … what?" I asked uneasily.

"Isobel's internal organs. Her stomach was so damaged, it looked as if it had simply exploded, and he's at a loss to explain why."

"Her organs *exploded*? Are you serious?"

He pressed a finger to his lips. "You're to tell no one, Emily. Not even your grandmother. Not until we receive the final report."

"But ... Oh, my God. How can anyone's organs just explode?" I gasped with incredulity. "And if she was flirting with major organ malfunction, how could she *not* fill out her medical history form?"

"A stomach doesn't normally explode on its own, bella, which is why the medical examiner is having to seek outside assistance with the diagnostic panels. Isobel's death is apparently far outside the realm of what modern medicine considers normal."

I looked up at him, not liking the sound of that. "So if organs don't explode on their own, does that mean some external influence *helped* them explode?"

"Shall we make an effort not to get ahead of ourselves?" he cautioned.

"But—"

He lifted my hand to his lips and kissed the hollow of my palm, causing my arm to tingle from fingertips to shoulder. "Your mother has just arrived with her laptop. Shall we continue this discussion later?"

The mood in the library was giddy.

"Is there anyone who hasn't seen my video of the *Highland Queen* crashing into the dock?" asked Dick Teig as he held his Smartphone in the air. "It's in high def, with stereo Sensurround."

"I have a picture of the rescue boat," offered Osmond.

"I have some nice footage of the paramedics starting the IV drip in the captain's arm," tittered Margi. "And a good still shot of the blood pressure cuff they were using."

The room was so crowded, Etienne and I couldn't find seats together, so he ended up standing by the windows, while I dragged a chair over to the table where Mom was setting up shop. The only person who wasn't riding high on emotion was Dad, who sat glumly in an armchair, looking as if the loss of his camcorder had caused him to lose his will to live.

Poor Dad. Maybe I'd have to buy him a new camera in Wick.

"Thank you all for being so prompt," Mom announced as she powered up her computer. "You did a wonderful job at the castle today, and I know you're anxious to hear the results."

All eyes riveted on Mom in anticipation of her next words. Breathing ceased. Fingers crossed.

"But first I'd like to tell you about the new system I devised that uses time as a mathematical function of—"

Groans. Boos. Hissing.

"Just tell us the results," yelled Bill Gordon.

"Yah," shouted Dolly. "We trust your math."

"Cut to the chase," encouraged Dick Stolee.

Mom looked dumbfounded. "You don't want to hear how I arrived at my calculations?"

"NO!" came the unanimous reply.

Muttering something under her breath, Mom hit a couple of keys that caused an incomprehensible grid to appear on her screen. She heaved a long-suffering sigh. "But the results won't make any sense to you unless I explain how I arrived at—"

"WHO WON?" bellowed Stella Gordon.

Lips twitching with irritation, Mom caved. "The winner of today's leg is"—she ran her finger across the screen as if to double-check—"the same team that is now at the top of the leader board and nosing ever closer to the grand prize of a free trip on Destinations Travel's next holiday adventure." She paused for dramatic effect. "Team Yes We Can!"

Team Five leaped off the sofa, shrieking like Justin Bieber groupies. "We won!" they cried, jumping up and down, bear-hugging, high-fiving, and peppering each other with kisses.

"Now we're cooking!" whooped Cameron as he banded his arms around Bernice, Lucille, and Dolly. "We're on a roll, ladies! There's no stopping us now! From last to first. BOO-yah!"

But as I regarded the expressions on the faces before me, it became obvious that not everyone was thrilled to see the emergence of the lowly underdogs as contest leaders.

Erik and Alex observed the celebration stone-faced.

Stella Gordon curled her lip into a menacing smile.

And Bill Gordon eased back stiffly in his chair, his eyes throwing daggers every bit as deadly as the one he'd stolen from the bus.

"I think Team Five deserves a round of applause," said Mom, clapping loudly, "or better yet, a toast!" She unzipped her fanny pack, retrieving a lime green mini bottle of Thistle brand water. She raised it in the air. "Anyone else?"

They pulled them out of shoulder bags, pockets, sporrans, purses, and tote bags and lifted them grudgingly into the air. Lime green mini bottles of Thistle brand water.

At least two dozen of them.

Nuts.

TWELVE

"THEY WAS HAVING A shoppers' special on bottled water in the hotel gift shop," Nana told me as we approached Wick the next day. "Buy one, get two free."

I frowned. "But why did you pay for water when you can get it free on the bus?"

"'Cuz the water in the hotel was on *sale*, dear. Gettin' somethin' for free don't got the same buzz as gettin' it dirt cheap."

We'd followed the coastline as we headed northeast on the A9. We visited the home of the Earls and Dukes of Sutherland at Dunrobin Castle, geocached at an obscure site near Hill o' Many Stanes, and spent the rest of the day crossing a flurry of firths and being wowed by sweeping views of the North Sea, which appeared to be stuck at permanent low tide despite our many hours on the road. I'd switched seats with George at our last comfort station, so this was the first time I'd been able to talk to Nana today.

"The clerk give us fair warnin' that the farther north we drove, the fewer shops we was gonna find, so we loaded up. I got three bottles, Tilly got six, and your mother got about a dozen." She gave me a hard look. "She probably wants to make sure I don't got no excuse for not takin' them dang pills she give me."

I hefted Nana's stubby bottle of Thistle brand water in my palm. Just my luck that Mrs. Dalrymple had stocked the same brand of water in her gift shop that Calum had stocked in his cooler. Talk about muddying the evidentiary waters. "Did you happen to see anyone other than the Iowa gang buying up the inventory?"

"Nope. But that don't mean they didn't get in on the deal. I wasn't in there too long 'cuz I wanted to run the bottles up to my room before the bus started loadin'."

"So when did you make your big purchase?"

"Yesterday mornin', after breakfast. Them two hunky fellas was in there tryin' on sweaters, so they probably seen the sale sign too." She glanced over her shoulder, then said in a low voice, "I don't know if you've noticed, dear, but them two young men aren't like the other fellas on the trip."

"No kidding?" I feigned surprise. "How so?"

She dropped her voice to a deathbed whisper. "They got real good fashion sense. I never seen nuthin' like it. I'm hopin' George'll pick up a few pointers. I don't got the heart to tell him what he looks like when he wears his plaid shirt with them checkered pants a his."

Signs for a hospital and railway station welcomed us to Wick. We crossed the stone bridge into the town, passing over a coastal river whose exposed bottom was a swill of black tidal mud cluttered with rocks, seaweed, and a blanket of neon green algae that was crawling up the support walls like a flesh-eating virus. Beyond the bridge was the town's business district, comprised of an orderly

155

assemblage of tidy stone buildings that housed the offices of local government. A giant sundial sat in a grassy recess in front of the largest building—a floral creation fashioned from so many flowers, it might have been the prize-winning float in the Rose Bowl parade. Farther down the street sat a slew of banks, real estate agencies, medical offices, vacant storefronts, boarded-up storefronts, painted-over storefronts, and Indian takeaway restaurants whose specialties were listed as curries, kebabs, and pizza.

Wick looked like a sleepy little town, but as we navigated to our hotel, I realized it wasn't actually sleepy.

It was deserted.

"You s'pose anyone lives here?" Nana asked, sounding a little creeped out.

"Maybe stores close early on Wednesdays." I regarded the empty sidewalks, the darkened storefronts, the absence of pedestrian traffic.

"But it's only three o'clock."

I felt a tingle of unease. "Maybe that's late in Wick." Dragging my eyes away from a butcher shop that was offering unbeatable prices on fresh haggis, I began gathering up my belongings. "Did you ever get a chance to skim Mrs. Dalrymple's Hamish Maccoull book?" I asked as we hung a left just past a fish and chips place.

"Finished it."

"You finished it?" I stared at her, bug-eyed. "It was like . . . four hundred pages long."

"Five hundred twelve."

"Oh, my God. Were you up all night?"

"Nope. Only took me a couple of hours."

My amazement increased. "How?" It had taken me three months to read the first Harry Potter book, and that had only been three hundred and twenty pages long.

"It's on account of the course they was offering at the Senior Center. *Speed Readin' for Geezers*. It targeted us old folks who wanna get to the bottom of our To-Be-Read piles before we die."

Five hundred pages in two hours? Man, at that rate, I could speed-read my way through the whole Windsor City Public Library in less than a week. I could become the human equivalent of Google! "*Uh*, will they be offering a course for say, younger adults?"

"Don't think so, but if they do, run the other way."

"Run? Why?"

She gave a little suck on her uppers. "'Cuz bein' able to read stuff at lightnin' speed isn't all it's cracked up to be. You just end up gettin' the bad news twice as fast."

"What bad news?"

"Don't really wanna talk about it, dear. It's too disturbin'."

"Are we still talking about the Hamish Maccoull book?"

"You bet. And all's I gotta say on the subject is, if them folks in that book are s'posed to be my relatives, I hope it turns out I'm adopted."

"We've got an emergency here," yelled Bernice as she waved her arm frantically to alert the entire bus. "There's no cell service!"

I heard horrified gasps as they went for their phones.

"How come my phone isn't working?" cried Margi.

"It's down," wailed Dick Teig in a near panic. "The whole system's down!"

"Does that mean we can't text?" asked Alice.

"How can we take pictures if our phones won't work?" fretted Lucille. "I knew buying these off-brand models was a mistake."

"How are we supposed to communicate with each other?" demanded Dick Stolee.

I guess engaging someone in conversation face-to-face wasn't an option.

Wally fired up his microphone and stepped into the aisle as we eased to a stop in front of the hotel. "The cell service in Wick can be a little spotty."

Hissing. Razzberries.

"They haven't constructed enough cell towers yet, and the wind can be a problem."

"How come no one warned us about that *before* we signed up for the trip?" railed Bernice.

"Because on some days, there's no problem at all. Tomorrow, it could be just fine."

"What if it isn't?" asked Helen. "We're looking at a lot of empty photo albums here."

"A couple of suggestions," he said without skipping a beat. "Pick up a disposable camera in town if you don't have access to photographic equipment other than your camera-phone. The grocery store across the street might even carry them. And if you need to phone family in the states, buy an international phone card and use the pay phone in the hotel."

Groans. Grumbles.

"Welcome back to the Stone Age," groused Dick Teig.

"Pay phone?" puzzled Osmond. "Do they still have pay phones?"

"How can I call home?" fretted Margi as she pined over her blank screen. "All my numbers are on speed dial."

"Are you telling us you can't remember your own sister's phone number?" taunted Dick Stolee.

"I don't have to remember," she snapped. "Didn't you hear me? It's on *speed* dial."

Before the invention of the computer chip, people prided themselves on being able to commit dozens of phone numbers to memory, most of which remained lodged in their heads until they died. With the new technology, people program all their numbers into their *phone's* memory so they can free up space in their brains to remember more critical things, like passwords and Pin numbers.

"How can we prove we've found our geocache containers if we can't take a picture of them?" Tilly called out.

Wally hesitated. "We'll have to—" He paused again. "Look, we don't have to deal with that until tomorrow, so let's put it on a back burner until then. If service gets restored, we won't have to deal with it at all."

As Calum lumbered down the stairs to begin offloading luggage, Wally addressed a few housekeeping issues. "Room keys will be available at the front desk when we go in, but the hotel doesn't employ a lot of staff, so you might have to wait awhile before your luggage appears outside your door. I'm going to switch up the schedule a little to allow you plenty of time to buy your cameras and phone cards, so let's plan to meet in the lobby in a half-hour to announce the winner of today's geocaching leg. Dinner's at six o'clock in the hotel dining room, and downtown stores will be open until nine this evening in case you diehard shoppers want to buy souvenirs. Lucky for us we're in Wick on a Wednesday when things are bustling. I'm told it's pretty dead around here the rest of the week."

The hotel lobby was an unremarkable space with a stone fireplace, threadbare rug, and furniture that might have been purchased from the local resale shop. My guys occupied the tatty armchairs near the windows, hands cradling their cell phones and eyes locked on their screens in the hopes that service would soon be restored. Bernice and Lucille bookended Cameron Dasher on the ledge fronting the fireplace, looking thrilled to have beaten out Dolly by a half-step for the plum seats beside him. Dad sat off in a corner by himself, shoulders slumped, staring at his shoes. Everyone else was scattered around the room in conversational groupings, squirming incessantly to maintain traction on the vinyl upholstery. I'd seated myself strategically across from Bill Gordon, because even though my bottled water theory had been blown to bits, I wasn't dismissing the idea that he could still be guilty of swiping the dagger. I just needed to isolate him from the crowd for a few minutes so I could do a little investigative probing.

"Is everyone here?" Mom stepped into the center of the room.

"Etienne and Wally are missing," I advised. "They're helping the valet staff deliver luggage." Since the "valet staff" consisted of a one-armed pensioner with a hunched back, bow legs, and one tooth in his head, it seemed the practical thing to do, especially since there was no elevator.

"Well, I can see you're all as excited to hear today's results as I am to announce them," Mom clutched her tabulations in her fist. "So without further ado—"

"Us folks on Team One wanna request a change," Nana spoke up as she raised a polite hand in the air.

"No changes!" Dolly Pinker decreed. "The rules are set and we're sticking to them. End of story."

"Hold it right there." Stella Gordon narrowed her eyes at Dolly. "The lady wasn't talking to you, so you can shut your trap."

"I don't care who she was talking to. We're not changing the rules."

"Bugger that." The words burst from Bill Gordon's mouth like sonic booms. He stabbed his finger at Dolly. "My Stella has as much right as anyone else in this room to have her say, so *you* shut *your* trap."

"Don't you dare speak to me that way, Bill Gordon. None of us is interested in what you have to say anymore." Dolly hiked her sleeve to her elbow, baring the colorful bruise on the underside of her forearm. "You see this? It's here because you were *sooo* cocksure of yourself on that boat yesterday, you nearly got us killed. It's a hematoma. Do you know how dangerous hematomas are? I could develop a blood clot and die!"

"Gee, that'd be a shame," Bernice said out the corner of her mouth.

Bill shot a defiant look around the room. "You mean to tell me, this is the thanks I get for trying to save all you people?"

"If you hadn't been so grabby, you wouldn't have broken the throttle," Dolly accused. "And if you hadn't broken the throttle, we might have been able to stop *before* we hit the damn dock!"

161

Head-bobbing. Nods of agreement.

"So that's the way the wind's blowing, is it?" His face grew ugly. "Ingrates. If it ever happens again, you can just sit there and suffer."

"We already are." Alex braced his palms on either side of his jaw and gently turned his head. "My neck is killing me, and if it gets any worse, guess whose butt is going to end up in a sling?"

Oh, God.

George raised his hand. "What does that mean exactly?"

"It means Alex is going to sue Bill's ass," Erik said helpfully.

With order starting to fray around the edges, I made a preemptive move and let fly a piercing whistle that silenced the group like an industrial-size mute button. I didn't dare wait for Mom to restore order.

She couldn't whistle worth beans.

"Thank you, Emily," Mom said when she stopped wincing. She smiled at the crowd. "Maybe you can take up the exciting issue of litigation after I announce the results. But first, the chair recognizes Marion Sippel and her request for a change."

Dolly tossed her head back and groaned. "Have you heard *nothing* we just—"

"Oh, put a sock in it," Bernice crabbed at her. "You had your say, now it's someone else's turn. Go ahead, Marion."

Whoa! Bernice was actually defending Nana's right to speak? She must really dislike Dolly to compromise her values so much.

"Our team's decided on a new name," Nana informed us. "We're Number One."

Mom waited expectantly. "I know you're Team Number One. What's the new name?"

"We're Number One," Nana repeated.

Mom's smile thinned. "You've said that twice already, Mother. Is there something about the question you don't understand?" Her eyes rounded in sudden alarm. "Oh, no. Have you stopped taking your herbal supplements?"

Nana lowered her eyelids and fixed Mom with a long, unblinking stare. "Don't make me come over there, Margaret. 'We're Number One' *is* the new name."

"You can't be number one," Bernice objected. "We're in the lead, so *we're* number one."

"No you're not," said Margi. "You're Team Number Five."

"But we're still first," Bernice shot back.

"I don't care what Team Number One calls itself," fussed Dolly. "We're still ahead. We're a lean, mean, searching machine, and it's our team who's going to end up saying, 'We're number one.'"

"I thought that name was already taken," said Helen.

"Show of hands," instructed Osmond. "How many people think—"

"QUIET!"

All eyes riveted on Mom. She might suck at whistling, but she was finding brand-new ways to employ her library skills.

"Here are your results. The times are a little slow today, because some of you are coping with the after-effects of yesterday's accident, but when your pain and soreness wear off, I'm sure you'll make up for it." She smiled broadly. "Imagine a little drumroll here. Okay then. In ascending order, Team Do It or Lose It is on the bottom, followed by Team Two, Team There Is No Dog, Team We're Number One, and Team Yes We Can."

Lucille Rassmuson launched herself off the fireplace ledge and executed a full-fledged jump-around, complete with bouncing, jumping, and jiggling. "We won again!" she hooted as she pulled Cameron, Bernice, and Dolly off the ledge to join her. "We won, we won, we won."

"Don't get too arrogant," Bill Gordon grumbled. "We're in second place and breathing down your necks like a heat-seeking missile. Tomorrow we'll pull ahead. You just wait and see. I guarantee it."

"Service is back on!" cried Alice. "I have a signal!"

Cheers. Whoops. Spontaneous keystroking.

So while the gang celebrated this uptick in their fortunes by text messaging the person who was probably sitting beside them, the other guests milled around, commiserating with each other about their inability to remain competitive with Team Five.

And it wasn't pretty.

I hadn't realized how banged up they really were until Mom mentioned it, but she'd been spot on. They were dragging themselves around like the walking wounded—limping, stiff-necked, rubbing their backs, massaging their shoulders. I could only imagine what condition I'd be in today if Cameron hadn't thrown himself on top of me to prevent me from sliding across the deck into the bulwark.

"I need to talk to you," Bill Gordon said in a raspy voice as he came up beside me. "Not here." He bobbed his head toward the opposite end of the room. "Over there."

"You bet." I could hardly contain my excitement. I didn't even need to come up with a dopey excuse for wanting to have a conversation with him. *Yes!*

"Can that pinhead really sue me?" he asked when we were out of earshot.

I gave him a withering look. "He has a name."

"Yeah, yeah, whatever. You know who I mean."

"The boat company bears full responsibility for damages, so even if *Mr. Hart* decided to sue, I doubt he'd be able to extract any money from you."

"So he can't take me for everything I'm worth?"

"I doubt it."

He exhaled a long breath. "Okay, that . . . that makes me feel better. My investments haven't been doing so well lately," he said in a surprising show of humility, "so the old portfolio has taken a major hit. You could say it's left me a little cash poor."

Aha! Could I pivot to the perfect segue or what? "A lot of people are cash poor right now . . . which is why we decided to offer our guests free bottled water on the bus instead of making them pay outrageous prices for it elsewhere. Have you had a chance to sample—"

"If Stella knew, she'd have a cow," he said, cutting me off. "There's no pleasing that woman. No matter what we have, it's never enough. I want, I want, I want. Buy, buy, buy. I swear she's got one aim, and that's to see me in ruins."

I waited a beat. "So does that mean you've taken advantage of the free water on the bus or not?"

He looked beyond me, his expression turning sour. "Damn."

"So what are you two discussing over here all by yourselves?" Stella inquired as she joined us.

"Nothing," he bristled. "I've gotta pee." And with that, he stalked off like a toddler on his way to a time out.

"He does that a lot," she said dully.

"Storm off?"

"Pee. It's one of those prostate things, but it doesn't stop him from testing out the equipment whenever he finds an opening, if you catch my drift."

Holy crap. Was she accusing him of being a serial adulterer?

"So what *were* you two talking about?" she asked, regarding me as if I were a cat with telltale canary feathers sticking out of my mouth.

"*Uhh*... litigation. I think Alex really rattled him, so—"

"Are you a lawyer?"

"No, but—"

"Then why would my husband need to approach you with legal questions?"

Hmm. This was a little awkward. "He, uh, he wanted an unprofessional opinion about liability, so I gave him one."

"And you expect me to believe that?" She took slow measure of me, looking me up and down. "You're planning a tryst, aren't you?"

"No! I don't want to try out Bill's equipment. I have my own equipment!" I paused. "Well, it's my husband's equipment, but I'm the primary user, and very happy with the operating system, so I'm *not* in the market for secondhand models."

"Sure, you're not. Women are attracted to Bill like turkey buzzards are attracted to roadkill."

I gave her a squinty look, wondering if that was supposed to be a compliment.

"It's the Gordon curse," she said matter-of-factly. "Gordon men bear the burden of being absolutely irresistible to women. It's because of their big, meaty hands"—her voice grew sultry, her eyes dreamy—"their broad, barrel chests. I've seen the way you look at Bill—you and that Pinker woman."

I blinked in shock. "Dolly practically accused him of involuntary manslaughter a few minutes ago. If she was looking at him funny, it was probably because she was imagining what he'd look like in a witness box after Alex slapped a lawsuit on him."

"Don't think I don't know what you're up to," she fired back. "And don't think I don't know how to stop it. You better watch yourself, missy, because I'm onto the two of you."

Cries of woe from the tatty armchairs by the window.

"Dang!" hollered Nana.

"What happened to our signal?" wailed Alice.

"Shoot! I was just about to send my message," Margi whined at Grace. "Now you'll never know what I was going to tell you."

"And one *more* thing," Stella griped as the noise and grumbling over lost cell service increased in volume. "You better check the quality of your beverage inventory, because that bottle of water Bill took out of your cooler yesterday? It leaked."

THIRTEEN

I forced myself to remain outwardly calm, but inside, I was doing cartwheels. "So... Bill took advantage of the complimentary water on the bus yesterday?"

"Of course, he did. You don't think he'd pay for it in the gift shop when he could get it for free, do you? He might be a sexual magnet, but he's still a skinflint."

"We're going shopping," Dick Teig announced as the gang paraded past me.

"We're gonna look for some of them disposable cameras on account a we can't take no more pictures if our phones are dead," said Nana.

"Did anyone notice a camera shop on our way through town?" asked Tilly.

"How are we supposed to find the right store if we don't have GPS to guide us there?" complained Dick Stolee.

"You could find it the old-fashioned way," I suggested.

They paused en masse, hanging on my next word.

"You could explore on foot."

Eye rolling. Snorting. Snickering.

"Oh, sure," squawked Helen. "Do you know how fast we'd get lost?"

"You're from Iowa," I reminded her. "Iowans don't *get* lost."

They exchanged questioning glances with each other. "That's right," Dick Teig marveled. "I forgot about that."

"Iowans don't get lost?" George looked skeptical. "Are you sure?"

"George!" I scolded. "Don't you remember navigating us single-handedly back to our hotel from the Carrick-a-rede Rope Bridge in Northern Ireland?"

He regarded me blankly. "Nope."

"I remember George doing that," Osmond agreed. "I just don't recall being in Ireland. Did we have a good time?"

"Hey, guys," I asked as I saw our bellman dithering over the best route to get around all of us. "Can you clear a path so the bellman can get through?"

They dutifully scattered to left and right, forming two orderly contra lines that the bellman trudged between, wheeling a huge tartan plaid suitcase behind him. "That's Bill's suitcase," Stella observed from behind me, "but"—she had the grace to lower her voice—"how's that poor schnook going to drag it up three flights of stairs with only one arm?"

"Say." Dick Teig stopped the bellman as he passed. "Can you tell us where the nearest camera shop is?"

"Aye," said the bellman, letting go the luggage handle to free up his hand for direction giving. "Ye hae nae sookie"—he gestured toward the town center—"and goon ma hook fer loony."

"Right," said Dick with a hesitant nod. "Everyone got that?"

Self-conscious looks. Desperate glances.

Margi plugged a finger into her ear and rattled it around for a couple of seconds. "Would you ask him to repeat it? I think my eardrum is punctured."

"Ye hae nae sookie," he repeated pleasantly, "and goon ma hook fer loony."

"Okay," said Margi, "it's not my eardrum."

"Could he draw us a map?" asked Alice.

The bellman shook his head. "Oi nae sinne doonan," he said, rotating his lone hand in the air.

"What'd he say?" asked Nana.

"He says he can't write with his left hand," volunteered a glum voice from the lobby.

I stared at the gang. The gang stared at me. We all turned around to stare at Dad, who was still huddled in an armchair in the far corner of the now vacated room.

"You can understand him?" I asked with no small degree of astonishment.

"Sure," he said without pomp. "Can't you?"

"*Uhhh*—No?"

"Dick understood him, didn't you, Dick?" prodded Helen Teig.

"Quiet, Helen," he grumbled under his breath.

The bellman smiled cheerfully as he bobbed his head. "Dooky ma poon," he said as he flexed his misshapen fingers.

Nana lengthened her eyes to tiny slits. "Are you sure he's not speakin' in tongues?"

"He says he could never hold a pen correctly in his left hand, so he gave up trying decades ago," Dad translated.

"He said all that in three words?" gaped Osmond.

Dad looked slightly sheepish. "Well, I added a few prepositions for clarity."

"Aww," Margi commiserated, offering the man a sympathetic look. "The old Palmer handwriting method was a bear to learn, wasn't it? I hear they're not teaching it anymore, and people are so happy to be rid of it, they're not even complaining about being illiterate."

"So what'd he say about the camera shop?" urged Dick Stolee.

Dad boosted himself out of his chair and walked over to us with the hint of a spring in his step. "Out the front entrance, left to High Street, then a right. The camera shop is halfway down the block, next to the jewelry store, and they'll be open late tonight. And if you tell them you're guests of the hotel, they'll give you an extra discount on all sale merchandise." He made eye contact with the bellman. "Sound about right?"

"Dung ma hooey fer tootie poo tae glaum an furk a loon ma fanny."

"What'd he say?" asked Nana.

"He said, 'Yup.'"

"All right then," Dick Stolee announced. "Let's hit the road. If we hurry, we'll be able to make it back in time for dinner."

"How much time before dinner's served?" Alice called out as they rushed the front doors.

"Two n' a half hours," said George.

"Dang," Nana wailed as they shot out the doors. "That don't give us no time at all."

"That suitcase belongs in room 312," Stella told the bellman with an air of condescension in her voice, "and it's filled with some irreplaceable stuff, so you better take extra care. My husband will have a bird if you damage anything on your way up."

Irreplaceable stuff? Irreplaceable, as in, a three-hundred-year-old dagger?

I fired a glance at the suitcase, noting the easy-glide zipper and absence of a security lock or TSA strap. *Gee.* Unimpeded access. How handy was that? "I'll help him," I offered, trying unsuccessfully to hide my excitement.

Stella regarded me, deadpan. "If I were you, I wouldn't be so thrilled about the prospect of tearing your shoulder out of its socket. I hear the surgery to repair it is a bitch." Hoisting the strap of her pocketbook higher up her arm, she marched through the outer lobby and out the front door, leaving me in sole charge of Bill's luggage.

Almost.

"How about I give you a hand?" I chirped at the bellman as I gripped the handle of the bag. "This'll free you up to deliver someone else's."

He clapped his hand on top of mine and let fly a happy stream of jibberish. I deferred to Dad for the translation.

"He says he's got it."

"But look how many other pieces he has to deliver." I nodded toward the outer lobby, where our remaining bags were corralled in a roped-off area. "If I pitch in, we'll have this stuff delivered in no time at all."

The bellman shook his head. Dad offered a quick translation. "That's a no."

"What floor is that one headed for?" Wally called out as he strode toward us from the corridor.

"Third," I said as I tightened my grip.

The bellman exerted his authority and tugged the handle away from me. I exerted mine and tugged it back.

"Out of the way," Wally insisted as he knocked both our hands away, commandeering what amounted to a hostile takeover. "I'll take it."

"You can't do that!" I protested.

"Fug yer gooney!" cried the bellman.

Wally paused. "What'd he say?"

"'You can't do that!'" Dad repeated.

Wally arched his eyebrows. "You can understand him?"

"Look, Wally," I said in a breathless rush, "I can handle this. It's very important that *I* handle this."

"You have a good ear, Mr. Andrew." Wally gave an approving nod, clearly impressed with Dad's interpretive language skills. "How long have you been able to decipher the Scottish tongue?"

Dad marked the time on his wristwatch. "About three minutes."

"How many bags do we have left?" Etienne asked as he sprinted down the corridor in our direction.

"Miceli! Did you know your father-in-law can understand the language, burr and all?"

"Seriously? I wish you'd said something sooner, Bob. I've been going around and around with the people at the front desk, and I still don't know what they're saying. You want to give it a try?"

Dad's face brightened. "You bet."

Etienne kissed my forehead on the way by while Wally charged down the corridor in the opposite direction, pulling Bill Gordon's luggage behind him. "Hey, Emily," he called back to me, "if you want to help out, there's a couple of smaller bags in the corral that you could probably handle."

"Thanks," I said flatly as he wheeled the suitcase out of sight. "I'll get right on it."

With Etienne preoccupied with hotel personnel and two whole hours to kill before dinner, I decided to bite the bullet and look into buying Dad a camcorder to replace the one he broke.

After taking a quick shower and freshening up, I purchased insect repellent and a fly swatter at the grocery market across the street, then hanged a left at a knitting store and walked a couple of blocks until I reached High Street, which seemed even more deserted than it had been before, if that was possible. Window shopping was obviously not one of the main pursuits of Wick's elusive populace.

I found the jewelry shop halfway down the block, and next to it…a hardware store? I peered at the garden implements and boxes of casual china on display in the window, realizing this was the right place only after I saw Nana standing behind a sixteen-piece set of Corelle dinnerware, waving me away.

What?

I gave her a questioning look, to which she responded by raising a finger for me to wait.

"Is this the latest trend in merchandising?" I asked when she exited the building to join me. "Disguising a camera shop as a hardware store?"

"They got them disposable cameras all right, dear, and some real nice digital ones, but you don't wanna go in there right now on account of the clerk's a little overwhelmed. He don't speak English real good, so we had to send a runner to fetch your father. And now we got another delay 'cuz your father's a little winded."

"Oh." I craned my neck to watch the flurry of activity inside. "Well, if Dad's inside, I'd better wait until he leaves because I want to surprise him with a new camcorder. Did you notice any camcorders for sale?"

"Yup. But folks was more interested in the hot ticket items."

I smiled. "What's considered a hot ticket item in Wick, Scotland?"

"SaladShooters and Chia pets. Back home, you can't find 'em no time but Christmas, but here, you can buy 'em all year round. Isn't that somethin'? Grace and Helen are lookin' to have some shipped home to have on hand for family birthdays."

"Have you bought your camera yet?"

"Nope. I couldn't get near the checkout counter 'cuz the Dicks are hoggin' the calculator, tryin' to help the clerk figure out volume discounts."

"So, you want to stroll down High Street with me until the dust clears in there?"

"You bet."

"Do you need to tell George and Tilly where you are?"

"Nope." She dug out her phone. "When the signal comes back on, I'll text 'em."

I regarded her oddly, noting a distinct improvement in her posture. "How come you're not lopsided anymore?"

She steepled a finger against her lips and threw a conspiratorial look right and left. "Don't tell your mother, but I lightened my load."

Crossing to the opposite side of the street, we followed the sidewalk toward a neatly paved pedestrian mall flanked by buildings that evoked images of what the world would look like if its entire population suddenly disappeared. There was no line at the Lloyds Bank cash machine. No moms buying children's clothes at M & Co. No customers fighting over free vouchers for cell phones at Woolworths. There *was* a certain charm to the place in an abandoned kind of way—the chimney pots crowded atop chimneys, the dunce-capped turret on the Crown Bar, the Victorian streetlights interspersed between wooden benches and baskets of summer flowers.

Nana looped her arm through mine as my stack-heeled slides *clacked* on the pavers, echoing through the emptiness. "You s'pose this is where them fellas at the History Channel filmed that series, 'Life After People'?"

No customers at the news agents. No patrons seated around the outside dining tables at the freehouse.

"I've never seen that show."

"If you got a notion that the planet's in bad shape now, you oughta see what happens when no one's around to screw it up no more."

We peeked through the windows of an establishment called Morag's, which seemed to play a dual role as a gift shop, selling boxed jewelry and animal figurines, and a restaurant, serving food other than Indian, Chinese, or takeaway. Their *We're Open* sign hung inside the front door, but I assumed it was too early yet for the dinner crowd, because the place was empty.

"Morag's," Nana mused as we passed by. "I was readin' about a Morag last night."

"In the Hamish Maccoull book?"

"Yup. She was kin. The daughter of one of Hamish's brothers, and she didn't want nuthin' to do with no marriage her folks was gonna arrange, so she threw a tantrum."

"Did she have a crush on someone else?"

"Nope. She was just bein' what you'd call a teenager."

"So how did parents deal with difficult teenagers three hundred years ago when they couldn't threaten them with loss of car or cell phone privileges?"

"They sent her off to fend for herself in the middle of winter with nuthin' but the clothes on her back."

"*Ew*. Harsh, much?"

"Yup. They found her body after the snow melted. Looked like she'd starved to death on account of she couldn't find nuthin' to eat."

"Oh, my God." We sauntered past an abandoned bakery shop and a real estate office, whose available listings were prominently displayed in the window. "That's"—I shivered—"unconscionable."

"You haven't heard nuthin' yet. You wanna know what Hamish done to a fella what he caught poachin' on his land?"

I bolstered myself with a calming breath. "Does the story involve blood, violence, or keenly honed weaponry?"

"Don't know. Depends on how sharp his broadsword was when he lopped the fella's arm off."

"Nana!" As we strolled beyond the real estate office, I passed a glance down the narrow lane that veered off to our left—which is when I saw the legs poking out from behind a black metal trash barrel. "Ohmigod."

I rushed over to the body and dropped to my knees. "Oh, God. It's Dolly."

She was curled in a fetal position on the pavement, eyes wide and fixed, mouth gaping open, fists still clutched against her stomach. I tried to find a pulse on her neck, her wrist.

Nothing.

I shot a look at Nana. "Do you have a signal on your phone yet?"

She checked the screen. "Still out."

"Try Morag's. They must have a landline. Nine-nine-nine. And tell them to hurry."

"Check her pocketbook, dear," she said as she turned back toward the restaurant. "Maybe she's got meds that can help."

Help bring her back from the dead?

I stared at the steamer trunk of a handbag lying beside her.

And yet...

I grabbed it off the ground and tore open the zipper. Wallet. Passport. Baby aspirin. Breath mints. Mini bottle of water. Cosmetic bag.

I riffled through the contents, hoping to find at least one bottle of pills. What I found instead, hiding at the very bottom of the pile, wrapped in a plush terry washcloth, was Hamish Maccoull's missing dirk.

FOURTEEN

He introduced himself as Detective Constable Nigel Bean, and the hotel was kind enough to offer him the use of the manager's office so he could question me in private, away from the rain that had started to fall.

"So when I couldn't find a pulse, I sent my grandmother to Morag's to call an ambulance. I guess you know the rest."

Officer Bean made a final notation in his notebook before looking across the manager's desk at me. He was middle-aged and stocky, with abnormally large ears, a space between his front teeth, and a voice that started at his toes and rumbled all the way up his body. I figured he was an import from another locale, not because he looked any different than the hotel staff, but because when he spoke, I could actually understand what he was saying.

"I'd like ta thank ye fer yer actions, Mrs. Miceli. I just wish it could hae made a difference." He drummed his finger on the medical form Wally had supplied him. "I'm a bit baffled. According ta her own account, Ms. Pinker was fit as they come, other than a bruise I noticed on her arm."

"She received that yesterday in a boat mishap." Her prediction echoed in my head. "Is it possible she died from a blood clot that formed because of the bruise?"

"It was justa wee bruise." He shrugged. "So whit would cause an otherwise healthy female ta suddenly collapse and die?"

"Our tour director told me the only drug she was taking was a daily baby aspirin."

Bean grinned. "I've heard that people can be less than truthful on these forms, which is why I've sent an officer ta search her room fer prescription bottles." He rechecked his notes. "I don't know if we've checked her handbag yet."

"I, uh, I already went through her pocketbook. My grandmother thought she might be carrying something that might help us revive her, but all I found was the baby aspirin." I slid my hand into my shoulder bag. "And this." I placed the dirk on the desk.

He raised a bushy eyebrow, his gaze lingering on the dagger for a long moment before he leaned back in his chair and said in an almost too calm voice, "If there's a good reason why Ms. Pinker's personal effects are in yer handbag and not her own, I'd like ta hear it."

I winced. "It's kind of a long story."

He folded his arms across his chest. "I'm listening."

I opted for the abridged version, explaining about the geocaching element of our tour, Isobel Kronk's part in the dagger's appearance, my inheritance of the thing after her sudden death, its mysterious disappearance yesterday, and its unexpected reappearance in the washcloth at the bottom of Dolly's pocketbook. "I should have known better than to remove it from her bag. I mean, my husband is a former police inspector. He'd be appalled if he knew what I did. But I was afraid if I left it where it was, it might get lost in bureaucratic red tape, and I'd lose track of it completely. Obviously, not one of my better decisions."

"This is the second death you've suffered on yer tour?"

I nodded.

"And ye've been in the country fer how many days?"

I lowered my voice to a self-conscious whisper. "Three."

He scribbled a notation. "Do ye know the cause of Ms. Kronk's death?"

"The medical examiner hasn't been able to draw any conclusions yet. He needed to farm out some tests to a lab with higher tech equipment, but his initial analysis apparently indicated that Isobel's stomach kind of … exploded."

He fixed me with a look that caused his eyes to shrink to the size of pebbles. "Exploded?"

I nodded again. "He told my husband that it was a pretty unusual case. I guess exploding stomachs are a rarity in Inverness."

"I believe they're a rarity anywhere. Whereabouts in Inverness were ye? I grew up just outside the city, on the banks of the River Ness."

"*That's* why I can understand you."

"Beg pardon?"

I leaned closer in and lowered my voice to a hushed tone. "We didn't have any trouble understanding the people in Inverness, but we're all having trouble understanding the hotel staff here. Their burr is a little … challenging."

He smiled in agreement. "It indeed takes some getting used ta. My wife is from Wick, and I still don't know whit she's saying half the time." He pondered that for a half-second. "Which isn't always a bad thing. Please, go on with whit ye were saying."

"*Uh*—we were staying at the Crannach Arms Inn on Loch Ness when Isobel died."

"Is that a fact? And did ye meet the proprietress whilst ye were there?"

"Mrs. Dalrymple? I certainly did. Do you know her?"

"She's my aunt."

"No kidding? Well, it was your aunt who insisted I take the dirk."

"Why was that?"

"Because, according to her, it has a rather checkered history, and she didn't want it lying around her hotel, contaminating the air with bad karma."

He grinned. "Aunt Morna was always one ta get yer blood pumping with her talk of spells and incantations. When I was a lad, I spent many happy days digging through the picture books in her library, scaring the bejeebers out of myself." He leaned forward in his chair and dragged the dagger toward him. "So let's have a look at this dirk."

"Your aunt had a book that documented its entire provenance."

He held it beneath the banker's lamp on the desk, angling it right and left as he examined the scrawl beneath the hilt. "Hamish Maccoull?" His voice cracked like that of a fourteen-year-old entering puberty. "Are ye telling me this is the dirk that belonged ta *the* Hamish Maccoull?"

"That was your aunt's opinion."

"It's been missing fer centuries!"

I shrugged. "Isobel Kronk found it in a hollow tree in Braemar."

"This is incredible. The inscription is still perfectly legible." He trailed a fingertip across the string of ancient words as he squinted to see them more clearly.

"You speak Gaelic?"

"I don't speak it, but I can read it. Aunt Morna made sure of that." He hesitated as he translated the words, his complexion losing some of its color. "Well." He quickly set the dagger back on the desk, regarding it as if it had suddenly sprouted fangs and a rattler.

"I'm apparently descended from a long line of Maccoulls on my mother's side, so Hamish's dirk has some historical significance for our family."

He inched the dagger across the desk with the tip of his forefinger. "So Isobel Kronk removed the dirk from its hiding place, and you later found her dead."

"Yup."

"And Dolly Pinker stole the dirk from another hiding place, and ye later found *her* dead."

I sighed glumly. "Yup."

"All right then." He wrote something in his notebook before flipping it shut and slipping it into his shirt pocket. "Thank ye fer yer cooperation, Mrs. Miceli. I've no other questions at the moment, but I'd like ta speak with yer grandmother."

"She's out in the lobby." I eyed him skeptically. "So ... I can just leave?"

"Aye."

"You're not going to throw the book at me for absconding with possible evidence?"

"Not at all. In fact, it's yers fer the taking." He slid the dagger the rest of the way toward me.

"No kidding?"

"Departmental rule: a weapon not used in the commission of a crime is not evidence. Besides, I'm thinking that Ms. Pinker had no right ta take it from the outset, so I'm giving it back ta ye. But I'd suggest ye keep it away from the rest of the group this time."

He circled the desk and swept his hand toward the door. "I'll follow ye out, Mrs. Miceli."

I stowed the dirk in my shoulder bag, gathered my belongings, and extended my hand to him as I stood up. "I appreciate your being so reasonable about the dirk, Officer Bean. Thank you again."

He pumped my hand. "No worries."

"I was really afraid you were going to lock it up in your evidence room at the police station."

He laughed as we reached the door. "I couldn't very well do that, could I?"

I gave him a questioning look. "Why not?"

"Wouldn't dare take the risk. I'll not hae that thing anywhere near my department, Mrs. Miceli. Didn't Aunt Morna translate the inscription fer ye? It's cursed."

The sound of angry voices beyond the door caused Bean to spring into high alert. With an apologetic grunt, he rushed past me, leaving me to follow hot on his heels as he maneuvered around the clerks at the front desk and charged into the lobby.

"Knocking off *one* of our team members wasn't enough?" Cameron Dasher bellowed at the guests crowded into the room. "You decided you had to knock off *two*?"

Bill Gordon shot to his feet, face red and finger stabbing the air. "Just who the hell are you accusing of whacking your teammates, Dasher?"

"Someone in this room!" Cameron pulled a fierce face, his eyes shooting fire as he ranged a look at his tour companions. "You think I'm dumb enough to believe that two deaths on my team are pure coincidence? One of you is so afraid we're going to win the whole shooting match that you're bent on killing every member of our team to make damn sure it doesn't happen!"

Officer Bean cleared his throat with enough force to cause heads to swivel around. "Please continue," he encouraged Cameron as the room suddenly fell silent.

"Ask them!" Cameron tossed his hand out to indicate the room at large. "Ask them where they were when Dolly collapsed."

"Forget *us*!" Bill spat. "Where were you?"

Lucille Rassmuson bounced to her feet so fast, she nearly knocked Cameron over. "I resent that implication, Mister," she snapped at Bill. "We were hiking across that bridge at the far end of town when Dolly decided to head back to the hotel."

"Yeah," said Bernice, jumping up beside her. "We figured the edge of town was the only place we could plan our next strategic move without the rest of you losers trying to eavesdrop on us."

"What prompted Ms. Pinker ta leave?" asked Bean.

"She was complaining of a headache," said Cameron.

"Whining about a headache is more like it," groused Bernice. "Are you familiar with the term 'drama queen'?"

"I suggested she come back to the hotel and take a hot bath," said Lucille, crimping her brow as she added, "I haven't had a headache since The Change, but I'm pretty sure that's what I used to do to get rid of one."

"I think I used to hold my breath and count to ten," Alice reminisced.

"No kidding?" marveled Osmond. "You're not gonna believe this, but I do the same thing to get rid of hiccups!"

"I assume Ms. Pinker took yer advice?" Bean pressed Lucille.

"Yup. Her head hurt, and she was starting to get a little queasy, so she took off. We offered to walk back with her—" She fisted a hand on her hip and shot Bernice a tart look. "At least, Cameron and I offered, but—"

"She had a freaking *headache*," Bernice defended. "It wasn't as if she was on her deathbed…even though she apparently was."

"We shouldn't have listened to her," said Cameron, his voice brimming with regret. "We should have insisted on walking back with her."

"I think she was suffering from a killer migraine," Lucille theorized. "Can killer migraines actually kill?"

"Well, something killed her," said Cameron. He slanted a suspicious look around the room, his gaze lingering on Bill Gordon. "Bernice, Lucille, and I were hiking along the river near the bay when Dolly died. So where were the rest of you?"

"It's none of your business where we were," barked Bill.

"I was in the camera shop," Margi volunteered. She bobbed her head at the people surrounding her. "Me…and all of my closest friends."

Nine finger-waving Iowans flapped their hands into the air— a number that decreased by one when Osmond suddenly peeked inside the shopping bag in his lap. He scratched his head. "If I was in a camera shop, what am I doing with a SaladShooter?"

"I spent a long time shopping in the market across the street," Stella offered without prodding. "I wanted to stock up on junk food in case the only choice on tonight's dinner menu is haggis."

Gee, that was curious. I'd picked up a couple of things in the market, too, but I hadn't spotted Stella.

"What's haggis?" asked Margi.

Tilly raised her voice to lecture room volume. "It's a mixture of sheep's heart, lungs, and liver, minced together with onions and oatmeal and boiled in a sheep's stomach to create a very tasty pudding. It's Scotland's national dish."

"I've eaten in yer hotel dining room," Officer Bean said proudly. "Ye hae my word that the haggis is excellent."

The color drained from Margi's face. She shot Stella an imploring look. "Did you happen to notice how late the market stays open tonight?"

"Could we talk about haggis later?" urged Cameron. "Don't you think it's more important right now to find out where everyone was this afternoon?"

I stepped closer to Officer Bean, because if Cameron kept forcing the issue, Bill's short fuse could easily erupt into a full blown—

"I took a walk," Bill replied calmly, his expression as smug as a champion chess player who was about to squash his opponent. "A nice long jaunt along the riverbank west of here. So if you're expecting an alibi from me, I hate to disappoint you, but I don't have one." He flashed an oily smile. "It was just me, and swarms of midges."

"They're particularly bad this time of year," Bean agreed, "especially if yer hiking along the river away from the bay."

Cameron stared at Bean, thunderstruck. "You actually believe him?"

Bean massaged his jaw for a long moment, his gaze drifting over the two-dozen guests crammed into the room. "I've no bone ta pick with any of ye. I'm not investigating any of ye. If the medical examiner says Ms. Pinker died from something suspicious, then we'll hae reason ta talk. But until then, I've no authority to slap irons on any of ye fer taking a stroll along the river."

"Do tourists often drop dead in the streets of Wick for no apparent reason?" Tilly asked him.

"Healthy people don't usually collapse on the pavement and die," Bean replied in a tight voice. "I expect the medical examiner will back that up with his report, unless he discovers that the lady died from something that … defies explanation."

"Like what?" Dick Teig called out.

Bean shuffled his feet. His voice grew strained. "I prefer ta leave that ta the experts."

Holy crap! I stared at him, bug-eyed. Was he hinting that Dolly might have died because of the curse? No twenty-first-century law officer could believe that, could he?

Cameron let out a long, frustrated sigh. "I'm happy you consider this an open and shut case, Officer. Two people on my team have died in two days. Can you actually stand there and tell me you think it's mere coincidence?"

"Yah," Lucille spoke up. "There's only three of us left." She pointed her finger at Bernice, Cameron, and herself. "One. Two. Three."

"Two of you left," Bernice said as she broke away from her teammates. "I quit."

"WHAT?" The word shot out of Lucille's and Cameron's mouths at the same time.

"You heard me." She folded her arms across her chest and plunked down onto the fireplace ledge. "Winning a free trip won't do me any good if I'm too dead to enjoy it."

"You *can't* quit the team," fretted Lucille.

"Oh, yah? Watch me."

"But what about Cameron and me? You're ruining our chances! How are we supposed to play the game with only two of us?"

Bernice fluttered her hands in the air as if washing them of the whole affair. "Don't know. Don't care."

Cameron groaned. "C'mon, Bernice. You can't give up. The team needs you."

"Tough. I'm abandoning ship."

"Just like a rat," sneered Lucille.

"Sticks and stones," hissed Bernice.

"Spoilsport," Lucille hissed back.

Bernice rocketed to her feet, spittle flying from her mouth. "You people are such morons! Wake up and smell the coffee. Don't you ever watch horror movies? Why do you think the members of Team Five are dropping like flies?"

Blank looks flew around the room. Margi raised her hand. "This is just hypothetical, but will our answers be counted if we don't watch horror movies?"

"It's because Team Five is cursed," yelled Bernice.

My mouth fell open. She *couldn't* know about the curse. No way. It had to be a lucky guess.

189

Gasps. Wheezing. Shock.

"That's just plain stupid," snorted George. "There's no such thing as a curse."

"What if it's voodoo?" said Grace.

"Is voodoo the one where you stick needles into things?" asked Margi. "Or is that pin the tail on the donkey?"

"Curses are more common in the British Isles than voodoo," Tilly informed us.

"I think all forms of cursing should be outlawed," declared Alice.

"Forgive the interruption," Officer Bean cut in, "but I hae a mountain of reports ta fill out back at my office, so I'd like ta ask Mrs. Miceli's grandmother a few questions before I'm on my way. Mrs. Maccoull, is it?"

"Mrs. who?" asked Dick Teig.

Bean paused. "Is Maccoull the wrong name?"

I felt my knees come slightly unhinged as I watched Bill Gordon's expression shift from bored, to roused, to feral. *Unh-oh.* This wasn't good.

"Maccoull?" echoed Bill Gordon in a booming voice. "There's a Maccoull among us?"

"She's not a Maccoull," I leaped in. "She's a Sippel. Mrs. Samuel Sippel. And she was probably adopted, so the family history doesn't really apply to her."

"SHE'S A MACCOULL?" Bill roared.

I heard footsteps suddenly pounding down the ground floor corridor. Mom raced helter-skelter into the lobby, gasping for breath, looking like an early explorer in search of a civilization. "I'm so sorry I've kept you waiting. I completely lost track of time. Have they rung the dinner gong yet?"

190

"Any minute now," said Dick Stolee.

Since we had forty-five minutes before dinner, I figured he was using the new math.

"Do you want to know what happened to Dolly Pinker?" Bill called out to Officer Bean. "I'll tell you what happened." He stabbed an accusatory finger at Nana. "*That* woman killed her."

Nana pivoted her head left and right before realizing Bill was aiming his finger at her. "*I* killed her?" She blinked her surprise. "No kiddin'?"

"She most certainly did not!" I cried.

"Maccoulls have been locked in a blood feud with MacDonalds for centuries," Bill ranted. "Dolly Pinker was a MacDonald." He fixed Bean with a hard look. "You know what a bunch of savages the Maccoulls are. *Every* Scotsman knows. Do I have to draw you a picture?"

"My grandmother is treasurer of the Legion of Mary," I defended. "She does not engage in blood feuds. She knows nothing about blood feuds!"

"Feuding is all the Maccoulls know," raged Bill. "It's in their blood. It's in *her* blood." He stabbed his finger at Nana again. "She killed Dolly as sure as I'm standing here. Ask her what was in those pills she was handing out at breakfast this morning. She gave them to everyone, but I bet she saved a very special one for Dolly. She gave her the one that killed her!"

Officer Bean's expression grew sober. "Ye distributed medications at breakfast this morning, Mrs. Sippel?"

"They wasn't medications, Officer. They was supplements. Herbal supplements."

Mom gasped so loudly, she probably collapsed a lung. "Mother! You gave away the supplements I bought you?"

"You bet," Nana fired back. "They was makin' me lopsided."

"They were not."

"Were so."

Mom let out a cry of irritation. "If swallowed with a full glass of water *as intended*, those supplements are supposed to strengthen your bones and *improve* your lopsidedness."

"My lopsidedness improved the minute I give 'em away. So there."

Alice raised her hand. "I swallowed several of Marion's supplements this morning. Am I going to die, too?"

Whispers. Chatter. Alarm.

"I wouldn't put it past a Maccoull to try to kill all of us," Bill accused. "How do we know she didn't slip Isobel a poison pill and kill her, too?"

"The *nerve* of you!" I snapped at Bill. "My grandmother is *not* a killer. Have you lost your mind? Look at her!" She executed a little finger wave as all eyes focused on her. "Is that the face of a cold-blooded killer?"

Officer Bean apparently thought it was. "Can ye tell me whit kind of supplements ye were passing out, Mrs. Sippel?"

"The stuff what's s'posed to keep us old folks livin' forever. Big honkin' capsules. Bark. Weeds. Warts."

"She not ingesting warts," Mom explained helpfully. "She's taking St. John's wort, which is an excellent herbal for fending off depression."

"It don't work," fussed Nana. "I get depressed just thinkin' about havin' to unscrew the caps off all them bottles three times a day. My wrists can't take the strain."

Officer Bean smiled gently. "Perhaps ye'd be good enough ta come down ta the station with me, Mrs. Sippel. I think we might need ta discuss this more thoroughly."

"You're arresting my mother?" shrieked Mom.

"I'm taking her in fer questioning," said Bean.

"You can't do that," Mom pleaded. "She's old and fragile. She could suffer a stroke at the mere thought of riding in a police car. My daughter is right. My mother is no killer. If you leave her at the hotel with me, I'll take full responsibility for her. I swear it. I'll move into her room with her, and I won't let her out of my sight."

Bean's jaw pulsed with indecision. He leveled a look at Nana. "Whit do ye think of that proposition, Mrs. Sippel? If I question ye here, do ye promise to remain under yer daughter's supervision until after the postmortem?"

"Of course she promises," Mom answered for her. "What other option does she have?"

Nana looked from Mom, to Officer Bean, to Mom again. Popping out of her chair, she marched over to Officer Bean. "I'm exercisin' my other option." She offered up her wrists for handcuffs. "Book me."

"Mother!"

"I don't need ta book ye, Mrs. Sippel. I only want ta—"

"You got a TV in that jail a yours?" she interrupted.

Bean's eyes twinkled. "Do we ever. A new, eighty-inch, flatscreen, LED-based LCD HDTV with a DVR that can record up ta five programs at one time."

"Cable?"

He grinned. "We just got hooked up ta satellite."

"That clinches it," said Nana. "I'm goin' with him."

George heaved himself to his feet. "If Marion goes, I'm going, too."

"So am I," said Tilly as she boosted herself out of her chair. "Good friends don't abandon each other, even when there's incarceration involved."

And on that note, the entire Iowa contingent stood up. Margi raised her hand. "Before I commit, could you tell me what your bathroom facilities are like?"

"Is this going to be a sleepover?" asked Grace. "We'll have to pack Dick's CPAP machine if it is. Have I ever mentioned how inconvenient it is to live with a man who teeters on the brink of death every time he falls asleep?"

"If we spend the night in jail, are we going to be back in time to catch the bus to the Orkney Islands tomorrow?" Dick Stolee inquired.

"What about breakfast?" asked Dick Teig. "What kind of grub do you serve at your jail? Buffet or sit-down?"

Bean waved off the crowd descending upon him. "I've no way ta accommodate all of ye. I'm sorry. Mrs. Sippel can choose one of ye ta accompany us, but only one."

"I'll go," I offered.

"Oh, no you won't," countered Mom. "She's my mother and my responsibility. I'll go."

Nana craned her neck to look up at Bean. "What's the sleepin' situation like in your cells?"

"We just purchased new single beds with memory foam mattress toppers. I actually tried one out myself and found it quite comfortable."

Her eyes lit up. "In that case, I'll take George."

"Mother!" cried Mom. "It's a jail cell, not a college frat house! What in the world are you thinking?"

Nana crossed her arms beneath her bosom and stared tight-lipped at Mom. "I'm not gonna tell you on account of I don't think you could handle it."

"Who can't handle what?" asked Etienne as he hurried into the room from the outer lobby, his arms clutching paper sacks from the grocery store across the street. "There's a police car parked out front," he said in a tentative voice. "That's not for us ... is it?"

"Hold everything!" I waved my arms over my head as I hurried across the room. "Etienne is the perfect choice to accompany Nana to jail. He volunteers, don't you, sweetie?"

"Excuse me?"

"You're going to jail with Nana," I announced as I grabbed the sacks out of his arms.

"Why is your grandmother going to jail?"

"I'm bein' held for questionin," Nana piped up. "But only 'til they get them results back from the postmortem."

"What postmortem?" He gave me a desperate look as I herded him toward Officer Bean. "Did someone die? Emily, what's going on?"

"Officer Bean will explain, won't you, Officer?"

"This is yer husband, Mrs. Miceli?" Bean eyed Etienne with the kind of universal respect that one officer of the law pays another. "The former police inspector?"

Etienne extended his hand. "Etienne Miceli, Lucerne Police Department, Chief Inspector, retired."

"I'll explain the situation on the way ta the station, Inspector."

"I'd prefer you explain—"

"C'mon, handsome." Nana grabbed Etienne's hand. "If we hurry, we might be able to catch one a them late-night reruns of *Law and Order*. Your satellite picks up TNT, right?" she asked Bean.

"Text me," George called out to Nana as the trio headed toward the front door. Disheartened, he turned worried eyes on me. "Do you think she'll be all right, Emily? I'm all for staging a sit-in at the jail if you think it would help. We could start an Occupy Wick movement."

"How many folks would have to show up for an occupy movement in these parts before it became a media sensation?" quipped Osmond.

"In Wick?" Dick Teig guffawed. "One."

Wally raced into the lobby laden down with more grocery sacks. "Why are Etienne and Mrs. Sippel getting into a police car? What's happened?"

I hung my head. *Oh, God.*

While the gang peppered him with disjointed snippets of our latest tragedy, I dumped the grocery sacks on the nearest chair before they dropped to the floor. What the devil was in them? Rocks? I peeked inside.

Nope. Bottled water.

Lucille hurried over to me, dragging Cameron behind her. "Go ahead," she urged Cameron. "Tell her."

"We're not going to be scared into quitting, Emily. Lucille and I are in it for the long haul."

"So please don't end the contest," Lucille begged me.

I sighed deeply, giving vent to all my misgivings. "I don't know, Lucille. I'm sure tempted. Seems all the contest is doing is stirring up trouble."

"We'll show that Gordon fella a thing or two about spunk," said Lucille. "A two-man team can win just as easily as a five-man team. Right?"

"Right," Cameron agreed. "We'll just have to stay focused and watch our backs."

"You can watch my back while I watch Bill Gordon." Lucille sidled a glance at him. "I don't trust that fella, Emily. His wife either."

I heaved a sigh. "I'm beginning to think this whole contest was the worst idea I've ever had. Let me talk things over with Etienne when he gets back from the police station. Maybe he can think of a way to modify the contest without leaving everyone in the lurch. I don't want to disappoint anyone, but—"

"You *can't* end the contest," pleaded Lucille, looking as if she were about to cry. "Please, Emily. I've never been much good at anything in my life, but I'm good at geocaching, so please, don't take that away from me. Cameron and I can actually win this thing. We're *this* close." She indicated a sliver of space between her thumb and forefinger. "I know I can afford to pay for my own trips, but just once in my life, I'd love to win something more exciting than another free scratch card at Hy-Vee."

I forced a sympathetic smile. "Whatever we decide, we're going to be fair. Whether we continue the contest or not, someone is going to end up with a free trip. That's a promise. Okay?"

Looking beyond Lucille, I noticed Erik Ishmael and Alex Hart in the outer lobby, making their way toward us.

"They've been gone a good long while," Cameron quipped as the kilt-wearing duo entered the room, looking oddly disheveled and out of breath. "I wonder what they ended up doing that the rest of us missed out on?"

I shook my head. "Don't know." But their arms were empty, so they obviously hadn't been power shopping.

"By the way," said Cameron, "I remembered where I've seen Erik before. Came to me last night. His stage name is Fast Freddie Torres."

I frowned. "Stage name?"

"Yah. He owns some of the fastest hands and feet in the world. I saw him perform in Vegas years ago. Fast Freddie Torres. One of the greatest kickboxers who ever entered the ring."

FIFTEEN

"DICK TEIG ADDED ANOTHER prescription to his drug list," Wally informed me. "It apparently slipped his mind when he filled out the form you sent him."

I'd arranged an after-dinner meeting with Wally to discuss whether we needed to make another appeal to the group for full disclosure on their medical history forms. Knowing guests were afflicted with thyroiditis or athlete's foot might not make any difference in a medical emergency, but it might make the medical examiner's job a little easier should anyone else suffer the misfortune of landing on his autopsy table.

"Nana mentioned Dick had stopped by the Urgent Care Clinic before we left Iowa. Something about an acid reflux attack at the Senior Center's All-You-Can-Eat Taco Buffet. So what's he taking for it? Ranitidine? Omeprazole?"

Wally handed me the form. "Viagra."

"Oh." I pinched my mouth tighter than a closed fist and forced my shoulder into a casual shrug. "Did you know Viagra has recently been found to have a dual purpose?"

He flashed me a wry look. "It can actually cure acid reflux?"

"No, but it apparently works wonders with altitude sickness."

Wally grinned. "I'll remember that if I ever plan an orgy on top of Mount Everest."

We were sitting in my room with its twin beds, wood paneling, late-model TV, and starving artists' landscape art hanging above the headboards. The rug was tatty, the space cramped, and there was no vanity in the bathroom to store things on, but we had an immersion heater that boiled water in less than a minute, and two cups that didn't have chips in them—a circumstance that had probably caused the rating in the official hotel guidebook to soar from one star to two.

Wally perused another form. "In the spirit of full disclosure, Margi Swanson adjusted her weight by a few pounds. Upward. She says she's retaining water. Your father adjusted his weight by a few pounds. Downward. He claims to have lost significant muscle mass over the last three days."

I grinned, disbelieving that Dad had wanted to appear more bulked up on paper.

"Osmond Chelsvig changed the year he was born."

"I knew it!" I slapped my palms triumphantly on my knees. "I *knew* he had to be a whole lot younger than ninety-six."

Wally shook his head and jerked his thumb toward the ceiling.

I froze. "He's *older?*"

"And trust me. You don't wanna know by how many years. Your grandmother switched her height from four-foot-ten inches tall to four-foot-nine."

"Oh, my God. She's lost a whole inch?" Mom was right. Nana was shrinking faster than a snowman in a heat wave. Which made me question the wisdom of her impulse to ditch her entire supply of supplements at breakfast.

"And that's it." He grabbed the wad and waved them in the air like day-old newspapers. "If some of these people have medical secrets, they're taking them to the grave with them."

"Neither of the Gordons expanded their information?"

He shook his head. "We'd be smart not to waste our breath on Stella and Bill, Emily. They've told me their personal information is none of our business, and they've no intention of budging. You can bank on it."

"What about … Erik Ishmael. Anything out of the ordinary in either his or Alex's medical histories?"

Wally riffled through the papers. "Erik takes a prescription pain reliever. A pretty powerful narcotic actually. No mention of what the problem is. He also takes a slew of dietary supplements and metabolites. Looks like he's downing every nutritional supplement the industry pushes at jocks to help them keep their competitive edge." He turned the page over. "No mention of his athletic background, but he probably excelled at some noncontact sport that didn't threaten to damage his cheekbones. Ping pong maybe?"

Erik must have been a skilled kickboxer indeed to have escaped the inevitable punishment of having his entire face rearranged in the ring. Either that, or his earnings had allowed him to spring for cosmetic surgery from some of the finest surgeons in the country. "How about Alex?"

Wally scanned the sheet. "He's on drugs for high cholesterol and hypertension. Pretty ordinary stuff." He chuckled as he slid the forms back into his leather carryall. "Did you know the guy is an honest-to-goodness rocket scientist?"

"I thought he was a nuclear engineer."

"Aren't they the same thing?"

I eyed him skeptically. "Don't nuclear engineers deal with nuclear energy and rocket scientists deal with … rockets?"

"Whatever. He told me rocket scientist, so I'm thinking the two terms are interchangeable."

Or had he simply forgotten what he'd written on the guest form? The same way he'd forgotten whether he lived in a condo or an apartment. I frowned, uncomfortable with the direction my thoughts were taking.

Wally leaned back in his chair and blew out a long, exasperated breath. "So what do you suggest we do about the contest? I hope you know it can't go on like this. Two people dead? Guests at each other's throats? It was a great idea in theory, but the reality isn't quite living up to the hype."

"Do you think we should throw in the towel?"

"In the interest of all involved, that would be the safest thing to do, but then you're left with the threat of litigation. You'd be breaking a contract with a heck of a lot of people, and they might take exception and sock you with a civil suit."

I sighed. "And then there's Lucille Rassmuson who'd be very gracious in defeat, but who's absolutely aglow that she's found an activity where she's more skilled than everyone else. How do I tell her to put away her GPS and enjoy the rest of the trip as a common tourist? Can you imagine her disappointment? She won't be a member of the number one team anymore, the object of everyone's attention and envy. She'll just be plain old Lucille Rassmuson again, invisible senior citizen from Iowa. My gut is already starting to wrench just thinking about it."

"It's life, Em. Not everyone gets to win."

"I know. But it seems so unfair."

He picked up his carryall and got to his feet. "So what about tomorrow? Are you going to let the teams loose on the Orkneys or not?"

"No decision yet. I need to ponder more…and wait for Etienne's input." I walked him to the door and stepped into the hall with him.

"It's too bad you couldn't come up with an Oprah moment and find a way for everyone to win. That'd be a great way to ease tensions and improve morale."

"And send Destinations Travel into Chapter 11 bankruptcy court. Good idea. Needs tweaking."

Laughter echoed through the corridor as Erik and Alex emerged from the stairwell. "People, people," Alex called out when he spotted us. "You should have stayed for the entertainment. Erik tried his hand at the bagpipes. I think he knocked every hearing aid in the room out of commission."

"My piping was a hell of a lot better than *his* dancing," said Erik as they walked toward us, stopping at the room next to mine. "He tripped over his own feet on a pathetically easy step and ended up in Bill Gordon's lap. You should have seen the old windbag's reaction. He went ballistic."

Alex smiled enigmatically as he removed the key from his sporran. "Bill put on a good show, but I wasn't fooled." He gave his finely clipped eyebrows a flamboyant waggle. "He liked it."

"Which explains why he dumped you on your keister," Erik taunted. "Will you just open the door and wish everyone a good-night?"

"Goodnight, all." Alex swept his hand toward his waist and sketched a deep bow before making a dramatic exit into his room.

Erik rolled his eyes. "What can I say? The radiation has finally affected his brain. Big day tomorrow, folks. Get some sleep." He executed a two-fingered salute before crossing the threshold and closing the door behind him.

I cocked my head, giving Wally a squinty look. "Are rocket scientists exposed to radiation?"

"Beats me. Why don't you ask Alex?"

I just might have to do that, I thought after I closed my door and locked it. I stared at the phone on the nightstand, wishing Etienne would call with news. *Any* news. He'd been gone for five hours already. He should know *something* by now, shouldn't he?

I turned the television on manually and flipped through the channels—all three of them. One was an international news network where the events of the day were being commentated by a bottle-blonde sex kitten with eye-popping cleavage. I was sure I was watching Fox, until my brain kicked in and I realized she was speaking a language that sounded suspiciously like Russian. The other two channels featured ghost figures delivering weather reports for the highlands and islands behind a veil of staticky snow. A weather channel marred by bad reception wasn't my idea of exciting TV viewing, but the static provided the kind of subtle white noise that often helped people sleep ... or think.

I stared mindlessly at the screen, casting about for something to boost my spirits, but all I kept hearing was Wally's words, playing back on an endless loop in my head: two people dead and guests at each other's throats.

Two people dead.

Nana would tell me that people die all the time, especially old people. Since our tours catered to seniors, the law of averages was simply doing its thing, so I shouldn't spend time fretting over mortality charts.

But Isobel and Dolly weren't that old, a voice inside my head argued. *They should have had a lot of years ahead of them.*

So why had they died? Why them? Was it happenstance—I turned my head in slow motion to eye the shoulder bag I'd dropped on the bed—or something else?

Dragging the bag toward me, I removed Hamish Maccoull's dirk and set it beside me, unwilling to buy into the mythology.

It was a knife. A very old and possibly bloodstained knife. Bad luck could not hitch a ride on an inanimate object by order of a man who'd been dead for over three hundred years. I mean, even if the whole curse thing had been powerful enough to actually frighten clansmen to death three centuries ago, the twentieth century had introduced a concept that people took far more seriously than ancient curses.

Expiration dates.

Everything expired these days—driver licenses, passports, anti-aging eye creams. Shouldn't curses follow suit?

I shot the knife a defiant look. "I'm revoking your active status and placing you on the inactive list. What do you think of that?"

I paused for a moment's reflection ... and hung my head.

Oh, God. I was talking to a knife.

I leaped half a foot off the bed as the phone rang out like a fire station bell on steroids. "Geez!" I ran around the foot of the bed to grab the receiver. "Hello?"

"They're allowing me no more than a five-minute conversation, bella, so I'll need to talk fast. Personal calls using department equipment are apparently frowned upon." He jacked his voice up a notch. "A problem that could be resolved if the existing phone system had more than one line."

I smiled. "Did the person that was directed at hear you?"

"Probably not. He's too busy staring at his gigantic flat-screen TV. Did you know they can pick up Fox News over here, Emily? But the really odd thing is, they're dubbing the female commentator in Russian."

"Have the officers finished questioning Nana?"

"For now. She answered all their questions honestly and without hesitation, but they're insisting she spend the night."

"Oh, no. Why?"

"Because the postmortem was inconclusive. They don't want to let your grandmother go until they have a better idea of what actually killed Dolly."

"And when is that likely to happen?"

"This is probably going to sound vaguely familiar, bella, but the medical examiner needs to send lab samples to a facility with higher tech equipment before he can fill out the death certificate."

I sucked in my breath. "Just like Isobel?"

"Unfortunately. And the similarities don't end there."

A nerve-rattling *crash* erupted from the room next door, followed by a brief exchange of angry shouts. I flinched. Man, I couldn't guess what Erik and Alex had broken, but if it was hotel property, they better offer to pay for it.

"The ME completed the autopsy in record time," Etienne continued, "but his initial analysis has caused a headache for Officer Bean. Apparently, Dolly died from a condition the ME has never had occasion to see before."

A chill darted up my spine and shot tingling sensations all the way to my fingertips.

"Her stomach appears to have exploded."

"Oh, no."

"Oh, yes."

"Do the police know about Isobel's exploding stomach?"

"They do now. Provincial labs might not boast cutting-edge technology, but they have an outstanding computer system with an easily accessible data base. Bean was all over it."

"What does that mean for Nana? Oh God. They can't be thinking she's responsible for *two* deaths, can they?"

"Let's just say, Bean isn't about to let her slip through his fingers."

"But she has no motive!"

"The contest," he said flatly. "He floated a theory that your grandmother wanted to slow Dolly's team down in order to give her own team a chance to catch up, so she slipped a debilitating substance to Dolly, all dressed up as a dietary supplement. Regrettably, it not only slowed her down; it ended up killing her."

"But that's ridiculous! Nana doesn't need to win our contest to finance her next trip. She's a bazillionaire. She can afford to go anywhere she wants without having to knock off the competition. And furthermore, his theory is totally warped. Isobel died when Team Five was at the back of the pack, not the front, so why would Nana feel compelled to kill a woman who wasn't even a contender at the time?"

He hesitated, lowering his voice to a seductive whisper. "Have I ever told you how irresistible you are when you're railing against injustice?"

"Etienne! This is serious!"

"I know it is, bella. I'm sorry. It's just that ... I miss you." With a sigh of resignation, he continued. "Officer Bean has also made some cryptic references to clan Maccoull and their legendary penchant for savagery and revenge. Do you have any idea what he's referring to?"

I rolled my eyes. "More nonsense. Nana can explain, if they'll let you talk to her. Is she nearby? Any chance I can talk to her for a few—"

"They're giving me the signal, so I need to hang up."

"Are you coming back to the hotel tonight or—"

"I'd prefer not to leave your grandmother alone, so I've requested a cot, and they're amenable to my spending the night. I'll call you tomorrow. Early. *Ti amo*, bella."

"I love you, too." The line went dead.

I placed the receiver back on the hook, my hand trembling with cold, my mind racing to make sense of the new information.

Two women. Two horrific deaths. Two identical pathologies pointing to a cause of death so violently lethal and rare, that it was unfamiliar to two separate medical examiners.

So what was the thread that connected the two deaths? Isobel and Dolly had obviously engaged in some activity or event that had condemned them to share the same fate. But what was it? Were they taking similar medications that might have been either contaminated or recalled?

Nope. Isobel had been packing an epinephrine pen; Dolly had been packing baby aspirin.

Did they share a genetic abnormality that might have manifested itself at the same time?

What were the chances? They weren't related. Isobel had been a Campbell; Dolly had been a MacDonald. How could they share similar genes?

In fact, the only bond the women seemed to have had in common was that they belonged to the same team and despised each other.

And lest I forget, they were both thieves.

As the disturbance next door escalated to a shouting match, I walked to the foot of the bed to stare at Hamish Maccoull's knife.

Isobel had told us why she'd stolen the dirk, but why in the world had Dolly? Had she intended to pawn it? Keep it? Use it? If she'd known about the curse beforehand, would she have stolen it anyway, or would she have been too superstitious to go near the thing?

I guess we'd never know now. But there were several indisputable facts we *did* know.

Isobel had stolen Hamish Maccoull's dirk and suffered a gruesome death.

Dolly had stolen the dirk and suffered an equally gruesome death.

Their autopsies revealed their deaths were eerily similar ... yet inexplicable.

So the question to resolve was, what would cause two human stomachs to disintegrate in exactly the same way, in a manner so alien to medical science, that it completely confounded local experts?

I hugged my arms to myself as I studied the knife, not daring to admit the inconceivable truth surrounding it.

Was it possible the knife really *was* cursed? I felt like a dimwit buying into such foolishness, but the evidence seemed so overwhelming that—

Damn.

What else could cause the kind of internal damage the women had incurred?

My shoulders slumped as I sank into the chair Wally had vacated. *I wasn't a doctor. How would I know?* But the body of evidence before me pointed in only one direction, forcing me to concede, with great reluctance, that there existed a slim possibility that Isobel Kronk and Dolly Pinker ... *might* have been felled by the power of an ancient curse.

There. I said it.

BOOM!

The landscape art suddenly flew off the wall and fell onto the bed, followed by the appearance of a booted foot as it punched a hole through the wood paneling directly above the nightstand.

"Sorry about that!" Erik called out. "Foot slipped."

I stared at the sole of his hiking boot as he wrenched it out of the wall, unable to drag my eyes away from the gaping hole.

I put my brain on rewind.

Felled by the power of an ancient curse?

Either that... or a roundhouse kick to the abdomen by a man once dubbed the greatest kickboxer in the world.

SIXTEEN

"John O' Groats is the northernmost settlement in Great Britain," Wally informed us early the next morning as we motored along the narrow A836, bucking crosswinds that caused every rivet in the bus to creak and groan. The terrain was flat as a tabletop, with sweeping vistas of the rockbound, wave-battered coast to our left. A profusion of purple heather blanketed the landscape, adding cheer to the gray rock and dull grass, but when the color faded, I suspected this treeless, wind-torn moor could be the bleakest place on earth. "The town was named for a Dutchman who petitioned King James IV for permission to run a ferry between the mainland and the Orkney Islands. His name was Jan de Groote, and his venture was one of the big success stories of 1496, because the ferry has been in service ever since."

"And it's still seaworthy?" Margi called out, stupefied.

"It's the same operation." Wally chuckled. "Not the same boat."

"It better have an engine," hollered Dick Teig, "because I'm not about to tear my rotator cuff by rowing across *that* channel in *these* winds."

"Then I assume you're planning to stay on shore," Alice chided, "because a boat built in 1496 is *not* going to have an engine."

"Yes, it will," argued Dick Stolee. "It just won't be diesel."

Oh, God.

I clutched the hand-grip on the seat in front of me as the bus swerved in the battering winds.

The gang was on edge this morning because their cell phone service was still down, so they were having to talk to each other instead of text. *I* was on edge this morning because I thought I knew what had happened to Isobel and Dolly ... but I was at a loss how to prove it.

"The ferry comes fully equipped with an engine, indoor and outdoor seating, a snack bar, and restroom facilities," Wally assured us, "so no one's going to have to stay behind. And just to finish my story, Jan is Dutch for John, but the O'Groats appears to reflect the ferryman's habit of charging each passenger one groat for the ride."

I'd stayed up past midnight trying to resolve the "hole in the wall" issue with the hotel's night manager. Since I couldn't understand a word he was saying, I'd had to wake up Dad from a sound sleep to translate. And Mom decided to join us since she was awake anyway, worrying about how to prevent news of Nana's incarceration from leaking to the Legion of Mary's Newsletter committee. Erik explained the mishap by pleading the Little Miss

Muffet defense: he'd spied an enormous black spider halfway up the wall, and he'd tried to kill it.

"With your foot?" I'd asked.

"Of course with my foot. You don't think I was going to smoosh it with my hand, do you? I mean, *euw*."

In the end, the manager apologized profusely for the insect problem and upgraded Erik and Alex to the bridal suite, bought Mom and Dad's silence about the infestation by upgrading them to the room Mary Queen of Scots would have slept in if the hotel had been around back then, and fixed the unwanted porthole in my wall by taping a piece of cardboard over it and giving me a can of bug spray, just in case the spider had been traveling with an extended family. So everyone went to bed happy.

Except me.

I was going to have to tell my husband that I suspected our contest had been infiltrated by a killer who was using his feet as deadly weapons.

"The ferry isn't scheduled to leave for another half-hour," Wally continued, "so you'll have plenty of time to grab a cup of coffee or use the comfort station before we board. And please remain in your seats once we're parked because Emily has an important announcement to make about the contest."

Buzzing. Whispers. Distrustful looks from the guests in the seats around me.

"What kind of announcement?" Bill Gordon yelled.

"We'll be arriving at the harbor in a few minutes, Bill. I suspect you can wait that long to find out."

I was a bit leery about how people would react to my idea, but Wally was on board, and I was pretty sure Etienne would be on board, too … once I told him, even though he'd probably never heard of Oprah. I would have told him this morning, if our five-minute time limit hadn't expired before I could get it out.

"Is anyone seeing what I'm seeing in the water over there?" George asked in a disbelieving tone. "What is that? A reef?"

I looked out the window to see a frothy swell of white water bubbling out of the sea like a tsunami wave, churning and roiling with volcanic intensity. Only, it wasn't breaking toward shore. It was just staying in the same place, like a permanent gash in the ocean's surface, bleeding out constant spume and brine.

"I've read about this," Wally enthused, "but this is the first time I've seen it with my own eyes. What you're witnessing, ladies and gentlemen, is the exact point where the Atlantic Ocean encounters the North Sea. There's no reef. It's just a friendly meet and greet between two powerful bodies of water."

"Meet and greet?" questioned George. "Looks more like a full frontal attack to me."

"Seas might be more choppy today because of the wind," Wally added, "so if you're predisposed to motion sickness, I suggest you take a prophylactic before boarding the ferry."

Snickering. Whispers. Snorts.

"*Psst.* Emily." From behind me, Osmond poked his fingers through the divide between the seats to tap my arm. "I got a condom with me, but I don't get how it's gonna prevent sea sickness. What am I supposed to do? Wear it, or swallow it?"

I looked heavenward and shook my head. *Really? I mean, really?*

The harbor at John O' Groats consisted of a parking lot filled with recreational vehicles and several single-story, whitewashed buildings spread out along a circular drive. After Calum maneuvered the bus into a vacant space and turned off the engine, I joined Wally at the front of the vehicle and took over the microphone, praying all the while for an outcome more favorable than total rebellion.

"Good morning. I thought this might be a good time to tell you about a new wrinkle I've decided to add to the contest."

All eyes were focused on me. Faces conflicted. Mouths stiff.

"I wasn't anticipating some of the problems we've run into, so to thank you for hanging in there with me and taking things in stride, I'm adding a few more prizes to the contest. Instead of giving away one free trip, Destinations Travel will be giving away"—I paused for effect—"five!"

Lips softened. Brows inched upward. Eyes gleamed with disbelief.

"One trip will go to the winning team, and the other four will be awarded to one member of each losing team." It would cost the agency a fortune, but I figured we could recover more quickly from a one-time output of capital than from the bad publicity that litigation would bring.

Studied silence.

"Are you telling us that you're chucking the competition?" Tilly asked in a stern voice. "That the geocaching skills we've honed over the past few months are being discarded in favor of a mindless and wholly random drawing?"

Uh-oh. I'd expected Bernice to give me flak, but never Tilly. "I wouldn't have expressed it in exactly those words, but I guess that's what it all boils down to." I flashed a self-deprecating smile. "Every team gets a pony."

She thumped her walking stick on the floor. "Good. Timed events completely unnerve me."

"Does this mean you're pulling the plug on the whole operation?" asked George.

"No, no. You can still search for the cache; I'm simply making it less stressful by eliminating the time limits, the scoring, the opposition, the—"

"The fun," hollered Bill.

The fun, the hostility, the resentment, the spitefulness.

He snorted with indignation. "Who cares about finding the next cache if it can't be dog-eat-dog?"

Two dozen hands shot into the air.

"Let me get this straight," said Helen. "Even if we don't find the cache, we're still in the running for the prize?"

I nodded. "You got it."

"This is great!" said Dick Teig. "We can screw up all we want and still score an all-expenses-paid trip. I like the way you think, Emily."

Smiles. Laughter. Gasps of relief.

Well. I smiled inwardly. That hadn't been so bad.

"If you're changing the rules, I want back in," demanded Bernice.

I shot her a withering look. *Of course she did.*

"You can't get back in," taunted Dick Stolee. "Once you're out, you're out. Right, Emily?"

"Well—"

Osmond popped out of his seat. "How many people think Bernice is entitled to participate in the contest again despite the fact that she threw the two surviving members of her team under the bus yesterday?"

Eyes narrowed. Jaws hardened. Hands remained folded in laps, except for Alice's.

"I think we should let her back in," she suggested in a tentative vibrato. "It's the only Christian thing to do."

"Taking up a collection is Christian," argued Dick Teig. "How 'bout we do that instead?"

"My cell phone is back on!" cried George, prompting gleeful outcries and general pandemonium throughout the bus.

"Mine, too," whooped Tilly. "And I have a message from Marion!"

"Me, too!" cried George.

Tilly adjusted her glasses. "'Greetings from Big House. Jail not so bad. Pizza from Chinese take-out place last night. Pepperoni, snow peas, and squid. Would have preferred thicker crust." Tilly grinned. "What did she send you, George?"

"Nothin'." He shoved his phone back into his pocket. Red-faced and flustered, he stumbled into the aisle. "I could sure use a cup of coffee. Are you through with us, Emily?"

"She better be," Dick Teig warned. "If that boat over there is our ferry, folks are lining up already."

That's all it took for the stampede to begin. The doors opened. Seats emptied. And before Calum could even clear the stairs to assist with deboarding, everyone disappeared through the rear exit.

Everyone, that is, except Bernice, who remained in her seat, staring at me without blinking, which disproved the popular myth that all septuagenarians suffered from dry eyes.

"I don't care about the stupid vote," she bellyached. "I want back in, and if it doesn't happen, you'll be hearing from my lawyer." She gathered up her things and stepped into the aisle. "And furthermore, if my name isn't in the pool for a free trip, I promise you one thing: you'll never see Bernice Zwerg's face on a Destinations Travel tour ever again." Pulling the hood of her slicker over her head, she marched down the rear stairs, leaving me to smile giddily at Wally.

"I'd hold her to her promise if I were you." He raised his hand for a high-five. "Make sure you get it in writing, signed and dated. Notarized if possible."

I hesitated just long enough for him to give me an anguished look. "Oh, come *on*, Emily! You're not seriously thinking about letting her back in. You're this close to being free of her." He did the thumb and forefinger thing. "We're *all* this close to being free of her."

"I know." My shoulders slumped as my gut tilted with my conscience. "It's just that … the part of me that doesn't want to kill her feels sorry for her. She has no friends, no social skills—"

"And no redeeming qualities." He glanced out the door as a howling gust of wind shook the coach. "Other than she can apparently fly. *Holy crap*."

He was down the stairs and out the door before I realized Bernice was being blown across the pavement with such force, she was practically airborne. Calum and Wally grabbed her as the wind splayed her against the front of a late-model minivan—a fortunate landing place considering the hood ornament on the Jag parked beside it.

I looked toward the waterfront, alarm twisting my stomach into figure eights. Wally hadn't been kidding about the seas being choppy. If the wind didn't let up, our ferry ride across the channel would turn into—I yanked a package of pills out of my shoulder bag and snugged the hood of my raincoat over my head as I charged into the parking lot—an absolute nightmare.

The terminal area was a practical little place that looked to have been constructed on a shoestring budget. Two spurs of a no-frills concrete pier hugged the waterfront like arms, creating a small inlet for rowboats and motorized rafts. Lobster pots and trash bins cluttered the side of the road. A sign advertising wildlife cruises hung from the hexagonally shaped ticket office, along with scores of postcards in metal dumps, and a painted mileage post informing us that the North Pole was 2,200 miles to our north and New Zealand 12,875 miles to our south. Our ferry was moored alongside the pier, and waiting to board it were the wind-battered guests of Destinations Travel, clumped together like a massive clog in a kitchen pipe.

"Does anyone need motion sickness pills?" I asked as I circled the perimeter of their huddle. My goal today was to keep a watchful eye on Erik and Alex, but when I didn't see them in the scrum, I figured they were probably shopping, which is exactly where I'd be if I didn't have to play pharmacist. "They're the chewable kind. And they're more effective if you take them at least a half-hour before departing."

Stella Gordon eyed me with suspicion. "Where'd you get them? In the same place where your grandmother got hers?"

My mouth fell open. "Stella! I would not offer you tainted pills ... and neither did my grandmother."

She shrugged. "How should I know? Maybe deviant behavior runs in your family."

Deciding not to dignify that with a reply, I moved on, waving the package in the air. "Motion sickness pills, anyone?"

"Dick and I could use a couple," Helen spoke up as she angled her head away from the wind. "But we'll wait for George. He's picking up a package at the gift shop."

"Take mine." I opened up the box. "They'll be in your system quicker if you take them now." I popped two tablets out of their foil-backed panels.

She stared at them self-consciously before driving her elbow into the small of Dick's back.

"What?" He shuffled around to face her.

"Emily has motion sickness pills."

Dick stood paralyzed for a moment, flattening his kilt against his thighs with both hands. "George is buying a new batch at the gift shop," he said guiltily. He nodded toward the long red building attached to the ticket office. "So … we're good."

Was it my imagination, or was I being boycotted? "Suit yourself." I turned next to Osmond, whose eyes widened desperately before waving off my offering.

"Thanks anyway, Emily, but … George is buying some hot off the shelf … in tamper-proof packaging."

Oh, my God. It wasn't my imagination. My own group didn't trust me any longer! "*My* pills came in tamper-proof packaging." I flashed the sheet with its eight bubbled compartments at him.

"There's two missing."

"They're in my hand."

"Aha."

"So would you like one?"

"Nope. I'll wait for George."

Rattled by this unexpected show of mistrust, I forced the pills back into their compartments and blared out an announcement for my own sake as well as the groups'. "You don't have to stand out here in the wind! You can wait in the gift shop until it's time to board!" Considering the wind was rippling the flesh across everyone's cheeks and cleaving permanent parts in hairlines, I thought it was a rather practical suggestion.

"Can't," balked Dick Stolee as he slapped his kilt down against his legs. "Don't wanna miss the boat."

"The gift shop is twenty feet away!"

Grace tilted her head toward her husband and lifted her eyebrows. "She just doesn't get it, does she?"

Frustrated by my failed attempt to save them from themselves, I shortened the cord on my hood to draw it closer around my face, and scurried up the stairs that fronted the gift shop.

The shop was called First and Last in Scotland, and was the official waiting area for ferry passengers not hailing from Iowa. It was a typical tourist trap that specialized in Scottish crafts, souvenirs, books, maps, umbrellas, T-shirts, flags, stuffed sheep, and ice cream served in either cups or cones. I wandered down the aisles, dismissing any idea of purchasing anything, until I ran across a clearance sale on scarves. They weren't the prettiest things I'd ever seen, but if Orkney turned out to be as windy as John O' Groats, guests who didn't have hoods on their jackets might be thankful to have them.

I grabbed a dozen and continued to the end of the aisle, spying George as I turned the corner, his back to me as he stood chuckling before a display of miniature thimbles and tea cups. "Aren't you afraid the ferry is going to leave without you?" I teased as I came up behind him.

Choking back his laughter, he fumbled to dump his cell phone in his pocket, dropping it on the floor instead.

"Balls," he said under his breath.

"I'll get it."

"No!"

But I'd already bent down and snatched it up. "Easy, George. It didn't break. In fact, I don't see as much as a scra—" I turned it over to check the screen. "*Yikes.*"

He tucked in his lip and lowered his little bald head.

I stared at the screen, wide-eyed. "Oh, my God. Is this from Nana?"

He nodded as best he could with his chin perched on his chest.

"She sexted you from jail?"

He nodded again.

The photo was an extreme close-up of flesh that was soft, and plump, and resembled a Brown 'n Serve roll before the baking process. I knew it belonged to Nana, but that's all I knew. I rotated it a hundred and eighty degrees. "Okay, I give up. Big toe?"

He raised his chin. "What?"

"Elbow?"

He leaned toward me and smiled affectionately as he mooned over the screen. "She probably shouldn't have zoomed in quite so close, but the macro setting on our camera's a real good one."

"Chin?" Though I wasn't sure which one of the three.

"It's her earlobe." He let out a tender sigh. "Your grandmother's lobes are so perfect, Emily. They're like little pillows. All soft and white and floppy. Sometimes when she's feeling frisky, I—"

"STOP." I stiff-armed his phone back at him and winced. "Too much information. Is the signal still up?"

"For now."

I pulled my phone out of the side pocket of my shoulder bag and powered it on. "If Etienne hasn't turned his phone off, maybe I can—"

"Come on, you two." Margi gasped out the words as she collapsed against the display table. "They're letting us board early because of the weather … and Wally's already handed out all the tickets … except yours."

"Margi?" I scraped her off the table and propped her back up on her feet. "Why didn't you let one of the Dicks come find us?"

"Couldn't." She sucked in a deep breath. "They don't know what the indecent exposure laws are in Scotland … so they're trying to lay low. I mean, there's kids in line."

I drilled a look at George. "Do you have the motion sickness pills?"

He shook his head. "All they have is breath mints."

Which would be fine if the aim is to prevent halitosis, but not so fine if the aim is to prevent yourself from hurling on the passengers sitting around you.

I quickly paid for my scarves and chased behind George and Margi as they headed for the boat. Wally handed me my ticket at the gangplank.

"You're welcome to sit inside or out, but I don't recommend 'out', unless you've become seriously unhinged."

I grinned. "Not yet, but I'm working on it."

The main passenger cabin was a large room with windows on all sides, a snack bar astern, and rows of permanently attached chairs all facing in one direction—kinda like a movie theatre, only without the movie. Dick Stolee intercepted me as I entered, his expression suggesting that something was terribly awry, and it was serious. "Can I talk to you?" he said in a gruff voice. "In private?"

Please don't make it about erectile dysfunction. Please don't make it about erectile dysfunction. "Sure, Dick."

As passengers lined up at the snack bar, we skirted around them, pausing near the last row of seats. "What's up?"

"It's about the cable programming back at the hotel. If there's a fee added to my bill for that adult entertainment network, I'm not payin' it. There was no prompt warning me that the program I was about to view was X-rated, and not only was it in Russian, it didn't even have subtitles. So...I'm not payin'." He crossed his arms, punctuating his tirade with an emphatic nod.

"Okay."

He dropped his arms. "Really?"

"Yup."

"Hot damn." He scrubbed his hands in anticipation as he scanned the room. "Wait'll I tell Dick." He paused. "Same thing applies to him, right?"

"You got it."

"Hey, Dick! Hubba-hubba, baby!"

I hoped the hot news announcer slipped into something revealing tonight to make their viewing worthwhile.

I pulled my phone out of my bag again. *Yes!* The signal was still up.

"I understand why you changed the contest," Mom said as she came up behind me, "so I just wanted to tell you that in spite of the fact that you kept me in the dark, annihilated the rules, nullified my time charts, rendered my graphs useless, and altered the entire focus of the trip, I'll adjust." She exhaled a long-suffering sigh.

"Aww, I knew you would." I circled my arm around her shoulders and gave her a hug.

"Do you still want me to hand out the coordinates, or have you decided to trash that step in favor of having teams run around in circles in a random field someplace?"

"I'd like you to do everything you were doing before, Mom—the coordinates, the time charts, the graphs. I just don't want you to let on to the teams that you're still doing them. Creating the charts and graphs—that's the fun stuff, right?"

"Well, it is for me."

"So there's no reason why I need to spoil your fun. Keep doing what you're doing. The only thing you need to do differently is keep the results to yourself."

She lifted her brows. "I suppose it's possible." I could see her brain kicking into gear behind her eyes. "I could even add another graph that plots time as affected by weather and temperature changes."

"Go for it."

"Maybe I could compile all the documents into a book." She grabbed my arm in excitement. "And assign it a Dewey Decimal number!"

"Mom?" I bobbed my head at the person who'd queued up behind her. "Lucille is waiting in line to speak to me."

"Sorry, Lucille," Mom apologized. "I don't mean to hog my little girl."

Oh, God.

Mom gave me a wink and mouthed, "Our secret," before hurrying away.

With a clanking roar from the engine, the ferry nosed away from the pier. I caught Lucille's arm as the sudden movement sent her lunging for the nearest seat back.

"*Whoa!*" I cautioned. "How about I escort you to your seat?"

"I'll be fine. I just thought I should tell you that I'm not in the least upset that you eliminated all the skill elements from the contest."

"You're not?"

"Nope. I'm not even upset that you've turned the whole thing into a sham by offering prizes to practically everyone—like we're all first graders who can't handle losing."

I swallowed slowly. "About that, Lucille, I thought if—"

"And the really odd thing is, I don't even know *why* I'm not upset." She laughed with the delight of a schoolgirl who'd just received multiple invitations to the prom. "I've done a lot of reassessing about the important things in life since my Dick died, Emily. In the scheme of things, this is just a minor blip, so I'm giving you a pass."

"That's very kind of you." If Bernice hung out with Lucille more, maybe we could get an osmosis thing going there.

She shrugged. "Just thought you should know."

"Okay then. Thanks for the heads-up."

Giddy with relief, I watched her return to her seat. Was I on a roll, or what? Three with one blow. Dick, Mom, and Lucille. Problems solved. Crises averted. Order restored. I squared my shoulders and straightened my spine. Emily Andrew Miceli. Tour escort extraordinaire. Like my updated *Tour Escorts Manual* said in glossy black and white—*Every guest's concerns should be confronted head-on and resolved as quickly as possible by exercising logic, compassion, and restraint.*

With the manual's directive fresh in my mind, and my success rate boosting my confidence, when I saw Bernice elbow her way through the line at the snack bar and head in my direction, I realized there was only one responsible thing I could do.

Spinning on my heels, I ducked out the cabin door into the cold wind of the afterdeck.

Okay, I was being a coward, but if the guy who'd added that nonsense about meeting every concern head-on had been in my shoes, I bet he'd do the same thing.

Scrambling around a large metal pod riveted to the deck, I read the sign that indicated "Ladies" on the door, pushed it open, and stepped inside the two-staller, hoping that Bernice wouldn't follow me. But just in case she did—

I locked myself inside one of the stalls and held my breath. If she barged in, would she know it was me behind the door? I stared down at my feet. Would my shoes give me away? I mean, was there anyone else wearing ridiculously impractical platform wedges with ankle straps?

The wind whistled. Anchor chains rattled. Waves smashed and shook the bulkhead, causing me to stiffen my knees and brace my back against the stall for support. I heard a door bang shut close by, on the "Gents" side of the pod, and then I heard a man speak so clearly, it was as if his voice were being transmitted by speaker phone rather than drifting through the air vent above my head.

"How much longer?"

"It better be soon, before you decide to draw any *more* attention to yourself."

I stared at the vent, recognizing the voices immediately.

"Cool your jets, bro. I've done nothing to implicate myself."

"Says you. I saw the looks in people's eyes last night. They think something funny's going on."

"Hey, if you stick to the script, no one's gonna suspect a thing. I've got news for you. This isn't my first time out. I know what I'm doing."

"Stu's going to be pissed about the collateral damage."

"Isobel and Dolly? Look, Stu's always pissed about something. He's a pig-headed SOB with a foul temper. But he knows what it's like in the trenches. He'll be singing a different tune once we pull the trigger."

I sucked in my breath. Trigger? *Oh, my God.* They were packing guns?

"No more mistakes. We have to strike, and get out. So ... we're doing it today."

"Change of heart?"

"Yah, the Miceli broad scares me. She's a ticking time bomb. I think if she gets a hair up her butt and starts snooping around, she could ruin everything."

Two toilets *whooshed* at the same time.

"Not a chance. If she sticks her nose where it doesn't belong, I know exactly how to deal with her."

"You must have a damned death wish to—"

"Not my idea, bro. It's Stu's."

Water running. The sound of paper towels being ripped from dispensers.

Erik Ishmael laughed a truly evil laugh. "Hey, I'm pumped. Let's wrap it up. I'm ready to put another notch in my belt."

I stood frozen in place as the door banged shut again.

OhmigodOhmigodOhmigod. Erik and Alex. They were *both* killers! There was no ancient curse. These guys were hired killers with a contract to take out someone *other than* the two women they'd already killed. And they were doing it today!

As the ferry *boomed* into a trough and climbed the next swell, the deck pitched beneath my feet, slamming me face first into the stall's metal partition, backward against the wall, then flat onto my butt. I smacked into the toilet bowl as we bucked another wave, and as I felt a stream of warm liquid ooze from my nose, I realized with horror that someone on our tour was being targeted for murder.

One of us was going to be taken out today.

The question was, who?

SEVENTEEN

We staggered off the ferry like the bedraggled survivors of the original *Poseidon Adventure*, only with drier clothes. The group had exhausted the supply of motion sickness bags halfway through the forty-five minute trip, but the staff promised to have a fresh supply on hand for the return journey. Not that it mattered. If the majority ruled, we'd be returning to the mainland by a method of transportation less traumatizing than the ferry.

"I don't know about the rest of you, but me and Helen are taking the train back," vowed Dick Teig as he and Helen shuffled onto dry land.

"Me, too," said Osmond, whose coloring was slowly starting to pinken up.

I walked beside them, arm in arm with Alice, whose complexion was still only slightly less green than creamed peas. "I hate to be the one to break it to you, guys, but there's no train."

"Are there any plans to get one?" asked Dick Stolee, who was pausing every couple of steps in apparent hopes that the pavement would stop shifting.

"It's kind of hard laying track across a six-mile stretch of ocean."

"That's all right," announced Helen. "We don't mind waiting."

I was fortunate not to have lost my cookies on the ride over, but my nose had bled all over my raincoat, and I could feel a lump forming on my forehead, so I looked as bad as everyone else, if not worse.

Our bus was waiting at the end of the quay. The wind was still gusting, the sky had clouded over with storm clouds, and the damp sea air was sending a chill through my bones. It was a miserable day to be anywhere other than in front of a cozy fire. And if it started to drizzle, I suspected we'd have a hard time convincing people to even step off the bus, which meant they wouldn't get to explore the Italian Chapel, or the Ring of Brodgar, or Skara Brae.

I glanced toward the sky and prayed for rain.

"Open seating today," Wally announced as I delivered Alice to the base of the stepwell. "So, sit anywhere."

As I waited for Alice to clear the stairs, I felt Bernice close ranks behind me. "Are you planning to climb aboard or are you waiting for a written invitation?"

I ascended the stairs and looked far down the aisle to where Erik and Alex were sitting. I nodded the usual pleasantries as I passed by, then staked out the seat directly behind them. The seat backs were pretty low on this vehicle, more like a city bus than a touring coach, so I was in a great position for spying. The guys wouldn't be able to blink at each other without my seeing them.

They didn't know it yet, but I was going to be on them today like bark on a tree.

I just wished Nana and Etienne weren't stuck in Wick.

I was suddenly feeling very alone.

"The quicker you take your seats and get settled, the quicker we can leave," Wally called out from the front.

Once settled, I pulled out my cell phone and held my breath as I checked the signal. *It was on*! Not trusting it to remain on, I typed a message to Etienne as fast as my thumbs would fly. "Need verification. Imperative u check background of Erik and Alex. Pleez hurry." I hit the send button.

The Iowa contingent must have noticed the signal was up, too, because the bus was suddenly filled with the familiar *dinging* sounds of text messages landing in phone inboxes.

Ding! From the front of the bus. *Ding*! From the rear of the bus. *Ding! Ding! Ding!*

Erik shifted in his seat to address me over his shoulder. "I hate to complain, Emily, but I really think you should outlaw cell phone use on the bus. It's not so bad outside, but on the bus, it's so annoying. It diminishes the impact of the whole tour experience. It doesn't even seem as if we're in Orkney anymore." A scowl settled on his handsome face. "It feels more like the men's room at Port Authority."

Alex tsked disapproval as the *dings* continued. "I agree." He pivoted around to look me straight in the eye. "Even if the messages are critically important, what can anyone do about anything from here?" His gaze dropped to the cell phone in the palm of my hand.

I forced a half-smile as I held it up like a booby prize in a spelling contest. "That's the beauty of owning a cheap model," I lied. "Their range is so limited, you can't actually use them." I slid it back into my pocket.

"Forget your cell phone, muffin," chided Alex. "What about your raincoat? You're never going to get that blood out if you don't treat it immediately." He fumbled about in the vicinity of his lap, where his sporran was resting. "I remembered to bring my stain removal pen today." He lobbed it at me over the seat back. "But, if we're dealing with dry clean only, don't even bother to open the cap because you'll have a major disaster on your hands."

"Actually, it's wash and wear."

"Hallelujah. Do you have water?"

I pulled a bottle out of my shoulder bag.

"And a cotton handkerchief?"

"I have a packet of tissues."

"That won't do at all." He thwacked Erik's forearm. "Give Emily your handkerchief."

"What if I need it?"

"Don't be a putz. When's the last time you had to blow your nose?"

"I—"

"Never," Alex scolded. "I don't even know why you bother to carry one. Hand it over."

"Why don't you give her yours?"

"Because, dear heart, I've already used it."

"This is very generous of you," I said as Erik sailed the perfectly folded square in my direction. These guys were so genuinely nice sometimes that it was hard for me to believe they were hardened

234

killers, but I realized that "nice" wasn't who they really were; it was only who they were pretending to be.

"Quick like a bunny now," instructed Alex. "Dab, dab, dab. Scribble, scribble, scribble. Then blot. Trust me. I've had a lot of experience removing bloodstains."

My hand froze on the cap of the pen.

"His father was a butcher," Erik piped up, giving him the eye.

Sure he was.

Wally's breath hissed through the mike as he drew our attention to the front of the bus. "Before we take off, I want to introduce you to our coach driver. He's a local lad who's been conducting tours through Orkney for a few decades now. Would you care to tell us just how many years, John?"

I boosted myself higher in my seat, my eyes widening as I caught sight of the shriveled skeleton of a man who was standing beside Wally. *Uff-da.* We'd hired the Crypt-Keeper as our local guide.

The old guy crushed his slouch cap to his chest and smiled broadly into the microphone. "Fin puddy nae goon a weenie."

My head fell to my chest in despair. *Oh, God. Not again.*

"What'd he say?" Bill Gordon yelled.

Wally paused. "*Uhh*—More years than he can remember. Okay, shall we buckle up and get this show on the road?"

I attended to my raincoat as we motored out of the harbor and onto a road so painfully narrow, there was no center line down the middle. Lush meadowland stretched across the flat terrain, providing a backdrop for a profusion of dazzling wildflowers. Hand-hewn posts with chicken-wire fencing marked property boundaries. Telephone poles marched in drunken formation across the perimeter of fields, delivering needed services to the occasional farmhouse. We passed a church, a herd of grazing sheep, and a red phone booth marooned near the intersection of two crossroads, smack dab in the middle of nowhere. To call the Orkney Islands "a little remote" was a bit like calling the Antarctic plateau "a little chilly."

"Fer nook a gootie nae brae ma doon hookie," John mumbled over the microphone.

"Tell him to speak up," yelled Bernice. "I can't hear him."

"I still can't understand what he's saying," shouted Bill.

"Neither can I!" griped Stella.

"Nuff nae bawdy?" asked John.

"He says that Orkney is made up of seventy islands," Dad spoke up, "even though there's controversy about the final number, because some of the islands are nothin' more than a single rock poking out of the water. Only sixteen of the islands are inhabited by people. The largest one in the chain is called the Mainland, and it measures thirty miles at its widest point. The entire chain measures fifty-three miles north to south. The island we're driving across now looks like a galloping horse on the map; the other sixty-nine look like a school of deformed fish." Dad forced a chuckle. "I guess that's a little Orkney humor."

Awed silence.

Bill Gordon burst out in laughter. "Good one, Bob! You got all that out of six words?"

Dad shrugged. "He threw in a few more statistics, but I didn't wanna bore you."

"I motion that we hand the microphone over to Bob Andrew," shouted Dick Teig. "He can tell us what we're supposed to be hearing. All those in favor say, 'Aye.'"

"AYE!" came the thunderous response.

"Opposed?"

"Wait a second," Osmond bristled. "You can't put a motion up for vote. That's *my* job."

"The ayes have it," said Dick. "Let's hear it for Bob."

Applause. Whistles. Hoots.

Wally leaned over to speak to our driver, then motioned Dad to the front and handed him the mike. "John is okay with the new arrangement ... I think."

More applause.

I settled back in my seat, my gaze shifting between Erik's and Alex's heads.

Who were these guys? Who did they work for? The Mafia? The mob? Could you work for both without getting whacked for double-dipping? And if they were professional hitmen, how could they accidentally kill two unintended victims? Could pros afford to make mistakes like that? Or were they actually amateurs trying to work their way up to the big leagues? Had they goofed up on their own, or had someone given them the wrong information?

"Orkney's been inhabited for five thousand years," Dad told us as he interpreted John's spiel, displaying the unexpected skill and aplomb of a UN translator. "And for five thousand years, the only way to get from one island to the next was by boat. But at the start of World War II, a German U-boat changed all that."

Dad's voice grew more dramatic, with a hint of breathless anticipation. "The sub sneaked past the channel defenses between the Mainland and Lambholm Island and entered the inner harbor, the Scapa Flow, where the British Royal Fleet was at anchorage. It sent three torpedoes into the HMS *Royal Oak*, killing eight hundred thirty-three men. So to prevent future attacks, Winston Churchill ordered the eastern approaches from the sea to be sealed off, and he did that by building a series of causeways connecting three of the smaller islands in the chain."

Dad let out a relieved breath. "Churchill's decision is credited with saving the Scapa Flow and the rest of the British Fleet from future attack, and in later years, with chopping several hours off a Sunday drive from Burwick to Kirkwall. We'll be hitting the first one just over the next rise."

Erik had mentioned someone named Stu. Was it Stu who'd given him the wrong information? Who was this Stu? Stu, as in Stuart? Stuart, as in Bonnie Prince Charles Edward Stuart, the wannabe king who'd deserted his troops and escaped his enemies dressed in eighteenth-century drag?

"This first causeway is called the First Churchill Barrier," Dad informed us, "and we'll be crossing two more just like it before we arrive at our first destination. North Sea to our right; Scapa Flow to our left."

As we drove across a narrow byway that was flanked on either side by a manmade seawall of massive concrete blocks, and enhanced by the spectacle of a World War II vintage ship lying belly up in the channel, I heaved a frustrated sigh, too puzzled to be able to make sense of anything.

I could understand how they might have isolated Dolly on the streets of Wick to kill her, but how had they isolated Isobel? She'd died alone in her bed with the door locked. If Erik had assaulted her earlier in the evening, wouldn't she have cried out for help? Or had she felt so ostracized by the rest of the group that she thought people would accuse her of making the whole story up? Had she crawled into her bed that evening in excruciating pain, feeling too disenfranchised to call for help? Were we all, in fact, responsible for her death?

A surge of guilt washed over me, followed by an incredible surge of anger: Guilt, that I hadn't addressed Isobel's personality issues with more expertise. Anger, that Erik and Alex had used her character flaws to prey upon and eventually kill her. And she hadn't even been the right target!

I angled a long look down the center of the bus, my eyes darting from seat to seat. So who *was* the right target?

Two women with nothing in common other than they belonged to the same team were dead. Did that suggest the real target was a woman?

Although, to be entirely accurate, Isobel and Dolly did have something else in common.

They were both Scottish. Sworn enemies, but Scottish nonetheless. And I couldn't dismiss a niggling suspicion that that was somehow significant.

The drizzle started as we crossed the third Churchill Barrier onto the tiny island of Lambholm. The rain began as we pulled into the parking lot of what appeared to be a converted Quonset hut. The downpour commenced as John came to a stop and cut the engine.

"This is the Italian Chapel," Dad chirped enthusiastically, "built by Italian prisoners of war who were captured in the North African campaign. They were housed right on this site, in thirteen huts known as Camp 60, and their main purpose for being here was to help construct the four Churchill Barriers."

Through the raging deluge, I saw the whitewashed, gabled facade of a country church superimposed over the homely entrance to the Quonset hut. It had gingerbread house appeal, with two Gothic windows flanking the central doorway, an ornamental belfry, architectural doodads that looked to have been squeezed out of a cake decorating bag, and simple pillars that added a touch of grandness to the portico. On the Continent, the main pursuit of POWs had been to practice their escape skills; on Orkney, the main pursuit had apparently been to practice their artistic skills.

John opened the door, sitting calmly in his seat as horizontal sheets of rain dashed against the stairs and handrail, driven by hurricane force winds.

"Close the door, you moron!" yelled Bernice. "You're flooding the place!"

"You are now free to leave the bus," Dad announced with flight attendant proficiency. "You have a half-hour to explore the chapel and surrounding grounds."

"Are you crazy?" shouted Stella Gordon. "It's pouring out there! *You* explore the grounds. I'm staying put."

"I'm with her," said Bill.

"Can we drive to the next stop?" asked Margi. "Maybe this is just an isolated squall and it'll stop raining by then."

"These conditions are supposed to last all day," said Dad in a strangely modulated tone that reminded me of a Stepford wife, "but they shouldn't affect your activities. In Orkney, this is what's referred to as a gentle rain."

Okay, Dad's ability to channel John was officially getting a little creepy.

Wally stood up, his gaze drifting upward as a barrage of raindrops pelted the roof of the bus. "Conditions might be a little prohibitive to fully explore the site at the moment." He turned toward John. "And it might be a good idea to close the door."

Whoosh.

"Would someone tell me why we came all the way over here to visit a Quonset hut?" griped Stella.

"When's lunch?" asked Dick Teig. "I'm starting to get hunger pains."

"That's because you left your breakfast on the ferry," said Helen.

Wally checked his watch. "We're not expected at our luncheon venue for another hour, so we're going to have to—"

"So let's arrive early and surprise 'em," encouraged Dick Stolee. "All those in favor say, 'Aye.'"

"AYE!"

"Stoppit!" Osmond leaped out of his seat, arms flailing and fists clenched. "Dick Stolee is not qualified to conduct a vote."

Alice grabbed his jacket and yanked him back down beside her. "Save your breath. It's because of this whole Internet blogging thing. Everyone thinks he's an expert now."

Deciding that traveling to our next venue might be less risky than having our tires sink into the mud in the parking lot, Wally gave John the nod to head out. Unfortunately, with road conditions reducing our speed to a crawl, we arrived not an hour early, but ten minutes late, which caused major panic and a mad scramble for the exit doors.

"You don't have to rush!" Wally assured them as they muscled past him into the rain.

I let out an amused snort. *Good luck with that.*

The building everyone was escaping into was a one-story structure perched on a hillock overlooking the storm-battered waters of the Scapa Flow. It was neither commercial restaurant nor fast food joint, but rather a community gathering space for locals whose villages weren't large enough to warrant restaurants or fast food. Luncheon fare for tour busses was prepared by members of a ladies guild, in their own kitchens, so we'd be treated to some tasty examples of local, homemade cuisine, at a cost of only five pounds per person. But even more exciting than that for our female guests, the ladies washroom was a ten-seater!

I followed behind Erik and Alex as they tramped through the entrance, sticking with them as they entered the dining room. The tables had filled up quickly, but there were three empty seats at a long table against the back wall, so we grabbed them, sharing dining space with Tilly, Lucille, Margi, George, and Cameron.

"It's a fixed meal, so there's no menu," I said as I shrugged out of my wet raincoat and hung it on the back of my chair. I nodded at a platter of finger sandwiches in the center of the table. "Appetizers, I presume. Shall we start passing them around?" I scrubbed my hands in anticipation, wondering what exotic fillings we'd be sinking our teeth into. Wild Atlantic salmon with cucumbers and boursin? Oyster pâté with pecans and cream cheese?

Margi peeled back the plastic wrap, stacked a couple of sandwiches on her plate, and passed the dish to her left. Lifting up the corner of her bread to peek inside, she smiled. "Oh, goody! My favorite. Peanut butter."

What?

"Egg salad," said George as he inspected his selection.

Cameron chuckled. "American cheese … with butter."

No, no. This couldn't be right. Where was the salmon? The oysters? "Just a few mundane trifles to whet your appetite," I assured them. "The main course should be along presently." But it was definitely a little odd that the wait staff hadn't arrived yet to take our drink orders.

"Would someone hand me the water pitcher?" asked Erik.

Cameron passed it across the table. "So when did you retire from the kickboxing circuit? I was telling Emily I saw you fight years ago in Vegas—the year you took home all the marbles. I knew you looked familiar, but it took me awhile to place you. What year was it that you won the championship?"

Erik froze mid-motion, his hand hovering above his water glass as if it were being held in prolonged suspension by a master puppeteer.

"Kickboxing champion?" Alex guffawed. He arched a questioning eyebrow at his partner. "Have you been holding out on me? Shame on you. Frolicking in Vegas and not bothering to invite me along?"

"Oh, right." Erik threw Cameron a dismissive look as he remembered to pour his water. "Wasn't me, bro. Musta been someone wearing my face. What's that really long German word for it?"

"I thought all German words were really long," puzzled Margi.

"You're referring to the term doppelganger," said Tilly. "A word in our modern lexicon that has come to mean 'a look-alike.'"

"It was no look-alike," Cameron insisted. "It was you. Fast Freddie Torres? Sound familiar?"

Erik took a long swig of water. "Nope."

Cameron laughed. "Why are you running away from it, dude? If I'd rung up as many wins as you, I'd put it out there for everyone to ooh and ahh over. Say, what'd you do with that last championship belt you won? You can't wear something like that to hold up your jeans. I mean, with all the gold and glitter, that thing must weigh fifty pounds."

"I told you." Erik's voice grew sharp, his eyes narrow. "I'm not your guy. So, can we drop it?"

"My Dick loved to watch those awful boxing matches," Lucille reminisced. "And pro wrestling matches. And mud wrestling matches." She bit into an egg salad sandwich, chewing thoughtfully before swallowing. "Now that I think about it, Dick was quite fond of watching people in skimpy outfits beat the crap out of each other."

"Are you skipping the appetizer course, Emily?" Tilly took the sandwich platter from me as I handed it to her untouched.

"Yah. I'll let you guys finish the rest. I'm going to save my appetite for the main course."

"If it's as good as the peanut butter sandwiches, we'll be in for a treat," Margi enthused.

"Comfort food," said Alex. He glanced at the blinding rain streaming down the windows. "We need comfort food in weather like this. Did you know NASA provides comfort food to the astronauts when they're in space? The only problem is, it comes out of a tube and looks like toothpaste, so what's the point? How much comfort can you eke out of eating toothpaste?"

Which reminded me. "Are you a nuclear engineer or a rocket scientist?" I asked Alex.

"Believe it or not, Emily, I'm a little of each."

"So, have you ever been exposed to radiation?"

"Certainly not," he said blithely.

"Oh. Then Erik was only teasing last night?"

"Teasing about what?" asked Alex.

Erik blew out a long breath. "It was a joke already! You know—ha ha ha? I was being facetious. His brain has *not* been affected by radiation. If his breath could light up a Geiger counter, do you think I'd be sitting here beside him?"

Margi looked aghast. "Oh, my goodness. You'd abandon the poor thing to fend for himself in his hour of need?" She tucked in her lips. "That's very disappointing."

"Has anyone read the new biography of Leonardo da Vinci?" Tilly jumped in. "He drew up plans for a flying machine as early as the mid 1400s. From the perspective of a rocket scientist, Mr. Hart, would you consider da Vinci's blueprints the first embryonic stage of aeronautical or astronautical engineering? And for those among us who are unfamiliar with the terms, perhaps you'd be so good as to explain the difference between the two."

Smiling inwardly, I settled back in my chair, waiting. Alex threw his head back and groaned.

"Rea*lllly*, Miss Hovick. I so appreciate the question, but I'm not about to bore these good people with a treatise on rocket science. It'd be more exciting for them to watch paint dry."

"I don't mind watching paint dry," confided George, "especially if it's one of those intense new colors, like marshmallow or clouds. But I wouldn't mind hearin' about rockets either."

I smiled brightly. "Me, too."

He gave his head an adamant shake. "Absolutely not. I never talk shop when I'm on holiday. Isn't that right, cookie?" He leaned toward Erik and batted his eyelashes.

"Hey," Erik droned. "Do you mind? We're in public."

"I don't mean to change the subject," Margi interrupted, "but shouldn't we be starting the main course sometime soon?"

I ranged a look around the room, looking for Wally.

No Wally.

"Why don't I just pop up and see what the holdup is."

As I hurried through the dining room, I noticed a lot of empty sandwich platters, which meant everyone else was waiting for the second course as well. So where was it?

I passed through the entry vestibule, headed down a connecting corridor, and ended up in a room with a refrigerator, stove, several butcher block tables, and three white-haired ladies wearing neatly starched aprons.

"Hi." I offered a friendly smile. "I'm part of the tourist group in the dining room. We have a schedule to maintain, because we have to catch a ferry back to the mainland later, so we're not in *that* much of a hurry, but we really do have to watch our time. So, will you be serving the main course soon?"

"Whit fock fer dool un fae ma pooky," explained one of the ladies with a quick bob of her head.

How could I *not* have guessed she was going to say that?

I held my finger up in a stalling gesture. "Don't move from this spot, okay? I'll be right back. We just happen to be traveling with our own translator."

I sprinted back into the hall, running into Margi in the vestibule. She held my phone out to me.

"It was dinging inside your raincoat pocket. I thought it might be important."

"Thanks. While I get this, would you run back and tell Dad I need him?"

It was a text. From Etienne.

"Background check disturbing. Subjects don't exist."

EIGHTEEN

I COULDN'T DECIDE WHAT freaked me out more—that our platter of finger sandwiches *was* the main course, or that Erik and Alex were honest-to-goodness imposters. The only comforting thing about the day so far was the unrelenting foul weather that was confining us to the bus.

It was raining so hard, tiny estuaries were forming rivers across the road.

Pretty bad when the only ray of sunshine in your day is rain.

The torrential downpour was the reason we were parked in the visitors' lot at the Ring of Brodgar, our noses pressed to the windows, *squinting* at an impressive circle of standing stones rather than wandering through them. This was to have been the site of today's geocaching search, but with no one willing to brave the elements, we canceled the event by unanimous consent, which was just as well, considering that Mom had forgotten to turn her computer off last night, causing the battery to run down. No computer meant no coordinates, and disrupted cell service meant no one's GPS was working.

It also meant that Bernice wouldn't be harping at me to let her back into the contest until at least tomorrow.

If I lived that long.

"If you rub away the condensation on your window, you can see that unlike Stonehenge, the monoliths of Brodgar still form a nearly perfect ring." Dad swept his hand in Vanna White style toward the spectacle. "Scientists think it was erected about four thousand years ago, which goes to show that Stone Age people didn't buy into the idea of built-in obsolescence."

"Could be they just didn't know how to spell it," suggested Osmond.

Something had changed drastically at lunch. Whether spurred by Cameron's insistence that Erik was Fast Freddie Torres, or Tilly's polite inquiry about the difference between aero- and astronautical engineering, Erik and Alex had shed their friendly exteriors to become tight-lipped and wary, like two men intent on completing a deadly mission.

And I didn't know how to stop them.

I stared at the blank screen on my cell phone, willing the signal to come back up. Etienne would know what to do. If only I could reach him.

Wally stepped into the center aisle, his expression apologetic. "We're supposed to be here for a full hour, but since you've decided to scrap this site, I'm going to suggest we head directly to our next stop, Skara Brae. It's a National Heritage Site with a museum, cafe, restroom facilities, and a top-notch reconstruction of a prehistoric dwelling. Once it stops raining, *if* it stops raining, you can venture out to visit the excavation site of an *authentic* Neolithic settlement. It was discovered in 1850 after a powerful storm swept over the bay and washed all the sand and topsoil off the beach. Ironically, until then, no one ever suspected it existed. Not even the family who occupied the mansion that sits practically on top of it. And the mansion had been occupied since the 1600s. It's just down the road a piece, so we'll be there in a few minutes."

Nuts. We were safe on the bus. It was when we split up into smaller groups that we ran into trouble.

I stared out the window, worrying the gloss off my bottom lip. If Etienne were here, he'd tell me not to do anything that would jeopardize either my safety or the safety of our guests. He'd tell me to be smart, remain calm, and stay frosty. But most importantly, he'd tell me not to be a hero.

My updated *Escort's Manual* was a bit more to the point: *When situations arise that are beyond your control, don't feel obliged to suffer silently. Share your misery. That's what your tour director is for.*

"We've got a problem with Erik and Alex," I blurted out to Wally the minute we hit the visitor center. I'd chased him down and dragged him to a quiet corner before he could run off to the men's room.

He regarded me sternly. "*Un*believable. I thought I might get complaints from folks like the Gordons, but never from you. Look, Emily, whether you like it or not, we're living in the twenty-first century, and relationships like the one Erik and Alex have are part of the emerging fabric of the times. So unless you're planning to limit your roster to couples who—"

"I'm not talking about their being gay! I don't care if they're gay. They're planning to kill someone!"

He stared at me, deadpan. "Of course they are."

"They are! I overhead them talking in the men's room on the ferry. They've already killed Isobel and Dolly—apparently accidentally, because the girls weren't their intended target. But they're going to make up for their mistakes today by hitting their real target, and then they're getting out of Dodge."

He lifted his brows. "You were in the men's room on the ferry?"

"I was in the ladies' room. There's an air vent between the two. But that's not the issue! They're planning to whack one of the guests on our tour. And I think they have guns."

That got his attention. "Did you see an actual weapon?"

"No, but Erik said something about pulling a trigger. And here's the other thing. I got a text from Etienne back at the community center. He ran a quick background check on Erik and Alex and he discovered *they don't exist.*"

He pushed a long breath out through his teeth, his expression morphing from disbelieving to grim. "Geez. You actually heard them admit they killed Isobel and Dolly?"

"Alex called it collateral damage and suggested that someone named Stu was going to be really ticked off about it."

"Geez." He gave his head a quick shake as if to clear his brain. "Okay, so how does Etienne say we should handle this?"

"He doesn't." I pulled my phone out of my pocket. "No signal. Do you think we should contact the police in the nearest town?"

He chewed that over, eventually shaking his head. "And tell them what? That you overheard two guys in the men's room say they were going to kill someone? It'd be their word against yours, and there's two of them to deny it."

I paused thoughtfully. "They didn't actually use the word 'kill.'"

"What word did they use?"

"They said they were going to 'strike.' But in the context they were using it, I'm sure they meant kill."

He planted his legs apart and crossed his arms. "They didn't say 'kill'?"

"They used a very acceptable synonym."

He shook his head. "You got nuthin', Em."

"But what about the fact that Erik Ishmael and Alex Hart don't exist?"

"It's not a crime to be an imposter."

"Are you sure? What about their passports? Isn't it a federal crime to put a fake name on a government document?"

"I don't know! But I *do* know that the local police aren't going to be able to do anything about your allegations. And I say that with some authority because I've been in the tour business a heck of a lot longer than you have, and I know how police in foreign countries deal with American tourists."

I looked him straight in the eye. "But ... what if I'm right?"

"You're never right."

"That's not true! I was right in Holland." I let out a breath. "Well, kinda right." I bobbed my head. "About a few things." I sighed. "Okay. I'm never right. But there could always be a first time."

"You had to mention Holland." He forced a grudging smile, admitting, "You did okay in Holland. Look, Emily, I think our main goal should be to get back to Wick and let Etienne and the police sort everything out. Sound like a plan? Because if we miss the ferry going back, I'm not sure anything will have prepared you for the headache of trying to find accommodations for two dozen people on Orkney."

"Okay, but if it turns out later that I'm right *now*, I'd like to think I did *something* to keep people alive. Everyone's in the café at the moment, but once they scatter, it's going to be impossible to keep track of them."

"Not if they stay inside the visitor center. You can tail Alex. I'll tail Erik."

"I can't tail him in the men's room," I objected.

"You can loiter outside the door, can't you? At least we don't have to worry about them exploring the grounds. Looks like the bad weather might turn out to be a blessing in disguise."

"Hey, everyone!" Dick Teig's voice echoed out from the café. "It stopped raining!"

Wally and I turned our heads in slow motion to glance out a bank of windows that revealed a sudden, inexplicable break in the weather. I compressed my lips. "Do we have a Plan B?"

Wally stared at the scene, seemingly mesmerized. "My mother told me I should have been a podiatrist," he said in a dazed voice. "I wish I'd listened."

"That clinches it then." I felt a rush of adrenalin shoot through my body like an electrical charge. "We need reinforcements."

He laughed. "And just where do you plan on finding them?"

I looked beyond the ticket counter to the café nestled at the front of the building. "Around the corner. There's a whole room full of them." I poked my finger in his sternum. "Here's Plan B: *You* put a bead on Erik and Alex. I'll take care of everything else."

They were scattered at tables throughout the room, enjoying hot beverages with slices of cheesecake and pie. I pulled a chair up to the table where Tilly, George, and Margi were sitting, and in a low, conspiratorial voice, explained what I needed them to do.

"What if they notice us?" asked Margi.

"I want them to notice you. That's the whole point."

"Would you mind telling us why you feel this is necessary?" asked Tilly.

"For now, let's just say I have a hunch, and if my hunch is right, your help will be like a strategic defense system."

"Marion's gonna be so disappointed she missed out," lamented George. "She even brought a wig along this time, just in case you asked her to tail some innocent shmuck you thought should be accused of murder."

"We can wear wigs?" Margi tittered.

I fired her a hard look. "No wigs."

"You want us to spread the word to everyone?" Tilly confirmed.

"All the usual suspects, except Mom and Dad. If Mom participates, she'll waste too much time trying to arrange all of you by height."

George retrieved his phone from its holster. "Too bad our phones aren't working. It'd be real easy to shoot one text off to everyone. I guess now we're gonna have to talk to them."

Tilly drained her cup and with an assist from her cane, boosted herself to her feet. "I must tell you, Emily. I was very unimpressed with Alex's response to my question at lunch. If NASA's rocket scientists are all as uninformed as he is, no wonder they cancelled the space program."

Margi made sad cow eyes at George. "So what color is Marion's wig?"

A shattering *crash* reverberated through the room, followed by a stinging epithet from Stella Gordon, directed at her husband. "Stupid ass! I told you to keep your elbows off the table!" She flagged down a clerk behind the customer counter. "Cleanup crew needed over here! My husband's fault. I had nothing to do with it." She got up from the table, leaving Bill to deal with the thousand shards of dinnerware scattered over the floor.

"Leave, already!" Bill retaliated. "See if I care."

Alex and Erik gathered their belongings and stood up, abandoning their plum spot by the window.

"Showtime," I said as I watched them head out the door behind Stella. "Okay, gang, time to roll."

I caught Wally's eye as I strolled back out to the ticket counter area. He nodded toward the restroom sign and gave me a thumbs up. Looking casually back toward the café, I saw Tilly, George, and Margi making the rounds at each table, sharing the plan in quiet whispers.

Yes! This was going to work.

I paused outside the restroom area, noting the half-dozen people queued up to use the pay phone. Now *that* was a rare sight— a public phone. I dug my camera out of my shoulder bag and snapped a picture, just in case my future grandchildren ever wanted to see an example of something that had become extinct ... besides penny candy and TV rabbit ears.

Stella Gordon wandered past me and headed down a wide hallway toward the museum section. Erik and Alex emerged from the men's room and strutted down the hall behind her, garnering a few admiring looks from female tourists, and a few giggles from the younger set. Wally sent me a purposeful look and struck out after them.

"Pretend I'm not talking to you," Alice said out the corner of her mouth as she paused surreptitiously beside me. "I just want you to

255

know that I've been hitting the gym at the Senior Center five times a week, so I'm up for the challenge." Without another word, she caught up to George, who was leading the charge down the hallway after Erik and Alex.

Osmond shuffled toward me, giving me the eye as he went down on one knee to tie his shoe. "Don't let on I'm talking to you," he said in an undertone, "but I've been taking special classes at the Senior Center to be ready for a day like this. I won't let you down, Emily. And don't worry about criminal charges. I'll be long dead before the case ever comes to trial."

What?

He let out a grunt as he struggled to get up. "Dang. Could you give me a hand? I'm stuck."

He hobbled off, falling in line behind the Dicks, who waved like pageant contestants as they passed by, and Helen, whose left eyebrow had fallen victim to the rain and was now entirely missing.

Bernice crab-walked in my direction, the humidity having made her hair so wiry it looked like a detonated Slinky. "Just so you know, I don't want back on Team Five. I want a team all to myself."

I kept an eye on the last of the gang as they paraded down the hallway. "Anything you say," I said distractedly. "Gotta run."

I chased behind the group, mingling with other tourists, stopping to read exhibit panels, admiring Neolithic artifacts displayed behind glass.

Helen waved her new digital camera above her head. "I want a picture of all the men who are wearing kilts," she announced as she pulled Dick Stolee toward Erik and Alex. "Anyone else want to try out their new cameras?"

The gang swarmed around them, even as Erik and Alex tried to escape.

"Oh, no you don't," said Helen, blocking their path. "You stay right there. DICK! GET OVER HERE! I wanna take your picture."

She arranged them in various poses. Made additions to the group. Moved them to different locations. Took advantage of several backdrops.

"That's it," snapped Alex after ten grueling minutes. "We're done here." After extracting Erik from the group, he made a detour into the area that housed the reconstructed prehistoric dwelling.

The gang swarmed after them.

So did I.

I passed beneath a low doorway and into a world that existed four thousand years ago.

The space was as big as a one-car garage and lined with rocks stacked one atop the other. A square fire pit sat in the center of the room. Slabs of rock, supported by upright stones, formed shelves along the wall, like a Stone Age pantry. Longer slabs angled out from the walls, forming the framework of what looked like primitive trundle beds. Animal pelts lay scattered about the room like throw pillows, adding a touch of warmth to the stark décor.

"What's this place supposed to be?" asked Dick Stolee. "A house or a condo?"

"Looks like a studio apartment to me," said Stella.

"Where do you think they put the fridge?" asked Margi. "There's no room in the kitchen."

"I bet they stuck one of those dorm models by the bed," said Osmond, inspecting the wall for an outlet.

"Anyone see the bathroom?" asked Dick Teig.

Tilly thwacked him with her cane. "It was a Neolithic society. Indoor plumbing had yet to be invented."

"No. Where's the bathroom, for real. I've gotta use it."

"Did you forget to take your pill again?" scolded Helen.

As Dick squeezed through the crowd, the rest of the gang pressed closer to Erik and Alex, keeping them mired in gridlock. I smiled. *Gee*, this was going well.

"Where do you suppose they would have hung the big-screen TV?" asked Dick Stolee.

"Nowhere," said Osmond. "There's no electrical outlets."

"Will everyone pose for a picture around the fire pit?" asked Helen. "Group photo!"

"I can't move until Grace moves," complained Margi.

"Me?" cried Grace. "I'm nowhere near you."

"Will whoever's on my foot, GET OFF!" sniped Stella.

Realizing the situation was well in hand, I slithered around the perimeter and exited the room, my stomach making gurgling sounds as I found my way to the back door of the visitor center. A lush expanse of wet grass stretched before me, and beyond that, a horseshoe-shaped bay, flanked by a crescent of sand beach. Paved walkways funneled tourists down two divergent mud-puddled paths—one leading to an excavation site near the beach, and the other toward a grand manor house constructed of perfectly chiseled stone. And with the rain on hold for the moment, visitors were actually stepping out to enjoy the self-guided tour.

My stomach suddenly growled long and loudly, reminding me that I'd stupidly refused the peanut butter sandwiches at lunch. Opening my shoulder bag, I riffled through the contents in search of an energy bar, knowing there were at least a couple left. I dug through the disorganized mess, sticking Alex's stain removal pen in a separate pocket to be returned to him, and Erik's bloodstained handkerchief—

I stilled my hand on the balled-up cotton cloth as I noticed a detail that had escaped my earlier attention.

I pulled it out for a closer look.

On the corner of the cloth, in thread as white as the handkerchief itself, was an embroidered letter.

A tiny capital T.

T? I couldn't drag my eyes away. T, as in Torres? Torres, as in Fast Freddie?

Oh, my God. Erik Ishmael might not exist, but it appeared that Fast Freddie Torres was very much alive. And I had his monogrammed handkerchief to prove it.

I checked my phone. Still no signal.

Damn. I had to tell Etienne. His background check on Erik Ishmael might have been a bust, but I bet there'd be a whole boatload of information on Fast Freddie Torres.

I retraced my footsteps back through the museum, running into the gang as they piled out of the prehistoric hut. "I think the fellas are gonna head outside to try and get rid of us," whispered George as he brushed by me. He winked playfully. "Ain't gonna work."

I hurried toward the restroom area, hoping the line to use the phone had disappeared.

No! It was twice as long and snaking around the corner.

I approached the ticket counter and smiled at a dour-looking woman behind the register. "Would you have a phone I could use?"

"Der pooblic fone es roon der kaner." She pointed to the sign.

"But it's really important."

She raised her eyebrows as if they were lead weights and pointed to the sign again.

I took my place at the back of the line and nodded to Dick Teig as he hustled out of the men's room.

"Where are they now?" he asked in a rush.

"At last sighting, they were heading outdoors."

He gave me a thumbs up and scurried down the hallway. I checked the time, located my energy bar, slouched against the wall, and began to munch.

Fifteen minutes and two energy bars later, the line had decreased by three people, and I was no closer to tightening the noose around Erik Ishmael's neck than I'd been before.

"Somebody!" Margi Swanson cried as she raced toward the ticket counter. "Call an ambulance! We've got casualties!"

NINETEEN

"I MOST CERTAINLY DID *not* say 'attack,'" insisted Helen.

"Did so," grumbled Osmond.

"I said *distract*. Emily wanted us to *distract* them."

While we killed time in a small conference room, Osmond sat with his pant leg rolled up and an ice pack pressed to his knee. "You mighta *thought* you said distract, but what I heard you say was 'a-ttack.'"

Which explained why an emergency vehicle was parked outside the building, ready to whisk Alex Hart off to the hospital in Kirkwall.

Osmond heaved his narrow shoulders as he cast an anxious eye out the window at the ambulance. "Looks like I ruined that fella's whole vacation."

But not as much as "that fella" had ruined Isobel's and Dolly's.

The initial diagnosis was that Alex had broken his leg, an injury sustained when he'd fallen backward into one of the pits on the excavation site.

"Tell me again what happened?" I asked gently. "I'm a little confused about the sequence of events."

"We were stickin' with them like peas in a pod," explained George. "Just like you told us."

"Then Helen suggested we take an outdoor picture of the 'kilted ones,'" said Grace. "Mostly because the wind was blowing their kilts up to their navels, so I could tell she was thinking, 'slide show.'"

"I was not!" defended Helen.

"You were, too," insisted Grace.

"Which is when Alice attempted to grab my cane out of my hand," said Tilly.

I looked at Alice. "Why did you want Tilly's cane?"

Tilly gave the stick a hard thump on the floor and in an imperious tone said, "She apparently wanted to be allowed an opportunity to shoot a picture of me landing flat on my arse."

Alice stared back at me, crestfallen. "While the boys were posing for a picture seemed a good time to pound on the two younger fellas, like Margi said we should do, but I didn't have anything to pound with, so I thought maybe I could borrow Tilly's cane."

"*Hound*," Margi wailed. "I said to 'hound' them."

Alice crooked her lips. "How many people think Margi's overbite is causing her to lisp?"

"No voting!" I snapped. "Do. Not. Vote."

Osmond lifted the ice pack to inspect his knee. "So while the girls had everyone distracted with their tug-of-war over Tilly's walking stick, I decided to attack. I mustered my courage and a head of steam, and I charged straight at those boys."

Awkward silence.

"And?" I prodded.

"He tripped over his shoelace and hydroplaned across the grass on his stomach," whooped Dick Teig. "You should have seen it, Emily. Water spraying in every direction. People leaping out of the way. George got a pretty good picture of the chaos."

I winced as I visualized Alex Hart going down like a candlepin in a bowling lane. "And that's when Alex fell?"

"Nope," said Dick Stolee. "That's when Dick and me and the two studs rushed over to scrape Osmond up off the ground."

I gazed from one face to another. "So when did Osmond take out Alex?"

"He didn't," said Tilly. "Helen did."

"Don't go blaming me!" fussed Helen. "I said I was having trouble with my zoom button and asked the four of them to scoot back a little farther so I could take the money shot. It wasn't my fault that fella couldn't figure out how close he was to the edge of the pit." She frowned. "Although, with his kilt flying up in his face like that, it could be his vision was a mite impaired. But the other three didn't fall in, did they?"

Whoa! "Are you telling me Alex's broken leg was an *accident*?"

"Of course it was an accident," said Tilly. "We're not inciters of violence." She slanted a long look at Alice. "At least, *some* of us aren't."

I offered Osmond a sympathetic look. "So why are you blaming yourself for Alex's mishap if it was an accident?"

He shrugged. "Dunno. I guess I figured someone should take the blame. I knew Helen wasn't about to volunteer."

The conference door opened. Wally strode in, grabbed a chair, and sat down. "Okay, people, here's the plan. The paramedics tell me Alex will probably have to stay in the hospital overnight. They're anticipating that the swelling in his leg will have to go down before they can fit him with a cast."

I sat up straighter in my seat, feeling a boost of energy. And while he was in the hospital, maybe someone could snag a DNA sample to help determine who he really was!

"When he's released tomorrow, he can catch the ferry back to the mainland and join us in Wick."

"But according to the schedule, we're supposed to leave Wick early tomorrow morning," Tilly pointed out.

"Not anymore. We're shuffling the itinerary around to make it easier for Mr. Hart to rejoin us."

"But there's nothing to do in Wick," pouted Helen.

"We could visit Marion if she's still in jail." George's eyes twinkled.

"We could go shopping," suggested Osmond. "I could use another SaladShooter."

"We could stretch out on our beds and die from boredom," droned Bernice.

"Let *me* worry about tomorrow," Wally advised, "and *you* worry about getting back on the bus. If we skip our scheduled stop in Kirkwall to see the twelfth-century cathedral, we should j*uuu*st be able to make our ferry in time. Any questions?"

Margi raised her hand. "Is Erik going to stay with Alex in the hospital?"

"*Uhh* ... no. The two of them decided it would be best for Erik to return to Wick with the rest of the group."

Margi clucked her disapproval. "I won't say I'm surprised, but I'm very disappointed. They seemed like such a devoted couple."

"All right then." Wally popped up and gave his hands a clap. "Let's get this show on the road."

"Before we leave, would anyone like to see my pictures?" Helen waved her camera in the air. "I've assembled them into a slide show."

Margi pulled a mirror out of her tote bag and held it up to her face, studying her reflection as she curled her lips back and clamped her teeth together. "Do I really have an overbite?"

Wally pulled me aside. "Nice plan. Did you actually tell your wrecking crew to kneecap the guy?"

"No. I told them to keep Erik and Alex surrounded. That's it. Alex's misstep was a total accident." A blast of prickly heat crawled up my neck. "Naturally, there was some miscommunication as they exchanged the information among themselves, and I accept full responsibility for that. I didn't account for the feedback on their hearing aids. But on the upside, Osmond self-destructed before he could implement his attack, and I don't think Alice ever did wrestle Tilly's cane away from her, which was probably pretty disheartening to Alice, considering how much time she's spent at the gym recently."

He opened his mouth as if to say something, squinted oddly, then turned around and left, herding everyone out the door in front of him.

Unlike Margi, I wasn't surprised Erik would be returning to Wick with us. They still had a job to do, and with Alex out of commission, there was only Erik left to do it.

The good news was, at least we'd managed to separate them.

Dealing with one killer would be a lot easier than dealing with two.

The stormy weather resumed as soon as we loaded the bus, and worsened as we made our way back to Burwick. When we pulled into the harbor, a collective groan went up from the group, because marine conditions had deteriorated even more, ensuring us a passage marked by savage winds and exceptionally high seas.

"I still have an untouched stash of motion sickness pills I can distribute if anyone's interested," I announced before we left the bus. "Any takers?"

They practically mobbed me.

As Dick Teig philosophized when he popped one in his mouth: "I don't care if they *are* tainted. If the ride back is as bad as the one coming over, I'm gonna wish I was dead anyway, so what's it matter?"

It was worse.

So bad in fact, that even *I* had to battle a slight twinge of queasiness, and I don't get queasy. As much as I'd been flabbergasted by the miraculous recovery of people on the outbound passage, I came to realize that two stomach-emptying trips in one day was one trip too many. Once back at John O' Groats, guests practically had to crawl to the bus, where they remained in their seats, pale and lifeless, until we reached our hotel. And since Wally was as incapacitated as everyone else, I dug out my annotated itinerary and offered the final announcements myself.

"Dinner is scheduled to be served at seven-thirty this evening, so I hope you'll take the next forty-five minutes to recuperate, and then join me in the dining room feeling bright-eyed and bushy-tailed."

They groaned, rolled off their seats in slow motion, and limped down the stairs like weary veterans of an after-Christmas sale at the Mall of America. I followed behind them as they climbed the stairs to their rooms, making sure everyone had the energy to complete the climb, then let myself into my room, squealing with delight when I discovered I wasn't alone.

"Nana!" I pulled her out of the armchair and wrapped my arms around her, squeezing her like an orange that needed juicing. "When did they let you out?"

"'Bout a half hour ago. They didn't have no charges to file against me, so they had to let me go."

"May I be included in the group hug?" asked Etienne as he boosted himself off the bed to join us. "Mrs. Miceli," he said, his eyes lingering on my lips, his voice a seductive whisper. Tipping my chin up, he kissed me full on the mouth, sending shooting stars across my vision. "I've missed you."

Unh. With my knees about to give way beneath me, I backed against the bed and sat down. Etienne sat down beside me, intertwining his fingers with mine. I exhaled a steadying breath. "Does this mean the autopsy report came back?"

"Nope." Nana settled back in her chair. "Them young fellas at the jail said some of them lab tests can take a long time to analyze, so we don't know nuthin' yet."

"We still don't have a cause of death?"

"For neither Dolly nor Isobel," said Etienne, doing a poor job of hiding his frustration.

I squeezed his hand. "I'm not sure every lab and toxicology test in the world will ever reveal what killed Isobel and Dolly."

"No kiddin'?" asked Nana.

"You say that as if you know something the rest of us don't," said Etienne.

I nodded toward the cardboard patch duct-taped to the wood paneling above the nightstand. "Did you notice the interesting art work on the wall?"

Etienne followed my gaze. "I noticed it this evening, but I don't recall seeing it when we checked in yesterday." A smile played at the corners of his mouth. "I blamed it on my usual excuse—man eyes."

"My Sam had them eyes, too." Nana gave her head a slow nod. "The only things you could count on them spottin' was three-quarter-ton pickups with V8 hemis and highway patrolmen with radar guns."

"Management hung up the cardboard last night to cover a fresh hole in the wall."

Nana snatched her feet off the floor and shot a terrified look at the rug. "Termites?"

"Spiders."

"THEY GOT SPIDERS WHAT CAN EAT THROUGH WALLS?"

"No, no! No bugs. It was Erik Ishmael's foot that made the hole. Can I explain?"

So I got them up to speed about what had happened in their absence: the hole in the wall that had prompted the upgrading of rooms, the Fast Freddie Torres allegation, the conversation I'd overheard aboard the ferry, my discovery of the monogram on Erik's handkerchief, our concerted efforts to prevent another death from occurring, and Alex's tumble into the excavation pit. "So does that give you any idea why I'm convinced all the lab results are going to come back negative? I think what killed Isobel and Dolly isn't something that can be quantified. I think it was Erik's foot."

"Dang," Nana lamented. "And them two fellas seemed so nice."

"If you'd heard them talking in the men's room, you wouldn't think they were so nice. Etienne checked their backgrounds. They're shadow people. They don't exist. And what's worse, by their own admission, they're not through with their killing spree yet." I studied Etienne's face, waiting for a reaction.

"They gave no hints about who their real target is?"

I shook my head. "They mentioned that Stu guy, but no one else. Oh, yah. And they might have guns."

"But what's the motive?" He heaved himself off the bed and began pacing. "Things don't add up. Two women with no apparent connection to each other are dead. Collateral damage, you say. Unintended deaths. Killed by a man with lethal kickboxing skills who was hired by someone named Stu. What kind of a hitman worth his salt kills two people unintentionally? And not with a gun. With his foot."

How come my theory sounded so much more far-fetched coming out of his mouth than my brain?

"George could accidentally kill someone with his foot," Nana chimed in. "It's on account a them steel-toed boots of his. And I oughta know 'cuz I been dancin' with him."

"Well, Isobel and Dolly did have one obvious thing in common," I spoke up. "They were both Scottish, but I can't figure out a scenario where that might be a factor in either one of their deaths."

Etienne grabbed a pen off the desk and began jotting notes down on a piece of hotel stationery. "Fast Freddie Torres. Unknown operative named Stu. Authorization for a DNA sample from Hart while he's having his leg set." He looked over his shoulder at me. "Do you still have the handkerchief? It's probably too contaminated to be of any use, but maybe some industrious technician can lift a partial print off it."

I plucked the handkerchief out of my shoulder bag and dropped it into a plastic sandwich bag that I dug out of my suitcase. "So now what?" I asked as I handed it to him.

"Now, I go back to the police station to make a pest of myself. Do you know what room Erik is in?"

"The bridal suite. In another section of the building."

"Okay. I'll see if I can arrange to have a plainclothes officer watch his room."

"Really? You can do that?"

"I can't, but Detective Constable Bean can. And I don't think he'll quibble. On paper, he's indebted to your grandmother to the tune of thirty-six thousand pounds sterling."

I shot Nana a long look. "What?"

She shrugged. "I was havin' one of them off nights, dear. I don't play gin rummy real good."

"So, what should we do while you're gone?" I asked as I walked Etienne to the door.

"Give Erik Ishmael a wide berth."

Which was probably a good idea since he was prepared to deal with me in a less than savory manner should I stick my nose where it wasn't wanted.

"Hurry back?"

He kissed my forehead. "Count on it, bella."

"There's somethin' else what them two girls had in common besides bein' Scottish," Nana suggested as I closed the door.

I regarded her narrowly, choosing not to complicate matters by quibbling about Hamish Maccoull's dirk. "There is no such thing as a curse," I reiterated as I slipped out of my raincoat.

She ranged a curious look around the room. "Where'd you hide it anyway?"

"I've put it in a safe place until I can figure out what to do with it."

"I'll tell you what to do with it. Throw it away. It's cursed."

"It's an historic artifact that could have significance far beyond anything either you or I could possibly imagine." I unstrapped my shoes and slipped into a more casual pair. I checked my watch. "Time for dinner. Should we mosey down to the dining room and pick at our food until Etienne comes back?"

She was zeroed in on the cardboard patch with trancelike focus, her face screwed into a wrinkled contortion, her eyes alternating between purposeful squints and rapid blinks.

I angled my head and asked slowly, "*What* ... are you doing?"

"Puttin' the evil eye on that piece of cardboard. I'm throwin' in the towel. It don't do me no good denyin' I'm related to Hamish Maccoull. If you got it, flaunt it."

"How about you hit the buffet line and practice putting the evil eye on the haggis?"

"Okay."

I fluffed my hood-flattened hair, touched up my lipstick, and followed Nana out the door, hearing a sudden scraping sound, followed by a noisy clatter and *CRASH!* from the room's interior.

I walked back into the room.

The nightstand lamp was lying on the floor, knocked off its perch by the cardboard patch that was now lying on the floor beside it, minus every strip of duct tape that had held it to the wall. I stared in disbelief and tried unsuccessfully to draw a normal breath.

Okay, but could she do something *really* impressive, like move a parked car, or make Bernice disappear?

"What was that?" Nana asked when I joined her in the hall.

I shook my head and smiled. "Nothing."

TWENTY

No one showed up for dinner.

Not even Wally.

"It was a pretty brutal crossing," I lamented again as we perused the desserts on the buffet table, "so I'm not surprised. I think the last thing on anyone's mind right now is food."

"Are we the only ones here?" Bernice's voice echoed across the room as she shuffled toward us, looking drained but determined to rain misery on someone else's dining pleasure. "Your motion sickness pills sure got the job done, Emily. Next time, maybe you should try another kind. The kind that actually work."

"People would have been a lot sicker without the pills," I fired back.

"Yah, yah. From your lips to God's ears. So what are they trying to kill us with tonight?" She drew back the retractable cover on a chafing dish. "Oh, good. More dog food."

Nana and I grabbed one of every dessert and returned to our table. To my dismay, though not to my surprise, Bernice joined us.

"So, about the geocaching event tomorrow." She unfolded her napkin and grimaced at her food. "I'll agree to be a part of any team … except Team Five."

Nana frowned. "Didn't you say yesterday you was quittin' the contest?"

"That's before Emily changed the rules. If she can change her mind, so can I."

"What'd you change your mind about, dear?"

"I expanded the giveaways. A prize for every team. Just to sweeten the pot a little."

"I like that idea," said Nana. "Kinda like what Oprah done a few times." She leveled a look at Bernice. "How come you don't wanna be on Team Five no more?"

"Are you people blind? Have you missed all the mooning and fawning going on between Lucille and Cameron? Really. It's nauseating. I have to be on a team where the members are committed to being focused on *me* instead of each other."

That sounded about right.

"Lucille's found herself a sweetheart?" gushed Nana. "Aw, isn't that nice? She's been alone a lot a years now."

"Yah, well, we'll see how that works out. Tax complications. Pain in the butt relatives. Housing headaches. Once their bubble bursts, they'll be in for a rude awakening."

Nana tucked in her lips and stared at Bernice. She began blinking … and squinting.

Oh, God.

"But you know who *should* be alone?" Bernice continued. "Bill and Stella Gordon. Have you heard the way she criticizes him? Up one side, down the other. She's fed up with his relatives. She's fed up with his bluster. She's tired of his temper. She's tired of all the women who chase after him. She wishes she'd married an Italian."

It was obvious Bernice spent a greater chunk of her time sniffing around tour members than photographing tour spots.

"If I was Bill Gordon, you know what I'd do?" She stabbed a stray pea with her fork and held it proudly in the air. "I'd get rid of her. I'd pray I wasn't living in a community property state so I could avoid having to share my life savings, and then I'd file for divorce. No one should have to live with anyone as cranky as Stella Gordon."

Nana screwed up her face and blinked faster.

"What's wrong with your eyes?" Bernice asked her.

I kicked Nana under the table even as a thought began to form in my mind.

Suppose Bill wanted to get rid of Stella. And suppose he'd be forced to split his assets with her, including his meager savings and extensive weapons collection. And just suppose he'd prefer to keep everything himself, especially his coveted Scottish arms. Would he opt for a long, drawn-out, disadvantageous divorce? Or would he decide to bypass the court system and deal with Stella in a much quicker, cleaner way, like … hire someone to take her out. A fellow Scotsman named Stuart, who subcontracted the work to two inept flunkies.

Uff-da! Was that it? Had Stella been the intended target all along? Was it *her* head that was riding on the express train to Erik's chopping block?

I popped out of my seat, leaned across the table to yank Bernice out of her chair, and planted a noisy kiss on her mouth. "Thank you! I won't forget this."

"*Yuuuck!* You … you … I don't swing that way!" She wiped her sleeve across her mouth, adding, "Not that there's anything wrong with it."

I pushed my chair aside and raced across the room.

"Bill and Stella Gordon?" I inquired at the front desk. I knew they were on the third floor, but I couldn't remember the room number. "Room number, please?"

They'd apparently been relocated to the ground floor after Stella complained about having to climb the stairs. At least, I *think* that's what the desk clerk said.

I found the room right off the lobby. I knocked on the door.

No response.

I knocked again, louder this time.

Still no response.

I pressed my ear to the door, hearing no sounds from within. No voices. No footsteps. No nothing.

My heart started racing.

I stumbled headlong into the room when the door flew open.

"*Geez!*" cried Stella. She wrapped her robe tighter around her body. Her hair was matted against her head and dark smudges circled her eyes. She was actually quite scary looking, but at least she was alive.

"How are you feeling?" I asked as I righted myself.

She gave me a tired look. "How does it look like I feel?"

"Not so good, hunh? Would you like me to ask the kitchen to prepare a sick tray for you and Bill?"

She turned away from me and banged on the bathroom door. "Do you want a sick tray?"

"*Bleeeeeeeeeeech*," came the involuntary reply.

She nodded. "That's pretty much a no."

"Is there anything I can do for you?"

"Yah. Leave so I can go back to bed."

"Okay, but if you should need me for anything, I'm in room—"

The door slammed in my face.

"—216." I rolled my shoulders. "I guess it's not really that important." What *was* important was that Stella was still very much alive, and if we could keep Erik away from her tonight, chances were she'd remain that way.

I ran into Etienne on my way back to the dining room.

"The balls have been set in motion, bella. The handkerchief is on its way to the lab. Officer Bean is contacting the FBI to help with the Fast Freddie Torres and Stuart information. He's making a petition for a DNA sample from Alex. He also enlisted a police officer from Kirkwall to question Mr. Hart in the hospital, but they've run into a spot of bother. Alex suffered an adverse reaction to an injected pain medication, so he's not anticipated to be in his right mind again until sometime tomorrow."

"Did you get your plainclothes officer?"

"That's the best news. The corridors are monitored by a surveillance system that has a direct feed to the police station, so they can monitor the halls without having to leave the department. I was a bit startled by the revelation. The cameras are so well camouflaged, I never noticed them. But if Erik leaves his room, they'll know. And they can send someone over literally within two minutes."

I frowned. "Is it a little odd that a hotel that's not modern enough to have remote controls for their TV sets would have a sophisticated surveillance system for their corridors?"

Etienne shrugged. "The UK may be a small country, but it has the largest number of surveillance cameras in operation in all of Europe."

"Well then, you'd better tell the police to pay special attention to the ground floor corridor," I advised.

"We don't have anyone staying on the ground floor, do we?"

"We do now. Stella Gordon, otherwise known as ... Erik Ishmael's next target."

He paused. "All right, bella, tell me everything."

So I did, and when I was done, he simply nodded. "It makes an enormous amount of sense. Let me put in another call to Bean." He smiled his admiration. "I do believe, Mrs. Miceli, you may have just cracked the case."

I basked in the glow of my success as he put in his call.

I preened as they sent an officer over anyway, in anticipation of Erik's making his move.

I slept like a baby that night knowing there was a police officer in the house, and that Erik Ishmael was as good as captured.

I awoke early the next morning to a rapid knock on our door.

It was Wally. "Erik Ishmael is missing."

"HE ESCAPED?"

"He's missing. Unfortunately, so are Cameron Dasher and Lucille Rassmuson. Officer Bean wants to see you at the police station. Pronto. Your grandmother, too."

"Why Nana?"

"She's the one who blew the whistle."

TWENTY-ONE

"IT WAS WHEN I was power walkin' a around the hotel, hopin' to avoid Emily's mother before the breakfast line opened. One of them windows on the ground floor was hangin' from its hinges, like someone had kicked it outta its frame."

"Erik escaped through his window?" I glanced at Bean. "Did that show up on the surveillance video?"

Bean's response was strained. "The surveillance equipment is on the inside of the hotel, Mrs. Miceli, not the outside."

"So we have no idea when he left." Etienne scraped his knuckles against his unshaved jaw. "What about Mrs. Rassmuson and Dasher?"

"They're on camera as having left the building just before seven o'clock last evening."

"And they just disappeared into thin air?" I asked.

"We're playing back surveillance tapes of the train station. We don't hae a car rental office in Wick, so it's the only logical place they could hae gone."

The department phone rang as if on cue. Bean answered, acknowledged the message, and hung up. "Mrs. Rassmuson and Dasher boarded an evening train heading south. Unfortunately, there was a problem with the track farther down the line, so it was forced ta delay its departure, which allowed Mr. Ishmael time ta board as well."

I gasped. "Erik is pursuing Lucille and Cameron? Why—why would he do that?"

"If we knew, Mrs. Miceli, we wouldn't be standing around here discussing it. The train has already reached Inverness, so if that wasn't their final destination, they've transferred ta another train and are heading somewhere else."

Would they be returning to the inn on Loch Ness, wanting to nurture their romance in solitude, away from the tour? Or had Erik somehow revealed his hand, prompting them to flee before he could strike? "Where else could they go from Inverness?"

"Anywhere in Scotland," said Bean.

That was a big help.

"Why does Erik want to kill them?" I fretted. "Why Lucille? What could she possibly have done to earn herself a death warrant?"

"You want I should text her and ask?" offered Nana. "I got a signal."

We regarded her, gobsmacked. Bean shrugged. "Go fer it."

Nana sent off a message.

The reply came almost instantaneously. "B happy 4 me. xo."

Nana smiled. "Don't sound like she's bucklin' under the stress."

"Ask her where she is," I prodded.

Nana typed the message. "Where r u?"

"A wonderful place 2 B," came the reply. "In love."

I forced myself to remain calm. "Ask her where they're headed." Nana sent the text.

"It's a secret," came the response.

"She has *no* idea she's being pursued by a crazed hitman who might be carrying a gun," I cried. "You have to do something."

"I'm trying ta put together a strategy, Mrs. Miceli, in case ye hadn't noticed."

"Her phone's got one of them fancy chips in it," Nana chimed in. "All the phones what Pills Etcetera sold us got 'em. I don't know what you call 'em over here, but back home, we call 'em ... trackin' devices." She lifted her eyebrows and shoulders in unison. "Just sayin'."

Bean held out his palm for Nana's phone. "Who's yer wireless provider?"

While Bean disappeared into a connecting office to make official inquiries in private, I wandered over to a huge map of Scotland that was tacked to a bulletin board. I poked my finger at Inverness and let my gaze drift to points south. "Too bad the train lines aren't marked on the map. Where could they possibly be running to? Perth? Back to Edinburgh? Somewhere in between?"

Nana came up behind me. "If they notice that Erik fella chasin' after 'em, maybe they'll have to get off someplace they don't want to."

"I'm afraid they might be too wrapped up in each other to notice Erik." I let out a wistful sigh. "After all these years of widowhood, Lucille is in love again."

Etienne hovered behind us, looking over our shoulders. "Perhaps we should include 'matchmaking services' on our travel brochures."

"So *that's* where that place is!" Nana tapped a spot on the map. "This here's the town what I read about in my Regency romances. It's where all them frisky English folks what need to get hitched real quick run away to so's the blacksmith can pronounce 'em man and wife. It's kinda like that Weddin' Chapel in Vegas, only without them Elvis impersonators. See it here?" She pinpointed the spot for me. "Gretna Green."

"Gretna Green?" I knew about Gretna Green. "Isn't Gretna Green like . . . the marriage capital of the world?"

I stared at Nana. She stared at me. We stared at each other. I grabbed her shoulders. "*Oh, my God!* They're running away to get married!"

I burst into Bean's office. "We think we know where they're heading."

"Would ye hold, please?" Bean clapped his hand over the phone. "Where?"

"Gretna Green."

"Why?"

"To get married."

"Why would they travel all the way ta the Scottish border ta do that when they could be married by a justice of the peace in Wick?"

I stared at him as if he had two heads. "Because Gretna Green would be more romantic, of course."

"Romantic." He rolled his eyes. "Mrs. Miceli, we're not going ta know anything fer sure until we initiate the tracking process."

"But—"

"*Please*, Mrs. Miceli." He returned to his call. "I'm sorry. Whit were ye saying?"

I stepped out of the office and closed the door behind me, shrugging at Etienne and Nana. "He doesn't quite understand the romance angle."

"I got a bad feelin' about this, dear. What happens if Erik breaks up their plans? What happens if Lucille's left all by herself someplace? She don't got the street smarts like what Bernice's got. What'll she do?"

I sank my teeth into my bottom lip and threw Etienne a pleading look.

"I know what you're thinking, bella. We're responsible for her welfare, and yes, we should be there for her if she needs us, but we're facing an impossibly challenging transportation problem. We have to make up the twelve-hour lead they have on us. So how do you propose we arrive at Gretna Green before them?"

"Well, would you lookit that?" marveled Nana as she pressed her face closer to the map. "An airport."

During England's Regency period, the blacksmith shop at Gretna Green had probably been an isolated stone building surrounded by pastureland and sheep. Two centuries later, it was a whitewashed stone building surrounded by a mini shopping center that touted souvenirs, food court, historical museum, and token piper.

We were blending into the crowd at the outdoor food court by huddling around a table, eating ice cream cones. The blacksmith shop with its marriage room was about twenty-five feet away, located amid a tasteful backdrop of greenery and circular stone fountains. A bagpiper in full regimental dress commanded the attention of an audience nearby, a plate sitting near his feet to collect donations from appreciative onlookers.

"If and when they arrive, *do not* allow your emotions to get the better of you," Etienne instructed us. "You will calmly escort Lucille and Cameron into the blacksmith shop, and if Erik shows up, *I'll* be the one in charge of handling him. Agreed?"

I gave him a thumbs up. Nana nodded as she shoved the last of her sugar cone into her mouth. The piper's audience burst into applause as he finished the last strains of "Amazing Grace."

"Mi hance ur schicty," Nana mumbled, touching her fingertips together to show us how sticky they were. She pointed to the sign for the toilet and stood up. "Be wight back."

My stomach twisted into knots as I scanned the tourists milling around the property. I hung my head and groaned. "How much longer, do you think? The waiting is killing me."

"If this is where they were heading, and they didn't miss any connections, they should be here momentarily. If not…"

I slumped against the table and hung my head lower.

"Emily."

"Just give me a minute. I'm feeling the need for a brief pity-party."

He gently squeezed my forearm. "They're here."

"What?" I jerked my head up.

There they were. On the far edge of the bagpiper's audience, listening to him begin his next tune. They were snuggled cozily against each other, hand-in-hand, smiles lighting their faces, Lucille looking happier than she'd looked in years.

Aw, that was so sweet.

"Are you ready, bella?"

We cut across the food court at a brisk pace. "I just thought of something," I said to Etienne as we approached them from behind. "Since we're already here, maybe they'll ask us to be witnesses at their wedding."

I sidled a glance at the street to find Erik Ishmael stepping out of a taxi. "Oh, my God." I grabbed Etienne's arm. "He's here."

"Don't panic. Just follow the plan."

As the air rang out with the slightly off-key drone of a lively march, Etienne detoured down the walkway to the taxi while I marched up beside Lucille. "Hi, there."

Lucille startled as she gaped at me in disbelief. "Emily?" Her mouth worked soundlessly. Her eyes looked about to fly out of their sockets. "What are you doing here?"

"Rescuing you."

"What?" said Cameron.

"No time to explain. But if you'd follow me into the blacksmith's shop, we can sort it all out there."

Cameron seized Lucille's arm, his expression turning testy. "Don't listen to her Lucille. Your friends have put her up to this. They don't want you to be happy."

"Of course we want her to be happy. Why do you think we've gone through all this hassle to find the two of you?"

"I don't understand," Lucille puzzled. "How did you get here?"

"Helicopter."

Her mouth fell open. "You chartered a helicopter to fly you from Wick?"

"I wish. We couldn't find one to charter, so Nana had to buy it outright. I don't know how she's going to get the thing home."

I trained a look at the street, where Erik and Etienne were standing toe-to-toe, locked in a discussion that looked to be growing heated.

"Please, you two, it's my job to get you inside the building before—"

"*I'm* not a killer!" Erik's voice was so loud, it drowned out the piper. "*He's* the killer!"

I blinked stupidly. Why was he pointing at us?

With a sudden deft move, Cameron spun Lucille against him, bracing his forearm across her throat and forcing her arm behind her back. "Keep your distance!" he shouted at Erik. "Back off, or I swear I'll break her arm."

I cried out in protest. "What are you doing?"

The piper's tune faded into silence as the audience focused their attention on this alternative adult drama.

"Let her go!" I demanded as I made a move toward Cameron.

He wrenched upward on Lucille's arm, causing her to cry out in pain. "Not another step," he warned as he dragged her backward toward the intersection of two walkways, "or I promise, I *will* break her arm, and it'll be excruciating."

Erik and Etienne raced down the walkway, joining me as the crowd formed a wider semi-circle around us. "Your luck's run out, Dasher." Erik made a gimme motion with his hand. "Let her go."

"Cameron," whimpered Lucille, her face contorted in pain. "Why are you doing this?"

"Are you going to tell her?" asked Erik. "Or should I?"

Beads of sweat popped up on Cameron's brow. "I love you, Lucille. You have to believe that. I'm just trying to protect you from all the lies people have spread about me."

"That's the spirit!" shouted a woman in the crowd.

The audience cheered.

"Listen to me, Mrs. Rassmuson," Erik implored, "Cameron Dasher is a con man who makes his living by preying on unsuspecting widows like you. He marries them, kills them, then lives high on the hog off their estates. You want to tell her how many wives you've buried, Dasher?"

"Don't listen to him, Lucille," urged Cameron. "He's trying to drive a wedge between us to convince you not to marry me."

Boos and hisses from the audience.

"At last count it was five wives," persisted Erik. "They're healthy when he marries them, but they all die quite suddenly, under circumstances that leave a lot of unanswered questions. But Cameron has already made sure that his widows don't have inquisitive relatives who'd raise any questions, so he's home free, and free to roam around the country, repeating the process over and over again."

"Lies!" Cameron spat, his eyes darting left and right as if searching for an escape route.

"It's too bad the last Mrs. Dasher had pre-arranged her own funeral," Erik continued. "I wouldn't be standing here now if she'd opted to be cremated. And it was too bad about that long-lost relative of hers. It's not like you to be so sloppy."

Tears gathered in the corners of Lucille's eyes and floated down her face. "Is what he's saying true?" she choked out.

"I think the dude's lying," shouted a guy from the audience.

"Which dude?" asked someone else. "The good guy or the bad guy?"

"Which one's the bad guy?" asked the piper.

288

"Poison is his stock in trade," Erik thundered. "So what toxic brew did you use this time? The same one you used on wife number five, or something more lethal? You should consider yourself fortunate that Mr. Dasher took such a shine to you, Mrs. Rassmuson. You were spared the same fate as your fellow teammates."

An exaggerated gasp went up from the crowd.

"Cameron," Lucille sobbed. "*Please*."

"Do you want to fess up about what turned you off on Isobel and Dolly?" Erik pressed. "Not enough money to satisfy you? More than the accepted quota of relatives?"

Cameron shook his head, rattled. "Isobel was a leech. A troublemaker. If I didn't get rid of her—"

"It's true then?" Lucille choked out.

"Shut up." He wrenched upward on her arm again. "Dolly screwed up by Googling me. Finding my name in the obituaries of so many dead women really set her off. I told her it wasn't me, but I could tell she wasn't going to drop it, so she forced my hand. She has no one to blame but herself. If she'd owned a regular cell phone without Internet access, she'd still be alive. Damn iPhones."

"She can't breathe!" I cried as Lucille's face went white, her eyes exploding with something dark and terrifying.

"I was your second choice?" she rasped in a wounded voice.

"Third choice," mocked Cameron. "But who's counting?"

She drove her foot into his instep with such might that he dropped his arm from across her throat and howled like an injured beast.

"WOO! WOO! WOO!" chanted the crowd, egging her on.

As he hopped away from her on one foot, he bumped straight into Nana, on her way back from the restroom.

"Get him, Marion!" Lucille yelled. "He's our killer!"

"*EEEEEYAAAA,*" cried Nana as she made a wavy gesture with her hands. Leaping straight up, she whirled like a dervish, snapped her leg out, and—WHAM!—drove the top of her foot into Cameron's face. His limbs jerked wildly before he tottered, stiffened, then fell backward onto the pavement with a resounding *BOOM.*

The audience burst out in uproarious applause.

Whistles. Hoots. Cheers.

"Is this one of those interactive theater shows like 'Tony n' Tina's Wedding'?" a woman asked Lucille.

"You guys rock," a man complimented her. He took out his wallet and made a quick check of the ground. "Where's your donation plate?"

"Your whole entertainment was so realistic," a bystander told Nana. "Are you a professional or amateur troupe?"

I hurried over to Lucille and put my arms around her. "Are you all right, sweetie? Did he hurt you?"

"Nope," she said as she took a deep breath and straightened her spine. "Only my pride."

TWENTY-TWO

AT THE INVITATION OF Detective Constable Bean, we gathered at the police station the following morning—Nana, Wally, Erik, Alex, Etienne, and myself—to tie up a score of loose ends. Cameron remained in the Dumfries police station outside of Gretna Green, waiting to be transported back to Wick under armed guard.

"We'd been monitoring his activities ever since wife number five was exhumed," Erik explained. "What looked like an unfortunate car accident turned out to be murder, but we couldn't pin anything on him because we couldn't draw a connection between him and the toxin that killed her."

Alex nodded. "When the toxicology reports come back for Isobel and Dolly, I suspect they'll indicate that both women were poisoned."

"The results of Isobel Kronk's labs just came in," said Bean. "Arsenic poisoning. When Ms. Pinker's come back, I imagine it'll read the same."

"But how did he pull it off?" I questioned. "He could never go anywhere without all of those women absolutely smothering him. How did he poison two of them without the rest of them seeing him do it?"

"Maybe he done it when he had a minute all to hisself," said Nana. "You remember that first night in Loch Ness when your father seen the monster? Them four girls was all in the potty at the same time, 'cuz I was in there with 'em, waitin' for the stalls to open up. You s'pose that woulda give Cameron the chance he needed to slip somethin' into Isobel's dessert?"

"Wouldn't she have been able to taste it?" asked Wally.

Erik shook his head. "Not if he used white arsenic. Dissolved in a cup of coffee, I'm told it's virtually tasteless."

"Okay, he might have taken advantage of an opportunity there," I agreed, "but what about Dolly?"

Wally scratched the back of his head, looking pensive. "When we first arrived in Wick, Dolly complained about a headache coming on, so she asked me if I had any over-the-counter stuff I could give her. I told her I'd have to unpack my suitcase to get to it, but Cameron overhead us and told me not to bother because he had some extra-strength acetaminophen capsules on him."

The room grew quiet.

"I imagine the capsules were packed with arsenic," said Etienne.

Alex nodded. "You can buy white arsenic in powdered form over the Internet, so transferring it into pain capsules was probably the easiest part of the whole process."

"Poor Lucille." I shivered involuntarily. "She would have been next."

"I'm still unclear as to why Lucille's roommate didn't notice she was missing until the following morning," said Etienne. He offered me a perplexed look. "Isn't Alice usually more observant than that?"

"It's on account of that dang ferry ride," Nana piped up. "Alice told me she was so sick that night, she slept like the dead. She didn't even get up to go potty. Not once." She gave a little suck on her uppers. "Take it from me, that's pretty dead."

"In Alice's defense," Wally spoke up, raising his hand testimonial style, "when she realized Lucille's bed hadn't been slept in, she raised an immediate hue and cry. Alice conducted herself quite admirably."

"Maybe you should offer her one of them free trips you're givin' away, dear," suggested Nana.

Etienne frowned. "Free trips? What free trips?"

"I still can't believe how incredibly nice Cameron pretended to be," I reflected. "I mean, he was the one who tried to protect me when our boat hit the dock on Loch Ness. Isn't that a little out of character for a serial killer?"

"In Dasher's case, no," said Erik. "He loves women. Just because he had no scruples about killing them doesn't mean he didn't feel strongly about wanting to protect them. The brain of a serial killer can be very complex."

"Was he telling me the truth about having five sisters?"

"He has five sisters who adore him," confided Alex. "They'll no doubt be completely devastated when they learn the truth about what he's been doing all these years."

293

I sat back in my chair and leveled a look at both Erik and Alex. "And what about the two of you?" I said in an accusing voice. "You don't exist."

They exchanged a look. "We'd prefer you keep that to yourself," said Alex.

"Who *are* you guys?"

Erik laughed. "Have you heard the old saw, 'If I tell you, I'll have to kill you'? Our organization coined the phrase."

"No kiddin'?" said Nana.

"So it's all been one grand masquerade," I allowed. "The rocket science, the gayness, the shopping."

"We faked two out of three," admitted Erik, smiling drolly. "I'll leave it to your imagination to guess which one still applies."

"Do you two fellas always work as a team?" asked Nana.

Alex cleared his throat. "This was a first … as evidenced by our many glitches which Mrs. Miceli always seemed to be on hand to witness. You're a very nice person, Mrs. Miceli, but you can be a real thorn in a person's side."

I drilled a look at Erik. "Are you Fast Freddie Torres?"

"Absolutely not."

"What did you drop on the floor the night you drove your foot through the wall?"

He thrust his chin at Alex. "My butterfingered partner dropped the laptop. Completely fried the system and all our data."

"Where were you when Dolly died?"

"At the train station, checking on the schedule. We were already anticipating Dasher's next move."

"Who's Stu?"

Erik held my gaze. "Pretend you never heard the name."

"How were you going to deal with me if I stuck my nose where it didn't belong?"

The two men exchanged glances.

"I overheard your conversation on the ferry."

"We would have had to take you into our confidence about the mission," said Alex, "and that would have increased the possibility of more people getting hurt by a factor of a thousand."

"I thank you gentlemen for keeping her in the dark," Etienne said gratefully.

"So are you young fellas plannin' to finish up the tour with us?" asked Nana.

"I don't think so," said Alex as he wiggled the toes sticking out of the foot of his cast. "In fact, Mrs. Sippel, I'd prefer to be gutted with a grapefruit spoon than spend another afternoon with your maniacal friends from Iowa. You people are dangerous."

"We're nuthin' compared to my Maccoull kin. They coulda gutted you real good, only they woulda had to use something besides a serrated spoon, on account of they didn't have no grapefruit back then."

Wally stood up. "If you're through with us, Officer Bean, we should be heading back to the hotel. We kind of have this schedule to maintain."

Bean shook hands all around, as did Erik, who pumped Nana's hand with an extra degree of admiration. "Impressive roundhouse kick in your takedown, Mrs. Sippel. Have you ever considered the competitive circuit?"

At the door, Nana snapped her fingers and turned back to Officer Bean. "You got any use for a helicopter?"

"I'm afraid a helicopter is beyond our budget."

"You don't gotta buy it; I'm givin' it away. All's I need you to do is write me a receipt. I can use the tax deduction."

Back at the hotel, things were happily chaotic.

"Is there any reason we can't continue the contest today?" Mom asked me.

"Nope."

"Are Erik and Alex coming back?"

"Nope."

"Then I'll have several open slots where I could put Bernice. Now all I have to decide is whether she's a better fit with the atheist or the vegetarian."

"Go for it."

Etienne came up behind me. "Free trips?"

"Think about all the new business it's going to generate!" I grabbed Dad as he shuffled out to the bus.

"Did you know there are at least twenty-one lochs in Scotland where Nessie-type creatures have been sighted?"

"Really?" His eyes lit up.

"You bet. Twenty-one. And we're planning to rejigger our itinerary so we can visit at least two of them."

"No kidding?" His face suddenly fell. "But I don't have a camcorder."

Tilly approached us from the direction of the front desk and handed Dad a shopping sack. "The hardware store sent this over for you, Bob."

I smiled as he peeked inside. "You do now."

As I watched them stampede out the door, I prayed we'd have smooth sailing for the rest of the trip. I'd packed up Hamish Maccoull's dirk with the intention of delivering it to the University of Glasgow at the end of the tour, so if it was indeed cursed, it could stay cursed in the country of its origin rather than someplace new, like say, Windsor City, Iowa. Our killer had been caught, Bernice wouldn't have anything to whine about for a few days, and our room this evening was supposedly furnished with a king-size bed, so I had big after-dinner plans.

With our outlook appearing so rosy, what could possibly go wrong?

"Emily, dear, come quick!" Nana raced back into the lobby. "Dick Teig's kilt just fell off … and he's not wearin' no undershorts!"

THE END

ABOUT THE AUTHOR

After experiencing disastrous vacations on three continents, Maddy Hunter decided to combine her love of humor, travel, and storytelling to fictionalize her misadventures. Inspired by her feisty aunt and by memories of her Irish grandmother, she created the nationally bestselling, Agatha Award–nominated Passport to Peril mystery series, where quirky seniors from Iowa get to relive everything that went wrong on Maddy's holiday. *Bonnie of Evidence* is the eighth book in the series. Maddy lives in Madison, Wisconsin, with her husband and a head full of imaginary characters who keep asking, "Are we there yet?"

Please visit her website at www.maddyhunter.com, or become a follower on her Maddy Hunter Facebook Fan Page:

http://www.facebook.com/AuthorMaddyHunter

WWW.MIDNIGHTINKBOOKS.COM

From the gritty streets of New York City to sacred tombs in the Middle East, it's always midnight somewhere. Join us online at any hour for fresh new voices in mystery fiction.

At midnightinkbooks.com you'll also find our author blog, new and upcoming books, events, book club questions, excerpts, mystery resources, and more.

MIDNIGHT INK ORDERING INFORMATION

Order Online:
• Visit our website www.midnightinkbooks.com, select your books, and order them on our secure server.

Order by Phone:
• Call toll-free within the U.S. and Canada at
  1-888-NITE-INK (1-888-648-3465)
• We accept VISA, MasterCard, and American Express

Order by Mail:
Send the full price of your order (MN residents add 6.875% sales tax) in U.S. funds, plus postage & handling to:

> Midnight Ink
> 2143 Wooddale Drive
> Woodbury, MN 55125-2989

Postage & Handling:

Standard (U.S. & Canada). If your order is:
> $25.00 and under, add $4.00
> $25.01 and over, FREE STANDARD SHIPPING

AK, HI, PR: $16.00 for one book plus $2.00 for each additional book.

International Orders (airmail only):
> $16.00 for one book plus $3.00 for each additional book

Orders are processed within 12 business days. Please allow for normal shipping time.
Postage and handling rates subject to change.

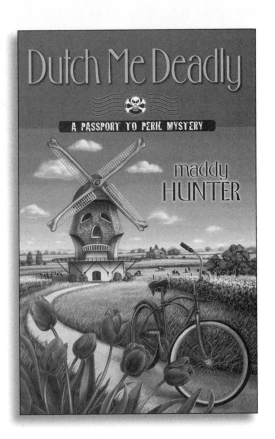

Dutch Me Deadly

☠

A PASSPORT TO PERIL MYSTERY

maddy HUNTER

Dutch Me Deadly
MADDY HUNTER

As a travel escort for seniors, Emily Andrew-Miceli has led her feisty Iowa clan all over the world. This time, they're off to see historic windmills and Dutch art in Holland—if they can ever unplug from their smartphones, that is. Joining them is the class from Bangor, Maine, celebrating their 50th reunion, which is divided by old rivalries. Emily's hopes for a 100% survival rate on this trip are dashed when an important member of the tour suffers a tragic (and highly suspicious) accident. Then the saucy seniors' wild night of drug-laced desserts and risqué shows in Amsterdam's red light district gets even more mysterious when one reunioner—the class bully—goes missing.

978-0-7387-2704-2, 288 pp., 5³⁄₁₆ x 8 $14.95